By: Author, Tosh Baker

Edited by: Beatrice Pavia

Published by: Eli's Lesbian Fiction

https://www.facebook.com/toshbaker64

Copyright protected with the U.S. Library of Congress

Case Number: 1-4309117001

Word count for
manuscript only: 75,948

Content:

- Synopsis
- Appreciation to friends and family
- Chapters One-Nine, Manuscript/Novel

Synopsis

Invite yourself and your greatest imagination into this extraordinary, fiction novel of two very real women, who came from different lives. In this gripping suspense thriller, follow them through their horrific journey of justified vengeance, as they recall their past and fight for their present. Enjoy the powerful and romantic bond that develops between Carmen and Sierra, as their story unravels into a twisting path of reality.

Imagine yourself as an EPA agent on a cold, autumn morning. You're hiking through the rough mountain terrain of Montana. While bent over, you can hear nothing but the sound of the powerful, flowing river. You're retrieving a water sample from it. In a matter of seconds, your life will change. You've been snatched up from behind, then blindfolded, brutally raped and left for dead. Your will to survive surpasses anything that you have just experienced. But your fear to expose this unfortunate reality to the public would have been a humiliation for you. You chose not to share this nightmare with the world. This is what happened to Carmen, and she decided to take matters into her own hands.

Now imagine yourself as a young girl, hiding inside a closet and peeking through the cracks. Your body is trembling with fear. You wet yourself at the sight of your mother being raped and brutalized. You see a loaded gun inside the closet next to you, and in a hopeful attempt to save her, you shoot her attacker dead. After running to your mother's aid, you witnessed the life leaving through her eyes, wondering, had you acted quicker, she still might be alive today. Sierra carried this painstaking reality with her throughout her entire life.

Sierra found Carmen that day on the cold mountaintop and rescued her. After developing a close relationship, they were able to confide in one another. The test of will and the decisions of right or wrong play a powerful role in this exciting tale of justified vengeance.

Unlike your average suspense thriller, you will enjoy getting to know Carmen. She reveals not only her strong nature to survive, but shall entertain the reader with her witty and humorous personality. Sierra, on the other hand, would be considered the all-American cowgirl, who is highly favored by the township in which she grew up. She is outgoing, with a loving but independent personality. She makes her living working as a tour guide through her native mountain terrain. Together, this team of women will deliver an amazing story with a twist. Buckle up and enjoy their adventure of friendship, love and justified vengeance.

Honor of appreciation, to friends and family.

John Buck:
- Local police detective of Bold Creek Township

Bill Doyle:
- Piper, the bad guy and laborer at Hilltop Drilling Company (oil fracking site in the Bold Creek area)

Jude:
- Owner of Jude's Café, a local diner in Bold Creek

Sadie Corda:
- Sadie Corda, Investigative reporter from Idaho

Paula Dietz:
- Sadie's friend from Idaho

Tyler Baker:
- Dr. Ty, Emergency room physician

Brittany & Billy:
- Sierra's cousin, who works in the crime lab and her husband Billy

Gary Post:
- Land buyer from Texas

Bryce Reynolds:
- Young ranch hand that lives near Sierra Wolfe in Bold Creek

Carole and Loren Hill:
- Owners of Bair-Hill feed store

Jason Zachariah:

- Beer tent attendant

Dwayne Darling:

- Excavator

Mike Thompson:

- Fire marshal

Steve Taylor:

- Local Rancher

Em Gee: Friend from Queensland, Australia

Scene set: A small mountain town somewhere in Montana

CHAPTER ONE

The cold autumn breeze pierced through a torn and tattered body. Her bare skin was exposed to the harsh elements of the rocky terrain. This helpless victim cringed with fear and was unable to see through the blindfold that covered her battered eyes. She was forced to lay face down on this secluded mountaintop, where she desperately clutched her bruised and bleeding fingertips in the hard ground. She struggled with her broken body, to scurry away from further abuse, while she pleaded for this nightmare to be over. His horrid body odor lingered, and his voice pierced through her. The constant, nervous tick of one man clicking what sounded like a lighter lid kept her attention, while the alcohol-drenched savage brutalized her. It felt like hours had passed when she heard one of them say, "Finish the bitch off, and let's get out of here."

The grungy, heartless man took a plastic bag from his jacket pocket and wrapped it over her face. This helpless victim struggled for air then with a powerful will to survive; she played dead by holding her breath. Each second left her desperate to breathe. In a compelling performance, she made a final choking sound and gagged up saliva. The drool ran from the corner of her mouth, and her body became non-responsive. She faked to be limp and lifeless in appearance and successfully led her assailant to believe that he had ended her life. With a ready sign of hope, she felt him release her. He stood over her, and then delivered a powerful blow, one last time, to her ribs. "This nosy bitch won't be stirring up any trouble for us, Boss; she's nothing but dinner for a hungry pack of wolves now; hell she's even been tenderized."

"Yeah, that's good to know," he replied, then flipped a lit cigarette butt on her naked body and left.

She listened intently to their footfall as they walked away. She then ripped the bag from her face and gasped for air. After removing her blindfold, and with every ounce of energy left, she crawled near the road's edge, where she collapsed in a patch of tall brush. She lay there lifeless, until she was startled by the sound of crackling footsteps through the fallen leaves. She feared the worst, and her heart raced. Then a wet, but curious, nose gently touched her face. *It's a dog*, she thought.

Then, like an angel sent from heaven, she heard a soft voice—it was Sierra Wolfe, a native of the Bold Creek area. She was out on a morning run with her dog when she noticed him circling a tall patch of grass. Horrified by what she discovered, she barely recognized the body as Carmen Storm, thinking, *I met her two days ago, down at the Village Hall.* "Carmen, honey, I'm here to help you. Let's get you warmed up." Sierra knelt down and took her coat off, then put it on Carmen. After gently helping her to stand, she softly spoke: "We need to get you to my truck. It's not far, less than a half mile to my cabin. I need you to be strong just a little longer."

With Sierra's help, Carmen found the extra strength she needed to survive this assault and whimpered, "We have to get out of here; they'll be back if they hear us."

"You're safe with me, Carmen. I always pack a gun. Do you know who did this to you?" Sierra asked.

"No, no I don't! How much farther do we have to go?" she asked with a quivering desperation in her voice.

"Not far now. You're going to be okay; I promise."

After what felt like a long struggle back to Sierra's cabin, Carmen was grateful she had been rescued and was safe inside the truck. She sat quietly on the ride to the emergency clinic, and with her arms protectively wrapped around herself, she whispered, "Thank you." Sierra's heart broke for her and imagined the worst. She hoped for some answers but knew now wasn't a good time.

While waiting to hear the doctor's assessment, Sierra went to the bathroom. She looked at her reflection in the mirror; she fought her own battle over this gruesome event. She tried to ignore vivid flashbacks that were erupting from her memory, of a horrific episode she had experienced as a child. She could only imagine what Carmen must have gone through on this dreadful autumn morning. With a million thoughts and unanswered questions erupting from her mind, she felt the room spin out of control. Her mouth watered as her stomach churned. She stumbled her way through a stall door, where she vomited uncontrollably.

Upon leaving the restroom, Sierra noticed an old friend, John Buck, standing outside of Carmen's hospital room. She was at ease, assuming he was the detective assigned to the case. After taking one look at Sierra, John knew she was obviously upset by this unfortunate episode and reached out to hug her. "Hey, girl; I just received a call from the E.R. I'm sorry you were the one to find her in this condition. I know this can't be easy." In a hopeful attempt to lift her spirits, he took her hand. "Hey, thanks to you, she's safe now. You're a hero. Are you okay?"

"Yeah, I'll be okay, John; it's not me I'm worried about. I found her on my morning run, not far from my cabin; she was alone and in this condition. I think she was raped and obviously beaten. I found her naked. I didn't have time to check out the crime scene, but I can take you to the location," Sierra replied.

"Yeah, Doc Ty thinks the same thing. He suggested I request a rape kit from the crime lab. She's heavily sedated right now. If you're up to it, maybe you can take me to the location where you found her. This should give her chance to rest before I question her," Detective Buck suggested.

"No problem John. I barely recognized her, but I know her—not well, though. Her name is Carmen Storm; I met her two days ago. She works for the Environmental Protection Agency and had some work to do up on the Northwest Ridge, testing the water supply here in Bold Creek. I'm the tour guide who escorted her to the cabin she'd be occupying during her stay. Who could have done this?" Sierra cringed with disgust.

"You never know, it's just crazy how some people could be so heartless. I haven't heard of anything this severe being reported since . . ." He paused in silence, as he looked at Sierra then lowered his head. "I'm sorry. I didn't mean to bring up the past. I'll catch this guy, don't you worry. Did she seem coherent when you found her, or did she say anything suggesting she knew her assailant?"

"No, I'm pretty sure she was in shock when I found her. By the look of things, I could only imagine what she went through. I didn't want to push her. It won't be easy finding the person who did this to her, unless she can identify her attacker. We have so many outsiders in our native territory now, with all the oil drilling and fracking. Can you contact Montana Board of Oil and Gas Conservation? I'm sure they have a list of all the oil-drilling sites in our area. Surely it's mandatory that they have permits for hydraulic fracturing. Hopefully you can run background checks and get some helpful information on the owners and operators."

"Yeah, that's a good place to start. When I get back to headquarters, I'll be sure to do that," John replied.

After a three-mile drive up the secluded mountain road, Sierra tapped John's arm. "Slow down, it's just up here on your left. Pull over right there." She pointed. "This is where I found her, just off the path, right over there, by that cluster of trees and tall grass."

While bagging various clothing items from the crime scene, Sierra was disturbed by the blood splatter on rocks; she took a couple of deep breaths and closed her eyes for a moment. She tried to shake off the visions flashing through her mind. She could almost feel what Carmen had gone through. Her stomach churned again, then she murmured, "Sick bastard, we'll find you," in a low tone.

John glanced up and noticed Sierra's back turned to him while she searched for other clues. He was distracted by her slender, well-kept physique and long, dark hair. He realized now wasn't a good time to make any flirtatious comments, so he quickly diverted his train of thought. "Hey, looks like we've gathered all the evidence; let's get out of here, and if I'm lucky, our victim might be ready to talk."

"Her name is Carmen, *Carmen*, John, and sounds like a plan to me. Just promise you'll take it easy when you question her; she's been through enough," Sierra replied.

"I promise. We'll run the evidence by the crime lab first. Hopefully your cousin, Brittany, will make this a priority. Then we'll check on Carmen, see if she's up to talking."

After arriving back at the hospital, Dr. Ty noticed the couple as they walked in and motioned for them to come over. "Hi, our patient is resting well, but she's suffering from two broken ribs on the right side. Looks like whoever attacked her probably kicked her several times. I've treated the contusions on her face. I assume she was punched repeatedly, as indicated by her broken nose and a slight fracture on her left cheek bone. Lastly, the rape kit came back positive for semen; the DNA still needs analyzed."

"Yeah, we just stopped by the lab to drop off some evidence. Brittany told us the news," Sierra replied and paused for a second. "So, do you think John and I can see Carmen for a few minutes? We'd like to have some questions answered, if at all possible."

"Mmm, I don't know. She is very uncomfortable with men in her room right now. I had a very hard time convincing my patient to let me help her. I had my assistant call for a female doctor to help out but was unable to get a hold of anyone. Luckily, with a nurse standing by, she decided to let me examine her. So I'd suggest you stay in the waiting room, John, while you go in alone, Sierra. If she shows any signs of stress during the questioning, please respect the fact that she may not be ready to talk."

"Thanks, and I'll keep that in mind," Sierra replied.

Upon entering the room, Sierra stood at her bedside. Carmen's eyes were closed. Sierra gently touched her hand and spoke softly. "Carmen, it's me, Sierra, the tour guide that found you. I really need to ask you a few questions about what happened out there." Carmen slowly opened her eyes and was startled. "Easy, it's okay, it's just me," Sierra responded with a gentle tone, and then held her hand for reassurance. "Carmen, I can only imagine what you went through, and I am so sorry you were a victim to such a heinous crime. I'm just glad you're alive; you're one tough lady. Look, I understand if you're not ready to talk about this or even relive the dreadful experience. However, we need to apprehend this savage so he never does this again."

Tears welled up in Carmen's eyes as she began to speak. "I can't do it. I don't want to press charges because nothing happened."

"I understand you're scared, but you deserve justice," Sierra replied. "This guy needs to pay for what he did."

"Justice, are you serious? He would only get five- to ten-year maximum in prison." Carmen scoffed. "The system is a crock of shit, and guys like this walk free every day, after time served. Besides, like I said, nothing happened."

"Carmen, you agreed to a rape kit. It came back positive with a semen sample. That means it's an official police investigation now."

"When they asked me if I was raped, I said yes. Truth is I don't know what happened to me. I think I was in shock but clearly remember now that I slipped down the rock slope. And regarding semen—I guess I'm just sexually promiscuous."

"Okay, Carmen, you get some sleep. Here's my number—give me a call if you want to talk. I'll let Officer Buck know you won't be pressing charges at this time." Then she touched her hand gently. "Again, I am so sorry you have gone through this; my prayers are with you."

After exiting the room, she glanced around to find John sitting on a bench in the waiting area. "How's she doing?" he asked. "Is she okay?"

"She has been through a lot in one day. Right now she's not pressing charges," Sierra replied.

"Are you serious? Did she say why?" John asked.

"She wasn't specific; maybe she'll feel different in the morning. Right now, she's not ready to admit she was attacked. If she does decide to stay and finish her work in the area, I may invite her to take the spare bedroom in my cabin.

I'd feel better knowing she wasn't on her own right now," Sierra replied.

"That's fine and dandy, Sierra. Just be safe, because whoever did this is still out there. If and when she does decide to talk, I want to know about it."

Sierra nodded her head. "You'll be the first to know, John."

On her drive home late that afternoon, Sierra kept replaying the events that surrounded the day. As she passed by the place Carmen had been assaulted, she became overwhelmed with an eerie feeling. Again, she suffered quick glimpses of a past childhood memory that she had spent most of her life trying to forget. The thought of Carmen's offender still being on the loose heightened her senses.

She was thankful for her longtime companion, Bear, who was a Newfoundland dog breed; he greeted her as he did every day with his loving personality. Unlike days prior to today, Sierra for the first time in years made a walk through the house. She double-checked that the windows were tightly locked and guns loaded. She noticed Bear could feel her tenseness; he followed her closely as she made her rounds. "Hey, buddy, I hope you know you're the only guy Mommy wants in her life," she said. Bear wagged his tail; he didn't really know exactly what she was saying but loved her attention. "Don't worry, we'll figure out who did this to Carmen. I'm so glad you found her today; she really needed us." Bear gave his happy smile, as he often did when Sierra spoke to him.

Despite not having much of an appetite that evening, Sierra forced herself to heat up some Ramen noodles. Before she knew it, the dinner had cooled down. She had barely touched her serving and couldn't bring herself to finish. She raked the remains into the dog dish. "Eat up, my friend. It's just not setting well with me tonight."

That evening, while outside on the porch, she took a couple of deep inhales off a joint. She had hoped to relax her mind but was startled when Bear grumbled a deep, low growl. He then bellowed repeated barks into the darkness of the night. Sierra reached for her handgun that she kept strapped to her hip and sounded off three shots from the deck. She yelled out, with an overactive imagination, "Whoever's out there, I won't hesitate to bust a cap in your ass! You hear me?" Then she commanded Bear to come in and locked the door behind them.

Early the next morning and still fast asleep, four loud, pounding knocks to the front door jolted her awake. Still on edge, she grabbed her gun and cautiously approached a window to see who was outside. She was relieved that it was John standing out there. "It's early," she groaned while unlocking the door. "Come on in and sit down. I'm going to take a quick shower."

"Well, good morning to you, too. I'm glad you're locking the door," he replied, then yelled out while she was walking away, "and you're welcome for the breakfast that you haven't eaten yet. I brought your favorite—biscuits and bacon gravy with hash browns." She paid no attention to his comment and continued to the restroom. He looked at the dog and asked, "Is she always like this in the morning?" Bear just moaned, as his attention was on the food. "Mmm, I see you're not a morning person, either."

A few minutes later, Sierra came out with hair wrapped in a towel and sat down to eat. "Yum, that looks good. Where's the coffee?" she asked.

"Here, you can have the rest of mine. I've had my fill," John replied.

"So, why are you here terrorizing me this early in the morning? You're a decent-looking dude. Hell, you even have a decent build. I'd think you'd have some woman keeping you tied to the bed," she taunted. "You should be cuddling with that special someone, making babies on this Saturday morning. But not you, you're banging on my door, before the rooster crows. Do you know you scared the crap out of me? You're lucky I didn't shoot you. I've been feeling a little trigger-happy since yesterday; this whole thing has me freaked out."

"I can imagine; sorry about that. And I do have girlfriends, just none I want to make babies with," he gloated, and then changed the subject. "I did some research last night. I checked out all the registered hydraulic fracking sites that are in a fifty-mile radius of our area. Most of them contain around four to fifteen laborers that maintain each location. I intend to get a list of each employee, then cross-reference for any sexual offenders. I even made a few calls to adjacent counties, and there have been no reports of sexual harassment or rape activity that resemble this case."

"Cool, sounds like you're on the right path. Good job, John. Times like these make me wish I would have settled in a career like yours. I just feel like my hands are tied, being a tour guide. I'd like to help more. If there is any research you'd like me to do, I'd be glad to assist in any way."

"You can help by keeping me informed on Carmen's state of mind, and if she decides to press charges, or if she remembers anything at all that could help the investigation," John replied. "And for the record, you know this area better than anyone else. I'm not so sure another guide would be able to do what you do here."

"Thanks, John; I appreciate the vote of confidence. I'll be seeing Carmen this morning. Maybe she's had a change of heart," she sighed.

"Yeah, let's hope so. Maybe you can stop by the crime lab, too. Perhaps Brittany has some information linking us to the perp. Do me a favor and call if you hear anything. I'll be at Mom's if you need me; she's been down with bronchitis."

"Oh, wow, that's too bad. Tell her I said hello and hope she gets better soon," Sierra replied. "And yes, I'll be sure to see Brittany and let you know about anything significant."

"Okay, we'll catch up later. Have a good one, Sierra."

"You too, buddy. Hey, by the way, thanks for breakfast; I love Jude's cooking."

"I know, right? Best food around for miles," John replied.

While driving into town, Sierra tried to decide if she should see Carmen or Brittany first. Then her phone rang, making her decision easy. "Hey, Sierra, it's me."

"Hi Britt, I was just coming to see you."

"I have some bad news, Sierra. All the evidence and testing samples for Carmen's case file are gone!" Brittany exclaimed.

"What do you mean, 'gone'?" a confused Sierra asked.

"Gone, as in 'gone.' There are no signs of a break-in, and my surveillance cams show no signs of anyone being in here. This leads me to believe it was somebody from our local

17

police force. I mean, who else could gain access or go unnoticed?"

"That doesn't make any sense. Are you sure you just didn't put it somewhere for safekeeping and forgot? I do that all the time," Sierra replied.

Brittany responded with a nervous giggle, "No, of course not. I wish it were that easy. I followed protocol; I handled the evidence, like I would any other case. All of it is gone!"

"Okay, Britt, if this was an inside job, we need to know. Don't talk to anyone until I call John. He'll know what to do. I'll be in touch soon, but first, I need to go check on Carmen."

"Just try to hurry, please, this is freaky weird, and it's making me nervous," Brittany replied with her quirky response, as she pushed her dark-framed glasses up on her nose, like she often did.

"He's at his mom's right now; she's been sick. I'll let him know before day's end. Just hold tight and be patient. He will be in touch with you soon."

"Okay, but do you think I'm in danger?" she asked.

"Just stay low and act normal, like nothing is wrong. John will be in touch later, I promise. Listen, I am at the hospital and ready to walk in, so I have to let you go. I'll be sure to check on you soon."

Upon her arrival at the hospital, Sierra was greeted by Dr. Ty. "Our patient, Ms. Storm, is demanding to be released earlier than I advise. I can't keep her here against her will, although she seems to be of sound mind. She suffered some pretty severe injuries, and I wanted to see her stay at least another day for observation."

"I see. Did she say if she had a ride?" Sierra asked.

"No. I just I assumed you were here to do that."

"Can I go in and see her?"

"Sure, that would be fine. You might want to knock, though; a nurse about her size brought in some clothes that she might be able to wear," the doctor replied.

Sierra nodded her head and thought that was nice. With a gentle tap on the door, she announced her presence.

"Come on in, I'm dressed," Carmen said.

Sierra approached her with a gentle bedside manner. "Hey you, how are you feeling today?"

"I could be better; just glad I'm getting out of here. I have a lot of work to do," she casually replied, as if she were in denial.

"The doctor thinks you should stay another day," Sierra said with obvious concern in her voice.

"I'm fine and just want to get out of here. I can't stand lying around like this; I'd rather heal on my own and in privacy."

"I can understand that. So you're still planning to stay in the area for work?" Before she could answer, Sierra said, "If so, I'd feel much better if you stayed in the spare room of my cabin."

"Yes, I need to finish my work, and I really appreciate your accommodating offer, as long as I'm not putting you out. At least until I'm one hundred percent again," Carmen humbly replied.

"Good, I'm glad to hear that, and I'd like the company. We'll run by your camp and pick up any supplies you'll need."

"Thanks, Sierra."

"No problem at all." Sierra found it hard to keep direct eye contact. The facial injuries were very bad and looked painful. Again, her heart broke for Carmen and what she must be going through.

A silence overwhelmed them on the ride up the mountain when they passed the crime scene. A tear trickled down Carmen's cheek; she tried her best to fight the flood of emotion boiling inside. Sierra noticed her anguish, then gently took Carmen's hand in hers. "My cabin is just up here on the left; we don't have far now. I make a pretty good cup of mullein tea, and with a shot of aged bourbon, you won't have any worries in the world," Sierra thoughtfully suggested in an attempt to divert Carmen's horrid recollections.

"Thank you, that sounds nice," Carmen replied and found comfort in Sierra's reassurance.

Upon arriving home, Bear anxiously bounced around the truck with excitement. "Wow, he's a beautiful sight. He's the one who found me, right?" Carmen asked.

"Yes, he sure did. His name is Bear, and he loves women; however, he's not so fond of men," Sierra smirked.

"Ah, that's a relief to know. You're such a handsome guy, Bear, and such a good boy," Carmen replied, while Sierra helped her into the cabin. She felt at ease in the comfort of Sierra's space. "Goodness, how nice and spacious this is for a smaller home. I see you have a flare for decorating. It has a very warming effect," she said as she admired the rustic living room that was covered in South American décor. "It's very nice."

"Thanks, I love it. Your room is right over there on the left, and we share a bathroom." Then she patted an old recliner. "When you're ready, you can sit down here, and I'll make us that spiced tea I was bragging about, if you're still interested?"

"I am interested, thank you. I'll take a spiked drink any day over this Vicodin the doc sent me home with. It makes me feel nauseous."

"No doubt, right. I don't care for it, either," Sierra replied. "After we finish our drink, if you're up for it, I can take you by your camp to gather up some of your things."

"That would be great. I don't have much, other than testing supplies and clothes that need washed. I'm sorry for any inconvenience," she replied.

"Don't be. I'm glad you're here. It can get lonely sometimes, even with my Bear."

Later that afternoon, while Carmen was taking a shower, Sierra stepped outside to call John; after two attempts and no answer, she lit a cigarette and thought, *Come on, John, answer the phone.* A few minutes later, she snuffed out her smoke, and just before she decided to go back in, she heard John's familiar ringtone. "Hey, buddy, glad you called back. Listen, a lot has happened today. I saw Brittany, and for some reason, all the evidence we brought in yesterday is missing from the lab. Worse yet, there is no security cam proof."

"Are you fucking serious? Did she report it?" John asked.

"No, she suggested that it could have been an inside job, due to the circumstances. I told her that I wanted to talk to you about this before we brought it to anyone else's attention."

"Yeah, I'm glad you did. Okay, I'll be back before four and will plan on seeing Britt," he replied.

"John, one more thing, I stopped by and picked up Carmen. She'll be staying with me until her work is done here."

"I hope you made the right decision, Sierra. Just do me a favor—be safe. I have a bad feeling about all of this."

"I'll be fine, John. How's your mom feeling?"

"Mom's good; she's got that Indian blood in her, remember. She told me to tell you hi."

"Aw, I miss her. I hope you told her hello from me, too. And who could ever forget she's a native to our land? I used to love listening to my mom tell stories about them being raised together on the reservation."

"Yeah, I know the stories all too well; they were the best of friends." Then he paused in silence for a quick moment. "How are you doing, Sierra? I know this is bringing back hard memories. If you need to talk, or if this gets too much, just know I'm here for you," John said.

"I know, John. I'm more concerned about Carmen than myself. She looks really bad; her black eyes and broken nose look dreadfully painful. Her face is really swelled up; I just hope she's going to be okay."

"I'm sure she'll be fine. Injuries like this take time to heal, but before you know, she'll be feeling and looking much better."

"Yeah, I suppose you're right. I just feel so bad for her. I have a few things I need to get done, but do me a favor, call me after you talk to Britt." A second after Sierra ended the call; she turned around to find Carmen standing at the screen door. "Hey, how was the shower?" Sierra asked.

"It was nice, thank you. Who were you talking to, if you don't mind me asking?"

"John. He's a longtime friend of mine and is a detective on the local police force here. Look, we had a problem this morning. All the evidence we gathered from the crime scene is missing from the lab."

Carmen shook her head, "Well, since I'm not pressing charges, I don't see the problem."

"Carmen, I have to ask, did you have someone from the inside obtain these articles?"

"No, absolutely not," she replied.

"Okay, well, John researched possible rape activity in the nearby counties. He found nothing of significant value. He is also investigating employees of the hydraulic fracking sites in a fifty-mile radius. There have been a lot of strangers in the area since the oil drilling began. Do you think it could have been laborers working the fracking sites?" Sierra asked.

"Look, I work for the EPA, as you're well aware. My research here could step on fracking sites that are illegally drilling for oil. If they're not following mandated rules and regulations, they could stand to be fined a large sum or even face imprisonment. Some don't even have proper permits to be drilling. Their actions are threatening your water supply. The chemicals are leaching in the ground and aquifers. The number of people that could suffer health issues is a big concern. Long-term exposure to these chemicals could cause cancer, diabetes, birth defects, the list goes on. So to answer your question, yes, if they are working an illegal fracking site, they could stand to lose a lot. Maybe they were sent to run me off."

"Carmen, are you sure you want to stay in the area? What if you're right, what if they don't stop until they run you off or, worse, kill you? You should take some time to heal, surround yourself with the people who love you. Now is not the time to make any decision that could change your life forever."

"My life changed when I was attacked; I'll never be the same again. If it was a laborer from an illegal site, then they'll pay for what they've done to me and all the people they're affecting by not following mandated rules or regulations. I'm not going anywhere. Besides, I have no family to go home to. I'm going on with my research as scheduled, and that's my final decision, Sierra."

"Then consider pressing charges. John and I will do everything possible to help bring this guy down, Carmen."

"Sierra, I understand your concerns, but I'm not pressing charges. If I were to do that, my private life would be exposed. The reporters would have a heyday. I was chosen to take this particular position because I am the best person for the job, and I won't miss the overdue bonus. If you want to help, then please start by respecting my wishes."

"I understand; maybe you should get some rest. I'm going to make a hot pot of chili for dinner this evening," Sierra replied.

"That sounds great, and thank you for not pushing," she sighed.

Later that afternoon, Carmen rested well in the comfort and safety of her new friend's home. Just after Sierra made that pot of chili, she turned it down to simmer, then thought quietly, *Hmm, while she's resting, I think I'll snoop around the mountain.* Before leaving the cabin, she grabbed her shotgun and placed a note on the kitchen table for Carmen, informing her that she'd be back soon. Bear begged to go along, but Sierra said with a loving tone, "You have to stay home and watch over our guest; she really needs you. I promise I'll be back soon. I'm just going to look around the mountaintop a little bit." Then she shut the door behind her and saddled up her beloved trail horse, Jessie, to assist.

She made several stops while heading up Glacier Pass. She took pictures of various fracking sites that were in operation just a couple of miles from the crime scene. One particular site caught her attention. She noticed a few burly guys standing around, drinking it up after work hours. They were loud and boisterous, and this drew her attention. Sierra stayed out of view while she zoomed through her lens for a better look. *I wish I could hear what they're saying better,* she thought. Then, for lack of better judgment, Sierra was unable to resist. With a curious nature, she dismounted her horse and brazenly crept closer. Coyly, she crouched against a filled-out spruce tree, just close enough to hear the drunkards boasting about who worked the hardest that day. She had an eerie feeling that she had found a couple of good suspects worth investigating. While intensely focusing on their conversation, Sierra was startled by a crackle of brush behind her. Before she could turn around and see what it might be, she was grabbed from behind. Her assailant wrapped his arms around her in a tight bear hug, then firmly placed his hand over her mouth and hoisted her off the ground; she violently struggled to free herself. Her heart pounded rapidly; she imagined her worst fears unfolding in front of her eyes. He carried her several feet before he released her from his grip. In a desperate attempt to run away, she darted forward. But he reached out and grabbed Sierra's arm and spun her around. He firmly shushed her by placing his hand over her mouth. She looked in his eyes and realized it was John; she viciously began swinging to hit him. "What the hell is your problem, asshole? Do you think this is funny?" she spouted in a low tone, as she adjusted her clothing back into place.

John tried to calm her down quietly and hoped the ruckus went unnoticed. "Stop, Sierra! Just stop for a minute. Why the hell are you poking around up here by yourself? I told you, we'd do it together. Geez, you're so damn hardheaded! You could get hurt or killed," he said, growling his concerns.

"Don't ever do that again," she warned. After brushing herself off, she tromped back to her horse, and then sarcastically asked, "Why the hell were you up here without me, then?"

"I'm trained for this sort of thing. I'm the cop, remember. I was doing a little ground work. That's what cops do, not you. I'm sorry I scared you, but don't pull this shit again," he replied.

"Whatever your reasoning was, don't ever surprise me like that again. I'm really pissed at you right now, John!"

"Sierra, it's dangerous to be up here alone right now. You saw what happened to Carmen; she's lucky to be alive. I'll follow you back home, and we can talk about this over a beer."

"No, not this afternoon. Besides, Carmen is resting, and I'm not sure she would welcome the presence of a man right now. I'll call you in the morning, and I assure you, I can make it home fine on my own." Then she patted her rifle and gave a smirk before she trotted down the mountain.

John felt thrown back by her lack of appreciation regarding his self-perceived noble gesture, muttering to himself, "I did the right thing; she should be thanking me. Shit! Fucking women, what a pain in my ass."

Sierra's mind was occupied on her ride back to the cabin. She was curious about the boisterous men that she had come across and wondered if one of them could have been the culprit who attacked Carmen. *Proving it will be hard unless Carmen recognizes any of them in the photos I took,* she thought.

After arriving back home late that afternoon, she turned her horse, Jessie, out to pasture, and then shivered from the brisk breeze. She held her rifle in one hand and threw her hat over her head with the other, then scurried up to the house. She glanced around for signs of Carmen, while the dog mauled her with happiness. "Yeah, I'm happy to see you, too, buddy. Hey, where's Carmen, huh? Have you been watching our new friend?" she said in a playful voice, as she spoke to her faithful, furry friend. After a quick scan through the cabin, Sierra realized Carmen was not inside. *Oh geez, surely she didn't leave the house,* she thought to herself. Her heart raced rapidly for a few seconds, wondering where she went. Then an instant calm settled over her after she caught a glimpse of Carmen's naked and sadly battered body getting into the hot tub that was on the back porch. A feeling of sadness overwhelmed Sierra. She felt helpless and unsure of what to say or even how to help this stranger through such a horrid time in her life. She lowered her head, and then diverted her thoughts by checking on the chili. While she was in the

27

kitchen, she saw a box of hot-chocolate packets that her grandmother had sent to her in the mail last week and thought a cup would be nice. Sierra was relieved when she glanced at the table and noticed Carmen had obviously gotten the note she had left earlier, informing her she would be back soon.

With a tray in hand, Sierra balanced her frothy, chocolate delights just right as she went through the sliding doors and onto the outdoor patio. Carmen's eyes were closed while she basked in the healing luxury of a soothing hot tub. Sierra gently placed the drinks in the cup holders and then quietly undressed. Just as she was slipping into the tub, Carmen's eyes slightly opened. "Ah, there you are. I wondered where you went. I hope you don't mind that I helped myself to your hot tub."

"Not at all. I call this my little piece of heaven," Sierra replied as she passed her a hot chocolate topped with whipped cream.

"Thank you, that's very thoughtful." After tasting her hot drink, her facial expression was heavenly. "Mmm, I haven't had a cup this tasty since last winter. I was at a small café in Washington state; I think it was called The Hops," she said then took another sip of her delightful treat.

"Thank you. Um, you have a little whipped cream on the tip of your nose," Sierra smiled.

"Oh, that's okay; I'll save it for later," Carmen giggled.

"I left a note on the table earlier, before I left. I wanted to let you know I'd be back soon. I'm just glad you felt at home enough to relax," Sierra said.

"I woke up a little tense, but I didn't see a note. I had a disturbing dream, though. I felt like someone was watching me, clicking a lighter lid—the same sound and feeling I had when I was being attacked. I was fine when I woke up, though, and realized Bear was snuggled up next to me; he's such a sweetheart. I knew it had to be just a bad dream. I assumed you were out running errands and would be here shortly. No worries."

Sierra looked puzzled. "Hmm, that's strange. I left the note on the table in plain sight, unless Bear knocked it onto the floor. I'll have to check when I get out of the tub."

"So, where did you go, anyways?" Carmen asked.

"I did a little snooping around of my own. I took some pictures of nearby fracking sites. I even got some video footage of a few drunk and mouthy laborers standing around a campfire. I assume they were on their own time," she replied. "You're welcome to take a look; maybe you'll recognize one of them," then paused for a hopeful reply or even a mere reaction from Carmen, but that didn't happen. She just lowered her head and hoped to avoid this topic. Sierra sensed her discomfort and changed course. "Hey, forget it. I'm sorry, no pressure. However, you might find this amusing. John found me there, hiding behind a tree, shortly after I started filming these guys and actually thought he was doing me a favor when he forcibly removed me from the site. I wasn't too happy about it and smacked him a good one."

"I could imagine. Did he feel like you were in jeopardy of being harmed?" Carmen asked.

"Yes, it freaked me out. He got me from behind, and I couldn't see who had me. After I realized it was him, I was just pissed. But he's always been like a protective big brother to me. When my mother passed away, his family practically raised me. I was always visiting with them, while I lived with my grandparents in this very cabin. Both our moms are Native

29

Indians to the area and were the best of friends, so we were all very close," Sierra replied.

"How old were you when you lost your mom?" Carmen asked.

"I was thirteen."

"I'm sorry; I know that must have been hard for you, Sierra."

"Harder than one could imagine." A tear slowly trickled down Sierra's face. "I'm sorry, the memory always feels like yesterday."

Carmen scooted closer and put an arm around her. "I'm here for you. Sometimes talking can be a great healing agent."

Sierra giggled as she fought back another tear. "Oh, that's calling the kettle black. Here I am crying about my past, and you have been through hell."

"I have plenty of time to talk about my feelings, Sierra. Besides, I still need to process all that has happened to me. So, how did your mom pass?"

Sierra looked down and said, "Very hard. She was brutally raped and beaten. I was hiding in the closet and saw the whole thing. I was only thirteen when I shot the man who raped and killed my mom. I was thankful that the shotgun was in the closet next to me. But I was too late. I didn't save her in time. I shot him after he stopped hurting her." Sierra sobbed, "Why did I wait so long? I could have saved her!"

"Oh, honey, I'm so sorry, but you were young; you had to be in shock. He could have done the same thing to you, had you failed to shoot him dead. I'm sure your mom is proud of you, and I can imagine she has been looking over you all these years."

Sierra was silent and nodded her head as she regained her composure. Carmen passed her a towel to dry her face. "I wish I could have killed my attacker. I want to kill him. I want to take back what he took from me—he and his friend who stood by, watching it all happen," Carmen said in a stone-cold voice.

"There were two men?" Sierra asked.

"Yes, the one who attacked me and then another who stood by, watching."

"I can imagine how you must feel. I'm so sorry I wasn't able to hear your cry for help. I would have shot them both for you," Sierra replied.

"Come on; let's get out of this tub before we shrivel up. Chili sounds really good, and we can talk more about that during dinner. How does that sound?" Carmen suggested.

"Sounds like a plan," Sierra replied.

The girls bonded that evening and shared the shocking elements of their past life experiences. They came upon a great understanding of each other that night. The things they had in common somehow tied these two together, as if they were kindred spirits.

CHAPTER TWO

Bright and early the next morning, John looked out from his kitchen window and shivered when he saw a beautiful blanket of snow covering the ground. He had always enjoyed the sight of the first snowfall and recalled how he could play in it for hours when he was a young boy. After pouring a stout cup of black coffee and smoking a cigarette, he grumbled, "Now it's just work." After shoveling a pathway to his truck and clearing the ice from his windshield, he drove into town. He felt unsettled and wasn't sure how he would handle the missing evidence situation that Brittany had brought to Sierra's attention yesterday.

When John arrived at the crime lab, he didn't see Brittany's car in the parking lot yet. He sat there a few minutes and finished his cigarette. He dreaded being there that morning and thought, *I really hate dealing with this shit. The woman doesn't want to press charges any damn way. It's just a fucking waste of my time.*

About the time he flicked his cigarette butt out the truck window, Brittany pulled up alongside him. "Hey, you're lucky you're my friend. Pitching butts in the parking lot is nasty— take note of that, please."

"Yeah, okay, noted," he replied.

"Sorry I'm running a little late. I've had so much on my mind since yesterday. It made for a sleepless night; I hope you can figure this out, John."

"Well, that's my goal, Britt. I actually have a couple of leads that I need to check into this morning. Do you think you can take an hour off and meet me at Jude's Café? I think it would be better if we met there; I wouldn't want to tip anyone off, if it was an inside job."

"Sure, I'll call headquarters now. I'll meet you over there in a few minutes, and if you get there before me, I like my coffee with cream and two sugars, please."

After the couple settled into a cozy corner booth of the diner, John didn't waste time getting to the point. "I'm thinking there's a mole working for someone on the outside," he said quietly. "I can't really share this with you right now, at least until I do a thorough investigation into the matter. Okay, can you do this for me—if anyone inquires about the evidence, just tell them the victim is not pressing charges and the case has been dropped, which is the truth."

"That's fine, I can do that. I can't imagine anyone asking about the evidence unless they're just stupid. It would be like telling on themselves," Brittany replied.

"Yeah right, but you'd be surprised how dumb some people can really be. Just stick to the truth—the victim is not pressing charges, so the evidence is not being processed or stored. I'll let you know when I find out anything significant."

"Okay, I got it," Brittany replied.

The meeting was cut short when John received a text from his sister, who told him their mother had been rushed to the emergency room and he should be there. "Look, Britt, here's some cash to cover our coffee and extra if you want some breakfast. I have to go. My mom is at the E.R. I'll catch up with you later."

"I hope she's okay; call me if you need anything," she replied.

Sierra tried to ignore an annoying, repeated text alert that woke her from a slumbering sleep. She moaned, "No, not now." With her hair tousled and a frown on her face, she grabbed her phone and mumbled, "This better be important," then with a single sweep, she tossed her blankets aside and sat up in bed to address the alert.

John: *Mom's in the E.R. It's pretty serious, if you want to come down to the hospital.*

Sierra: *On my way.*

"Shit," Sierra said out loud and without hesitation, she grabbed her blue jeans off the chair and hurriedly put them on. After slipping into her boots, she took a quick glance into the mirror. "Ugh, I need a shower," but knew she didn't have time. She tied her hair up, and then put on her favorite, well-worn ball cap, and just before she walked out the door, she remembered Bear. "Shit, come on, Bear, outside, and take care of your business quick; I need to get out of here." While she waited on him, Sierra made herself a thermos of black coffee, then went to peek in on Carmen. She wanted her to know that she'd be back in a couple of hours. After tapping on her bedroom door, there was no response from Carmen. Sierra cracked it open to find that she wasn't in there. She made a quick search through the house, but no trace of her. "Shit, shit, shit!" she exclaimed. After letting Bear inside, she noticed Carmen's boot prints through the freshly fallen snow; they led into the woods. "Oh, fucking great, no note. I wonder what the hell she's thinking. She's not even been home a day. She's in no shape to be traipsing through the damn woods alone!" Torn between going to see John's mom in the hospital or tracking after Carmen for her own safety was not a choice she wanted to make.

A few seconds later, Sierra was alerted by the back door opening, and in walked Carmen. "Hey, I got us some breakfast," she said, and with a proud smile on her face, Carmen held up two wild rabbits that she had successfully hunted.

Sierra was relieved to see her. "Oh nice, good job. Listen, I have an emergency in town. I'll be gone a couple of hours. Could I ask a favor? I'd like you to stay in the house while I'm gone. I'm just worried about you going in the woods alone. I'd like to be with you on any adventures like this until we catch your assailants. Besides that, you're still fragile and trying to heal."

"I'm fine alone. I have my gun loaded, I'm prepared this time, and I am feeling a little tender after that hunt," Carmen replied.

"Please, Carmen, just stay in while I'm gone, and we will talk about this when I get home. I really need to go now. John's mom is in the E.R. It's serious."

"Okay, I'll stay in. You go. I'll be fine."

"Thanks, and good job on the hunt this morning; we'll make a good dinner with that tonight. I'll call when I'm on my way back."

"Okay, be safe," Carmen replied.

"Thanks, and make sure to lock up."

As with most people, hospitals were never a favorite place for Sierra. She felt overwhelmed this morning with everything that had taken place and found the quiet drive to town peaceful. Sierra prayed for John's mother, Josie, and for Carmen; her heart went out to them. She recalled once, just days after her own mother had passed away, Josie had taken her for a drive to a secluded, beautiful river place, sacred to their Native heritage. "Here," she had said, "come, take my hand, child, wade in these waters with me; together we will wash away our pain and free ourselves to live on in peace." A tear streamed down Sierra's face as she remembered, then she took a deep breath and slowly released it, reassuring herself that everything would be okay.

John was relieved when Sierra showed up. "I'm so glad you could make it. Mom thinks of you as one of her own."

"I feel the same about her, John; what's going on with her?" she asked.

"It's not good. She was diagnosed six months ago with a late stage-four lung cancer; she didn't bother telling any of us about it. We just found out today," he replied.

"She probably wanted to save her kids from the pain of it all; I'm so sorry, John."

"I'm sure Mom has her reasons. She is certainly stubborn," he replied with a forced smile.

"Can I go see her?" Sierra asked.

"She's with a specialist right now; it'll be another thirty minutes before she can have visitors. I could use a cigarette; want to join me in my truck for a smoke?"

"Sure, but I want to say hi to your sister first."

Sierra approached Lori with a hug and whispered, "It will all be okay. Your mother is a very strong woman, whatever the outcome."

"Thank you, Sierra. You're right, Mom is strong. I just hope she is strong enough to fight the odds," Lori replied.

Sierra hugged her tight. "I'm here for you, Lori. Your family is very special to me. I'll be back soon, if you would like to talk more; John and I will be outside if we're needed."

"Thanks, Sierra, and don't you know cigarettes will kill you?"

Sierra nodded her head. "Yeah, something to think about," then smiled and walked out with John.

They felt the brisk air hitting their backs as they went through the parking garage. "I hope you fixed that heater in your truck," Sierra teased.

"I wasn't aware I had a problem with my heater, smartass."

"Ouch. Just kidding, John."

"I know, sorry. I'm just feeling a little touchy today with Mom and then everything else that's been going on," he replied.

"Yeah, I know exactly how you feel; it's been a bizarre week for all of us." Just as Sierra was getting ready to snuff out her cigarette, she noticed a crumpled piece of paper on the floorboard of John's truck; it resembled her personal stationery. With her inquisitive nature, she picked it up then pressed it out. John sat quietly as he watched her. Sierra was confused and surprised by what she found, as she read silently to herself, *Carmen I'll be back soon. If you wake up before I get back, make yourself at home.* "Um, why in the hell is this note in your truck?" a perplexed Sierra asked.

"I stopped by your place yesterday afternoon and nobody answered the door, so I used the spare key to let myself in. I totally forgot Carmen was there. I saw the note on the table and read it. I put it in my pocket and didn't give it a second thought. Just before I left, I noticed your horse was gone. I figured I'd find you doing exactly what I caught you doing—investigating without me," he replied.

"Well, don't walk in like that again, especially while Carmen is there! She would have freaked out had she found you without me. Geez, guys just don't get it; sometimes I'd really like to slap the shit out of you again!"

John flushed at her comments and couldn't reply. He got out of the truck and went back to his mother's bedside. Sierra followed him in and took a brief visit with Josie before they were asked to leave again.

"I have a lot to do today and should get going. Please call if there are any changes, or if I can do anything," Sierra told the family.

On the way out, she put her hand in her jacket pocket and felt the note she had found in John's truck. She was unsettled about his explanation, thinking, *it doesn't make any sense to me.* Then a funny feeling churned through her stomach when she recalled what Carmen had said late yesterday afternoon: *I had a disturbing dream. I felt like someone was watching me, clicking a lighter lid—the same sound and feeling I had when I was being attacked.* Sierra shook her head and said aloud, "No, not even possible. I must really be on edge."

Before making it out of town, Sierra remembered Bair-Hill feed store just as she passed it, thinking, *I'm such an airhead this morning.* She made a U-turn and went back to pick up grain for her horse. As she entered the store, Sierra was welcomed by a big smile from an old friend of the family. "Hey, Carole," Sierra said, as she approached the counter. "I'm glad to see you working today; I missed you. How was that vacation to Hawaii?"

Carole smiled. "Well deserved. We had a very nice time, and so did our dogs, Ace and Jack, but I'm glad to be back home, and so is Loren."

"I can imagine. I would love a vacation, but you're right, there is no place like home."

"So what can I do for you today, Sierra?"

"I need four fifty-pound bags of sweet feed loaded on my truck, and did you ever get that order of Wild Blue dog food in yet?"

"Let me check on that." She paused. "No, not yet but looks like it should be on Friday morning's delivery," Carole replied.

"Okay, go ahead and charge me for two fifty-pound bags, and I'll be back to pick them up."

"All right, hon. I'll call out to the warehouse and have one of the guys load you up."

"Thanks, Carole, you're a doll."

"Oh hey, I heard Josie Buck was picked up by the ambulance this morning. Do you know why?" Carole asked.

"Yes, I've been there to see her. It doesn't look so good. John said she was diagnosed with stage-four cancer. Her kids just found out about her illness today; she was keeping it from them."

"Oh, that's a shame; she's such a good woman. I'll send flowers, and hopefully it'll make her smile," Carole replied.

"That would be nice. You're very thoughtful, Carole. Not to be rude, but I need to get my butt back home and feed my horse. I'm sure she's wondering where breakfast is. Nice seeing you, and glad you had a good time away from the Big Sky Country."

"We did. Thanks, Sierra. See you later, hon."

"Oh, wait, I almost forgot. I'd like to get a hundred bails of alfalfa hay delivered today, if possible. I'll be home all afternoon, if you give me a time."

"I can do that. How does one o'clock sound?" Carole asked.

"Perfect. See you then."

On her drive home, she commanded her GPS to call a young man who often helped her with chores in the barn. "Hey, good morning, Bryce. Hope I didn't wake you up."

A groggy Bryce replied, "No, it's okay. I was just getting up. What can I do for you?"

"Can you come by my place; say around twelve-thirty or so? I have some hay that needs loaded into the loft and a few other chores that need done."

"Sure. See you then," Bryce replied.

Bear was alerted when he heard Sierra pull into the drive. He pranced and whined at the front door until Carmen let him out. He bolted to her with a bouncing excitement. "Hey, hi buddy. I missed you, too, you big old baby."

Carmen was standing on the porch and yelled, "Welcome home. Do you need help bringing anything in?"

"No, but thanks. I stopped by the feed store on my way home." Then she walked to the back of her truck, took a hunting knife from her boot and cut open a bag of feed. "How has your morning been?" she asked.

"Fine. I've been catching up on entries in my research journal; nothing overly exciting," Carmen replied.

After scooping out enough feed for the horse, Sierra jokingly asked, "Do you have those rabbits skinned yet, Ms. Wilderness Woman?"

"As a matter of fact, I certainly do," Carmen giggled.

After making her way up on the porch, Sierra gently hugged Carmen. "Thanks for waiting inside while I was gone."

"Oh, and I thought that hug was because you missed me," Carmen smiled.

"I see, well, I have another one just for that," she said, then gave Carmen another close embrace.

"By the way, that's a hell of a knife you took from your boot earlier. I could have used that to skin those rabbits," Carmen teased.

"Yeah, good old Uncle Sam-issued. I was in the Army when I got that, an Airborne Ranger. I am one of the few women who made it through the grueling training course," she gloated.

"Very impressive," Carmen replied with admiration.

"Thank you. I was proud to serve." Then she took a cute little bow, accepting the compliment. "By the way, Bryce, a young man from the Reynolds farm, will be coming by to help with some chores in the barn today—just thought I'd let you know."

"Thanks for the heads up, Sierra. I wouldn't want to shoot an innocent bystander, thinking he was a rabbit," she teased.

"Oh, Lord, that would suck," Sierra giggled. "He's a good kid and not afraid of a little hard work. His folks are both doctors up here at the local hospital. I heard they were out of town, at some seminar this week. I'm sure he could probably use the extra money."

"Well, the way I see it, Sierra, there's nothing wrong with having a strong guy around to take care of some of the heavier work. I love my neighbor Jack back home; he's perfect. He helps with large projects, just a friend that expects nothing in return."

"That's always nice," Sierra replied. "I've never been interested in guys. My first and only girlfriend, Sadie, and I signed up for the Army together. We dated for five years, and then after she served her three years, she went off to college, at a university in Illinois. She earned her bachelor's degree in investigative reporting and works somewhere in Idaho now. We stayed in contact for the first year then it slowly faded away. I haven't seen her since."

"I'm sorry, Sierra. Sounds like we have things in common—I lost my only girlfriend two years ago, but she was hit by a drunk driver on her way to meet me. We were celebrating our fifth-year anniversary. That was very tough time, to say the least."

"Wow that had to be hard. I'm very sorry," Sierra replied.

"Yes, it was very hard," she paused. "I thought I had been through the worst in my life when I lost Kara that day." She took a deep breath, and then lowered her head. "Until I woke up on a beautiful morning and the temp was a little brisk, but the sun was shining, and I thought if I could make it out before it starts raining, that I could spend the rest of the day analyzing my samples. The smell of the air was fresh and inviting. I drank my coffee, black with two sugars, then loaded my backpack and left for work. While I was bent over retrieving samples from the river, I was cowardly grabbed from behind and blindfolded. My clothes and dignity were ripped from me. I was beaten and kicked until I was forced to quit fighting. I was made to get on my hands and knees; the rough, rocky ground cut into my flesh, as he pressed his smelly body on me. I was beyond humiliated—I was broken. His friend stood there and coached him while he clicked his lighter lid. Then they left me for dead, but I was smarter than them," she said, stone-faced without any tears. "I survived; that was their worse mistake."

Sierra heard all of this loud and clear, disturbed by the picture that was painted. She was overcome by her friend's horrid experience. She cried the tears that Carmen couldn't. "Thank you for sharing that with me. I know it wasn't easy for you, Carmen."

"Sierra, help me."

"Help you? I don't understand."

"Help me catch these guys. Help me make them pay for what they did to me."

"I can call John if you're ready to reopen the investigation."

"No, not that kind of help. Never mind; forget I said anything. I will help myself."

"Talk to me, Carmen. What are you thinking?" Sierra asked.

"I want to find and kill them both. Watch them suffer the humiliation they put me through."

"Carmen, shush, no more talk like that. You could lose your career if ever caught, or worse, what if something went wrong and the tables turned on you? Those guys are obviously heartless and low-life. They don't have a conscience."

"Sierra, we have both been afflicted by cowardly men. You did your mother a great service when you shot and killed her rapist, whatever the circumstances were. He would be out walking the streets by now, had he gone to jail, and your mother would still be dead. I understand why you did what you had to do back then. You didn't have a choice in the matter. If we took our time, I'm certain we could make a foolproof plan."

"We?" She paused. "Oh God, I need a stiff drink," Sierra replied.

"Make that two, a double if you don't mind."

With all the talk of revenge, Sierra jumped when Bear started barking at Bryce's arrival. She yelled out the front door, "I'll be out in a minute. I need to get my boots on," then turned to Carmen. "I won't be long; go ahead and pour us a shot."

Sierra smiled when she saw the mounded truckload of hay coming up the drive. After showing Bryce where to put the bales, she pointed out the feed bags that were still in the back of her truck. "If you can move these to the bins in the barn, I would appreciate it, and be careful with this one," she said. "I had to cut it open earlier. Jess was past due for her breakfast. When you're done, come on up to the house, and I'll pay you."

"Thanks, Sierra. This shouldn't take too long."

"No problem, Bryce. I'm thankful for your help. When are your parents expected back anyway?"

"Saturday, I think," he replied.

"That's good. Well, okay then, I'll let you get busy."

Bryce couldn't help but steal a glance when she walked away. *Damn, she's hot for an older woman,* he thought to himself. Not that Sierra was that old, but to Brice, anyone over forty was old.

After stomping her boots off, Sierra was ready for that drink. "See, I told you I wouldn't be long. Wow, look at you. A girl after my own heart, with our shots already poured," she smiled.

Carmen giggled. "Yes, I guess I am." After passing Sierra her shot, Carmen raised her drink in a toast. "I'm thankful our paths crossed in these unfortunate times, and I'm thankful it was you who found me. Here's to us sharing a tie that binds us."

"You mean bonds us," Sierra replied.

"Yeah, bonds us," then they tapped the shot glasses together and with clenched jaws, felt the stout bourbon trickle down their throats.

The next few shots seemed to go down much easier. For many, whiskey can be a natural truth serum and a factor of boldness or bad judgment for others. However, the girls were enjoying themselves. "So, are you in?" Carmen asked.

"In?" Sierra questioned, then added, "I hope you mean another shot, or even a dip in the hot tub?"

"No, silly, although the hot tub sounds like a great idea. I'm talking about help, the type of help that will get these guys who attacked me. But yes, I can pour us another shot. I have that down pat," Carmen smiled.

"Ah, I see. Can we talk about that in the morning over coffee? I am really enjoying the mood right now and don't want a buzz kill, if you know what I mean."

"Yes, that's good. But promise you will hear me out."

After raising another shot, "I promise to hear your ideas through," Sierra replied. "Hey, how about some music? We need to get this party started!"

The cabin was full of laughter as the girls became more inebriated. They were relaxed, just living in the moment. Sierra reached for Carmen's hand after a favorite saucy song came on. "Come on, dance with me; it's by Paula Cole, called *Feeling Love*; I promise to be gentle with you."

Carmen laughed and replied, "Well, as long as you promise to be gentle; I'm still very sore. But yes, I'd be honored to dance with you anytime, Sierra; besides, it does have a really relaxing feel to it."

Sierra helped Carmen up from the cozy couch, and then gingerly embraced her. "I'm not squeezing too tight, am I?"

"No, you're fine. This is perfect."

It wasn't long before the couple made dancing together look like a poetic art. They slowly swayed to the mellow tune, while their slender bodies seemed to naturally fit one another. They rested their cheeks against the others. Sierra was enticed by the herbal fragrance in Carmen's long, blonde hair. "Mmm, this is nice, so nice. Your hair smells really good, but I'm pretty sure we need to take a break and just sit back down."

Carmen could sense Sierra's attraction but knew that she herself was not ready to cross any lines that might lead to a sexual encounter. She just wasn't ready. "I'm sorry."

"Don't be sorry; it was a very nice dance. Thank you for sharing it with me," Sierra replied. After they sat back down, Sierra placed a throw pillow on her lap then tapped it. "Hey, you're welcome to rest your head here. I give an awesome hair rub."

"Mmm, hmm, you don't have to twist my arm on that. I love my hair rubbed," Carmen replied.

The music faded into the background, and they enjoyed the moment, gaining a soulful bond. Carmen enjoyed the comfort of this harmless affection and the gentleness of Sierra's touch. Without words, Sierra hummed a quiet tune, as she continued to rub Carmen's hair, ever so tenderly. Carmen slowly faded into a slumber from the tranquil experience. She felt safe and relaxed for the first time in days since her horrid encounter. Sierra could feel her peace as she slept there so soundly and was glad she felt relaxed enough to trust her. It wasn't long after that Sierra became tired as well. She was thoughtful not to disturb Carmen and slowly stretched her legs out onto the coffee table. After covering Carmen up with a quilt, she then covered herself. They slept there in a blissful slumber, in the comfort of each other's presence. About four a.m., Sierra began to feel the repercussions of sleeping in a sitting-up position. She realized her neck was stiff after she glanced down to see Carmen was still fast asleep. "Oh shit, ah," she moaned.

After hearing Sierra's sound of anguish, Carmen woke up. "Hey, are you okay?" she asked as she sat up.

"Yeah, my neck is stiff, but not too bad. I'm going to head to bed and stretch out." Just as she stood up, Sierra looked at Carmen sitting there, so beautiful with her hair a mess. "You know, if it's not too weird for you, you're welcome to sleep in my room with me. I'll be good. We could just snuggle. It's been a long time for me—cuddling, that is. I think it would be nice."

Carmen smiled. "Yeah, for me, too. Cuddling, that is," then followed Sierra to her bed.

"You can sleep on either side. I usually sleep in the middle," Sierra giggled.

"Oh, you don't say. It just happens that I like the middle, too," Carmen teased.

"Well, then, it should make cuddling super easy, then."

After getting under the covers, they both complained about the cold sheets. Sierra said, "Hurry, roll against me, and I'll keep you warm. I've been told I'm like a human furnace."

"Oh my goodness, you really are warm," Carmen replied, as they spooned close together. "I must confess when I'm cold, I usually sleep with my socks on and sometimes my hoodie pulled up over my head."

"Oh my God, that would kill me. I would literally suffocate. My feet have to hang out from under the covers, and the thought of a hoodie would devastate me," Sierra replied.

Carmen found her comment entertaining. "You're just silly."

"I'm serious, though. I can't stand clothes on when I sleep: I feel like they are choking me," Sierra replied.

"Well, then, why do you have clothes on now? Get comfy, this is your bed. But I'm keeping my clothes on."

"That's cool, and thank you, I appreciate your understanding. I hope it doesn't make you uncomfortable."

"No, I feel rather safe with you," Carmen replied. The girls slept in with their legs and arms wrapped around one another on that lazy Saturday morning. They enjoyed the bliss of being together in the midst of a somber rest.

Later into the morning, the last thing Sierra wanted to do was to check an incoming text from John. She recognized the fact that it must be urgent, considering the number of back-to-back messages coming in. Careful not to wake Carmen, she gently got out of bed and went to the kitchen. After placing a frozen bag of peas on her forehead, she hoped to ease the discomfort from drinking the night before. Then she called John. "Hey, buddy, I see you texted me. I haven't read them yet. What's up and how's your mom?" Sierra asked.

"She passed away this morning at four-twenty." He paused in silence for a few seconds. "She went peacefully."

"I'm so sorry, John. How are you and the family holding up?"

"We are all doing fine. I think it'll take a day or two before it really sinks in," he replied.

"Have you guys talked about funeral services yet?" Sierra asked.

"Mom wanted to be cremated, so we'll honor her wishes and spread her ashes in the rivers of her Native land. I'll let you know more when the actual time arrives."

"Thanks, John. Is there anything I can do for you right now?"

"No, I just wanted to let you know about Mom and that I'll be gone a couple of weeks, handling her estate matters," he sighed then changed the subject before he became emotional. "So, how is Carmen coming along? Is she healing well?"

"Yes, she is doing very well. She is surprisingly strong-willed. I have enjoyed having the company."

"I'm glad you have someone there with you. I worry about you being out there alone with her attacker still on the loose. Has she remembered anything, or changed her mind about pressing charges?"

"No, she still has no interest in that. She is afraid it would ruin her career, so I'm not pushing the issue; it has to be her own decision."

"Well, for my own sake and yours, with my paid leave of absence, I would still like to get to the bottom of this."

"I understand that, John. But please respect Carmen's wishes in the meantime. She doesn't want or need to be pushed by anyone."

"Sierra, this is more for your protection. I don't want this happening to anyone, especially someone I consider like a sister to me."

"Thanks, you're very sweet, but you have a lot to take care of with your family right now. Don't worry about me too much; you have plenty of time for that stuff."

"You're right about that. I'll be in touch in a few days. I'll have a date and time that we'll be spreading Mom's ashes."

"Thanks buddy. Send my best to the family. Love you and talk to you later."

"Love you, too. Talk soon."

Sierra sat at the kitchen table for a few minutes, taking it all in. She remembered how hard it was to be without her mom, even to this very day. Then she felt the tender touch of Carmen come up behind her and gently touch her shoulder. She whispered, "Good morning, Sunshine. The frozen peas are telling me you have a hangover, and if so, are they helping?"

"Yes, they really are, and good morning back to you," Sierra replied with a smile.

"Then in that case, I might need a bag, too."

"I have some Tylenol in the cabinet above the microwave," Sierra added.

"No, I'm sure this will be fine. Would you like me to grab you a couple?" she asked.

"Sure, can't hurt. Thanks."

"So, Sierra, what's on your agenda today?"

"Food, to start. I'm starving. I'd like to make us some breakfast, then go out and feed my horse. After that, I'm not sure. It's going to be a beautiful day; maybe we could go on a hike together if you're feeling up to it."

"Yes, matter of fact, I am, and wow, you're my kind of girl. How about you go feed your horse, and I'll make us breakfast?"

"Hey," she smiled. "I like the sound of that. 'Teamwork is always better work,' my mom used to say."

"Sounds like you had a smart mom. I'm glad you have fond memories of her," Carmen replied. "I wish I could say the same for my dad."

"I sure do, and I'm sorry your father was a hard man. Not to change the subject so quickly, but I talked to my friend John early this morning. He said his mother passed away; she was like a second mom to me."

"I'm sorry to hear that. Are you handling it okay?"

"Yeah, I just hope they're able to handle it. They are all a very close family."

"I understand. It's hard to lose the ones we love, even if they were a monster. I'm just glad I didn't know about the lifestyle my dad lived. It was hard enough suffering the abuse he inflicted on me. Then to learn about the things he had been accused of, just broke my heart. It's sad to say, but he deserved what he had coming to him," Carmen replied. "But enough of all that. Let's get busy so we can get to that hike."

Sierra lowered her head. "I don't know how to reply to that. I'm sorry. However, I do need to get Jess fed. I'll see you in about thirty minutes. I need to spread some fresh straw and load the hay bin."

Carmen smiled. "You make that sound kind of sexy." Sierra just nodded her head and grinned.

After rummaging through the fridge, Carmen found some fruit salad, sausage links and whole-wheat bread, thinking to herself, *Okay, so fruit is always a good thing, and we'll need that extra protein for our hike, and yep, bread for fiber. I'd say that's a healthy breakfast.* She also found some trail mix and deer jerky and prepared to take along a bag for their adventure.

Sierra came in to a beautifully set table and such a sweet breakfast. "Whoa, this is amazing! You're amazing! Want to get married?" she teased.

"You're funny. I could be crazy, and then you'd be stuck with me," Carmen taunted back in retaliation.

"Crazy can be a good thing sometimes, but not crazy-crazy," Sierra replied in a joking manner.

"Yeah," Carmen smiled in return. "I agree, not crazy-crazy."

After a filling breakfast, Sierra cleared the table, and then approached Carmen with a warming hug. "That was an excellent breakfast, Carmen, just right. Thank you. I'll get on my hiking boots and grab a backpack. Are you ready for our morning excursion?"

"You're welcome, it was my pleasure, and yes, I'm ready. Hey, do you mind if I take along some testing gear? I'd like to grab some samples of the river water," Carmen asked.

"Sure, we'll be following the river most of the way. You might find some good sites for your research," Sierra replied.

"Excellent. I'll grab my stuff, and we're out of here."

After making a double check, Sierra felt prepared. "Okay, backpack loaded, gun loaded, water bottle loaded. Awesome; let's roll."

Carmen tapped her bag and smiled. "Lunch, gear and gun loaded. Glad you have water."

"Come on, Bear, let's go, buddy. So we'll head up the North Ridge here," she pointed. "It takes us through some beautiful, wooded sites. Then we'll head down the pass through the Native territory; that's my old stomping grounds."

Carmen nodded her head then took a deep inhale. "What a beautiful morning for a hike and the smell of the cool, brisk air is always so reviving; I love it up here—the lack of pollution in the atmosphere and the simple purity is what drives my passion for the work that I do. It's so important to preserve and protect our ozone from contaminates. Not to mention the people who are affected by polluted water sources."

"Wow, I love your passion and understanding. I couldn't imagine living anywhere else," Sierra replied.

Carmen was surprised the trail was rather easy to hike. "I have to compliment you on the beaten trail, and I can see you must travel it often."

"Thanks. Hiking is one of my favorite things to do; hence I chose the profession I am in. I usually enjoy leading most expeditions. I try to keep the path intact as much as I can, but the fallen leaves can hide branches and other timber that has broken off through the autumn season. I usually take my Gator and machete through the trails a couple of times a year, or after a bad storm, but haven't had much time lately. So do try and watch your step; I'd hate to see you trip."

"Sounds like a lot of upkeep and hard work," Carmen replied.

Sierra smiled. "It is, but worth it. This is like my playground. Hey, see up there past the two big pine trees? Just over that ridge is a waterfall. When we ascend down the pass, you should be able to get some good readings for your study."

"Great. That would be a good testing site. The water should be filtered well; let's hope it tests good, for all's sake," Carmen replied.

"I admire the work you do, Carmen. You put so much of yourself into this, and I can see you really care about the welfare and health of so many people. It's a shame that people fall victim due to such careless work ethics."

Carmen giggled. "Well, thank you for noticing, Sierra. It means a lot to me that you support and believe in my cause. There are far too many people who don't take it seriously enough—that is, until they lose someone they love to some disease due to neglect or careless business practices. It's hard enough to lose someone you love, but to see them suffer would be heart-wrenching."

"I totally understand that. Ah, here we are at the top of the mountain. I'm impressed you kept up so well." Sierra stood there and took her backpack off. "This is one of my favorite high points; you can see for miles over the forest. It's also a favorite break point to absorb the peace and tranquility." Then she took a rolled joint from her backpack. "Want to partake in a little buzz?" she asked.

"You can't be serious. Wow, it's been ages since I've done this, but why not?" she giggled.

"When I was a teenage girl, I'd come here and watch the bald eagles gliding over. They were in a journey of the hunt; I used to wish I could fly like that."

"And you don't wish that now?" Carmen asked with a straight face.

Sierra replied with a smile. "Hmm, good question, but I'm more a feet-on-the-ground-type girl now. I'd say my spirit animal would be a wolf—one that doesn't bite," she giggled.

"Hmm, a wolf, that's interesting. Especially knowing your last name is Wolfe. I especially dig the fact that you don't bite," Carmen replied.

"Of course, a nice wolf, dedicated and faithful, to be exact. A wolf also mates for life. Someday I hope to have a mate for life. They are also very family-oriented and protective of their loved ones."

"Ah, I see. I just never thought of it that way before. It's a noble thing to you and says a lot about your character. I like that."

"Yes, it's a good feeling or dream, I guess. But one day I will share my life with that perfect woman."

"I am certain you will," Carmen replied.

After traveling about an eighth of a mile, Sierra pointed out the waterfall. "If you want to go see it before we get to the bottom, I can take you there."

"I'd be crazy to say no to such a majestic beauty of life," Carmen replied.

"Good, well, let's get to it."

The powerful thrash and flow of the fall drowned out most sound. Carmen yelled, "This is magnificent, Sierra!"

Sierra yelled back, "Next summer, if you're still around, we'll come back here and take a real shower!"

"It's a date!" Carmen replied.

"Follow me, I want to show you something; it's just over here." Sierra fought her way through the brush just off trail and came to a small cave. "Check this out. When John and I were kids, we'd play here during the summer. Once a mountain lion surprised us, and John shot him with a slingshot, right between the eyes. It stunned him pretty good, and as soon as he gathered his senses, he scampered off. It kind of gives me the willies now that I'm older and know the risk of going into a cave in these parts. There could be anything staying inside for the winter months ahead."

"This is fascinating, and I'm glad John encouraged the lion to leave; that could have been a disaster. I have an odd but direct question, if you don't mind. Have you and John ever . . . you know?" Carmen asked.

"Hell no, John and I are like brother and sister. He has always known his boundaries with me."

"That's great, Sierra. I'm sorry if I pried."

"Don't be sorry, silly. I would have probably asked you the same thing, had the tables been turned. Are you ready to finish our journey down?"

"Sure, let's do this." Carmen found it tough to keep up with a vigorous and motivated Sierra, who was trotting down the mountain trail like a whitetail deer. "Hey, you think you can slow up just a dash? You have to remember I wasn't raised hiking mountains. I'm not as adapted to the terrain as you are, and my ribs are still very tender."

"Oops, sorry about that; are you okay? I wasn't thinking." Sierra then slowed her pace down. "Is that better?"

"Much better. This way, I can enjoy your company, too," Carmen replied.

Sierra smiled. "You're very sweet. I'm fortunate to know you, and if you don't mind, I have a question for you. Have you always known you liked women?"

"Yes, I guess so. When I was younger, I dated a couple of guys but never felt comfortable. After I met my first and only girlfriend, I knew I would never turn back. What about you?" Carmen asked.

"No, I've always known I was sexually attracted to women. Okay, careful on this decline; it can be tricky. We are almost there, and you'll be able to get those samples you want. It's just about a sixteenth of a mile down and to the east; it's a great clearing for the after-flow of the waterfall."

Carmen laughed. "Almost a sixteenth of a mile to the east, and that's almost there?" she asked. "Oh my girl, I see I have a ball of energy on my hands." After reaching their destination, Carmen successfully retrieved some appropriate samples from the water source. She was pleased, and then sat down on the bank for a break and to enjoy the blissful scenery. "I brought some deer jerky and a couple of apples, along with some granola, if you'd like to partake."

"Carmen, you truly are an amazing woman. I was just thinking breakfast has worn off. Thank you for thinking about this."

"My pleasure, but the motive was selfish. I get cranky when I'm hungry, so I rarely go anywhere without some type of food fix, either in my purse or my backpack," she giggled.

The girls were unaware of the clandestine eyes that were peering through the thick of the forest. A stranger moved closer to see the two women better, thinking, *That looks like the bitch I left for dead a few weeks back.* Then as he prowled closer, Bear caught his scent and began growling a low, deep grumble, which caught Sierra's attention immediately.

After drawing Bear back, she discreetly took a .45 handgun from her pack and stood up, then called out, "Hey, who's there?"

A man appeared. He was certain Carmen wouldn't be able to recognize him because he had blindfolded her during the attack, so he decided to yell out, "Just a fisherman, heading to the river. No harm intended."

"Then show yourself," Sierra called out.

The man approached the couple and stopped on guard at Bear growling. Sierra could sense his nervousness over the dog. "Bear, easy. I got this," she said.

With his fishing pole and tackle box in hand, he held them up. "See? Just wanting to fish."

"You do know this is private property—a Native reservation. There is no fishing here unless you have prior approval. Do you have a permit?" Sierra asked.

"Actually, no. I didn't realize it was private property." He noticed the gun then smirked, "I guess I'll just have to find a new place to fish then." As he started to walk away, he mumbled, "Fucking bitches."

After hearing his snide remark, Carmen was overwhelmed with the cold chills. She recognized his voice then she whispered to Sierra, "Ask him where he's staying and what he's doing in these parts."

"Hey, stranger, what brings you to these parts?"

The man stopped, and then replied, "Fishing, like I said."

"No, why are you in this area altogether? I don't recognize you."

"I run a fracking site just south of here, oil drilling, just like a hundred others trying to make a living," he replied.

"Do you have a name?"

"People call me Piper."

"Okay, Piper, if you want to fish, you can check out the river flowing on the south side territory. As long as you have a license, the game warden won't have any reason to stop you."

"I'll be sure to do that."

After the man left, Sierra noticed Carmen's hands were trembling. "Are you okay?" she asked with concern. "Talk to me, Carmen. Did you recognize him?"

"I don't know, I was blindfolded, but his voice was haunting. It sounded like my attacker's voice, but I can't be certain. I could smell him from here. His stench was familiar, too."

Sierra was concerned. "I'll probe around and find who he's working for. Piper is an unusual name; somebody will know him at the local bar."

"Please, Sierra, let's not talk about this right now. I just want to get back to your cabin."

"No problem, hon; let's get you back home."

After a long hike back, Carmen made sure to call dibs on the first shower. "Don't worry; I'll save some hot water for you—that is, unless you want to join me. You know conserving water is always a good thing, right?"

Sierra was shocked. "A shower together?"

"Yes, but I understand if my battered body scares you. It scares me, too."

"Nothing about you scares me, Carmen. I guess I'm just not sure what you're insinuating."

"Well, I was thinking it would be nice to have someone wash my back. It's hard to raise my arms or reach, without reminding myself that my ribs are tender."

"Yeah, I can only imagine the discomfort. Heck yeah, I'd love to shower with you," Sierra replied.

When Sierra saw the bruises all over Carmen's back, her heart went out to her. She washed her gently and thought,

That fucking bastard. He deserves to die. Then in a soft, caring tone, she spoke to Carmen. "I'm sorry he hurt you."

Carmen turned around to face Sierra, then hugged her close, and as the water ran steadily over their bodies, Carmen whispered, "I'm okay now and thankful you are in my life. He doesn't get to have my happiness. These bruises are temporary, and I will heal, but I'll never forget."

Sierra could feel Carmen's breath next to her. Their eyes locked, and they brushed their lips against each other. "I'm afraid if I kiss you that I won't be able to stop myself. I really like you, and the last thing I want to do is make you feel like you need to please me."

"I know I must look hideous. I'm sorry," Carmen replied.

"You're beautiful, Carmen, and trust me, I do desire you, in a very big way. I just don't want to rush you. I know you've been through a lot."

Carmen smiled. "Thank you. I'm sure you're right."

Then, just before Carmen got out from the shower, Sierra wrapped her in her arms and kissed her ever so gently on the lips. "You're amazing, and we will know when the time is right."

The girls were exhausted from the day's adventures. They discussed dinner plans, then Sierra picked a quarter up from the coffee table. "Let's flip for who will cook dinner."

Carmen giggled and snatched the quarter from Sierra. "No! No flipping, it's your turn. I made breakfast and a snack for us today, remember."

"Oh yeah, you sure did," then patted Carmen on the knee and said, "Okay, well, fair is fair."

Sierra prepared a lovely salmon dinner topped with sautéed mushroom and onions, cooked in garlic and soy sauce. She served it with a side garden salad. Before setting the table, she chilled a bottle of white Chardonnay wine. Then she lit two beautiful candles and stepped back to take a look at her accomplishment. She was pleased to present this special meal. "Dinner's ready, Carmen."

Carmen's eyes lit up when she saw such a nice meal. "Wow, breathtaking, and it looks delicious. I thought I was the master at setting a nice table, but looks like you have that touch of class, too."

"Well, only when I feel like it. Truth is, when it's just Bear and I, we usually pop a pizza or something simple in and sit in front of the television, feet on the coffee table and all," she smiled.

"Yeah, I know how that goes. It sounds very familiar, except I have never had my own dog before. I can see now how having one can be comforting, as far as having a companion. I really like Bear, by the way. He's a great dog with so much character," Carmen replied.

"Yes, he certainly is. I don't know what I'd do without him sometimes. He certainly keeps me entertained with his good nature. So, talk to me about today, Carmen. What if this guy Piper was the guy?"

"Then I would like to find out for sure; that would be my first step." She paused for a moment. "If I know beyond a shadow of a doubt that he is the man who raped me and left me for dead, I would kill him and dispose of his sorry ass somewhere deep in the wilderness. Besides, if it was him and he recognized me today, I'm certain he'll be looking to finish me off," Carmen replied with a nervous quiver in her voice. "But he had another guy with him that he referred to as 'Boss' that day—the fellow who was clicking the lighter lid or something that sounded like that—so if one goes, the other will have to go, too."

"Carmen that would be considered a double homicide, and, on top of that, premeditated. That would be life in prison or, worse, the death penalty if you were ever caught."

"Sierra, I understand that. My plan would be premeditated; I would think it through. Besides, if he did this to me, he's no doubt a brutal piece of shit that's done this before, maybe to several more innocent victims. Think about it, Sierra, if we were to find out—without a doubt—it was him, and we involved the law, he would do no more than five years at the max, with intent to kill. I refuse to have my face and name dragged through the public eye. My life and career would be ruined. That's such a waste, especially knowing he'd be free a few short years later," Carmen replied, then shook her head. "His awful body odor—it smelled hauntingly familiar today when he approached us."

"Yeah, he certainly stank, and I do understand your point about jail time. I'll help you investigate him as much as possible," Sierra replied.

"Thank you, Sierra. I'm glad you understand."

"My friend John will be coming around from time to time; we can't let him know about any of this. Carmen, it's vital we stay well under the radar when we start digging around. We can't leave any trails that would lead the law back to us, including network research. We can't use my computer. We'd have to research elsewhere if necessary."

"Yes, I agree with you. Just the two of us would know, and we won't speak a word of it to anyone, nor will we leave any type of trail. I won't rush a plan. I will think it through," Carmen replied.

"Okay, let's just sleep on it, and if you still feel the same way in the morning, we'll start our subtle investigation."

"Thank you, Sierra, from the bottom of my heart. You have no idea what this means to me."

"You're welcome, but remember, we have to make this right, better than right—it has to be perfect."

"I hope you know I probably won't get any sleep tonight. I'll be busy thinking about all of this, even after our long hike today," Carmen replied.

"Drink up on that wine; it'll help to relax those thoughts. Actually, we could both use a good night's sleep, especially after today." Then she paused for a brief second. "Hey, by the way, speaking of bed, I hope you want to share mine with me again tonight."

"Mmm, I was hoping you would ask. I enjoyed holding you last night; it was magical and felt so right," Carmen replied.

The girls enjoyed the rest of their evening together while snuggling in bed. They engaged in various conversations. They enjoyed taking the time to learn each other's favorite colors and the little things that matter. They spent time laughing and took turns sharing fun memories of their childhood past and the pranks they had pulled on friends when they were young. Their closeness allowed them to expose things they would have never shared with anyone else. Over the next few weeks, their relationship grew stronger, and so did Carmen.

CHAPTER THREE

Thunder rumbled on this brisk morning. The air was cold, and the relentless winds rocked a small fifteen-foot camper that was stationed at a remote fracking site near Bold Creek. Rain pounded the rocky, soiled ground, leaving the campsite a messy mud puddle. While nestled asleep on this early Sunday morning, Piper was awakened by a disturbing, constant drip that was pecking him on the forehead. Much like one could picture the Tasmanian devil; he grouched up from bed then peeked out the window to see a drenched, mud-covered mess outside. He grumbled, "I'm about sick of the shit, living like a freaking caveman, out in bum-fuck Egypt." He grabbed his phone. "Hey, Boss, I have a fucking mess out here. The camper is leaking from the downpour, and I need to get into town and pick up some tar to repair it."

"No problem just put it on the store credit. How is everything else going?" his boss asked.

"Well, a couple of weeks ago, I was taking my day off to do some fishing, and I can't be sure, but I think that nosy EPA agent is still alive. I thought I saw her with another woman near the river."

"Did she recognize you?"

"No, Boss, there would be no way in hell. I had her blindfolded when I took her down, remember?"

"Well, I guess this is what happens when you leave a boy to do a man's job," he replied with disgust.

"Sorry, Boss, I was sure she croaked when I suffocated her that day. I mean, she twitched, and her eyes were bulging through the blindfold. That bitch went limp, you saw her, she died. I'm certain whoever I saw was probably just some other whore that looked like her."

"You better hope it was someone different, Piper. And why the fuck would you even bother worrying me about this kind of shit if you yourself thought it could be someone else?"

"I don't know, but it had to be, Boss. I'm going to get off the phone and head to town for repair material. This place is a fucking mess."

"Forget about that woman, especially if she didn't recognize you, and if you run across her again, keep your dick in your pants this time and your mouth shut, moron! Any fuck-ups now could cost us our payday!" his boss replied.

"Yeah, yeah, okay."

"I'll be up that way in a couple of weeks. I've had some family business to deal with."

"Take your time, Boss, everything is fine."

Shortly after ending his call, Piper tromped through the muddy mess outside and to his truck. He grumbled to himself, "'Moron'? Who does he think he is? He's the moron who's not following code. Fucking pantywaist needs to clean up his business shit, if he's worried about losing money. Oh, I'm the big Boss Man! I'll be out of town for a couple of weeks, taking care of family bullshit. While I'm stuck in a fucking, leaking, tin can, doing all his dirty work. I'd like to slice his throat and run my eight inches up his tight ass, the little bitch boy."

Not real happy and with his face scrunched up, Piper walked into the local hardware store. "I need a five-gallon bucket of black roofing tar and something to mop it on with. You can put it on my boss's tab, Hilltop Drilling."

Just as he walked out of the store with his goods, Sierra recognized him as the man they had seen by the river a few weeks back. She and Carmen ducked down in the seat of their truck. "Carmen, wait here for a minute. I'm going to see what I can find out from my buddy Joe, the guy who runs the hardware store." She slipped out from her vehicle unnoticed and in to see her friend. "Hey, Joe, how have you been these days?"

"Oh, I could be better. The wife is having a hard time with Alzheimer's," he sighed. "How have you been, Sierra?"

"I've been busy as usual, never a dull day in the boondocks," she smiled. "I'm sorry to hear about your wife. I know that can't be easy."

"We manage. So what brings you in here today?" he asked.

"Well, the man that was just in here; do you know who he works for?"

"He just added some supplies to the Hilltop Drilling Company. I think they work the south end of the Bold Creek area, if I'm not mistaken. What's the interest?"

"No particular interest. Just thought I recognized him from somewhere earlier this week," Sierra replied.

"Well, if you're interested in meeting him, take my advice: He darn sure doesn't look like a keeper. He's a rude son of a bitch, if you don't mind me saying, and stinks from here to high heaven. I don't think that boy knows what a shower is."

Sierra laughed. "No, I'm sure he doesn't, and I'm definitely not looking or interested in meeting him. Like I said, I've seen him around a couple of times now, and just wanted to know who was occupying our neck of the woods."

Then she glanced at a tire gauge on the counter and said, "I need one of these, though."

Joe rang her item up and wished her a good day. "Hope your day is good, too, Joe, and please send my best to your wife."

"I'll do that, Sierra. Take care now."

After Sierra made her way back to the truck, Carmen's curiosity didn't waste a second. "So tell me, what did you learn about that creeper?"

"He works for Hilltop Drilling, and their site is in the Bold Creek area, just due south, a few miles from where I live."

"Hmm, well, that's a good start." Carmen smiled, then said, "Good job, pie face."

She smiled in return. "Pie face, huh? Hey, speaking of pie, Jude's Diner is just over there. How about some breakfast and coffee? She has the best food and desserts."

"Sure, I am famished," Carmen replied.

"Famished, you're funny today," Sierra teased.

"Wait, how do I look? I would hate for her to wonder about the bruises."

"There is barely any bruising left, Carmen. You've healed up beautifully."

Carmen nodded her head then looked into the passenger mirror. "Yeah, they are almost gone now. Another week and I'll be free of the reminder, at least that way, anyhow."

Sierra took Carmen's hand. "Come on, gorgeous, we're going to pig out."

After choosing a cozy corner booth in this country diner, Jude approached with menus. "Well, how in the heck are you, stranger? I haven't seen you in a coon's age, and who's this new face that's with you?" she asked.

"I've been good, thanks. I've been meaning to get here sooner but have been busy this autumn getting things buttoned up before winter. Carmen, this is Jude, our famous and beloved chef in the area, and highly respected by everyone."

"Hi, Carmen, welcome to my humble abode. I hope you enjoy the food."

"I'm looking forward to it, Jude."

After pushing her menu aside, Sierra placed her order. "I'll have biscuits and gravy with hash browns and bacon on the side. Plus, I'll have a cup of coffee with orange juice."

Carmen's eyes lit up at Sierra's choice. "I'll have the same, please. It certainly sounds delicious," then gave Jude a warming smile. Then she turned to Sierra. "When we leave here, do you feel like going south and snooping around? I'd like to find their drilling camp. Are you up for that?"

"I'm all for that, but I think we should give it a couple more weeks. We need to give him plenty of time to forget about seeing us. We don't need to alarm the creep," Sierra replied.

"It's already been several weeks, but I'm sure you're right. I'm just anxious to nail his ass to the wall."

"I can understand, Carmen, but we have to be patient and take our time, so there are no mistakes."

"Okay, we'll come up with a foolproof plan when we get home," Carmen replied.

After enjoying a filling breakfast, Sierra tapped her tummy. "That sounds good. Oh my goodness, I am stuffed," then pushed her plate back and flagged Jude over. "That was delicious, as always. Would you mind bringing me a go container for my leftover?"

"Sure and glad you enjoyed it. Would you like me to add pie? I have fresh peach today."

Carmen couldn't resist the temptation; peach had always been her favorite pie. "Yes, I would love some, and could you bring me a go container too, please? And Jude, it was an excellent breakfast. Five-star, without a doubt."

"Well, you made my day, Carmen. It's always nice to make another happy customer. I hope to see you girls back soon."

"My pleasure," Carmen replied.

Sierra placed her tab and tip money on the table. "You'll definitely see more of us, now that autumn chores are done. I hope you have a beautiful day despite the cold, icy rain. Burr."

"You girls do the same; thanks for coming by."

On their drive home, Carmen placed her hand on Sierra's lap. "I love how you know people; they seem to really like you as a person, too, and that's something to be proud of. I can see you have built yourself a good reputation in the community. Those types of things are worth never taking for granted, almost like a kinship."

"Thank you, Carmen. I have never really thought about it like that. I have been here all my life. Like I said before, my grandparents raised me in the cabin that I live in now. I owe them thanks, for the good people they are. They made life easy for me, to make my own way. Everyone loves and respects them."

"Aw, that's nice. Where are they now?"

"They're in Florida. After my grandfather retired from the mines in early 2000, they bought a condo in the Sunshine State. I was relieved they left me the cabin. I wouldn't know how to live amongst the retired already," she giggled. "Besides, I don't think I'd know how to live anywhere else."

"Yeah, I could imagine. The couple who took me on after I lost my dad was pretty good to me, I guess. I never knew my grandparents. Dad always said they were bad people, imagine that. I'm just glad yours were there for you after your mom was gone. If you don't mind me asking, do they know you're gay?"

"I am very grateful for them, and yes, they know about and accept my lifestyle. I'm also very grateful I have you in my life now," Sierra replied.

Carmen smiled and squeezed Sierra's hand. "We rock!"

Sierra smiled and then yelled out the window of her truck, "Hey, we rock!"

Carmen couldn't resist the childlike behavior and did the same out her window. "We rock!"

The girls' spirits were uplifted that day, and the mood was lighthearted. After they made it home, Bear checked out the bag of leftovers with his big nose and hoped they were for him, like most of the times before. "Hey, Bear, baby, you know Mommy didn't forget you," Sierra said, then gave him her leftover portion.

"Do you mind if he has my leftover, too?" Carmen asked.

"I'm sure he'd love it," Sierra replied.

Alerted by an incoming call, Sierra noticed it was John. While she sat down in the kitchen to talk with him, Carmen disappeared and turned on the hot tub, thinking, *After that great breakfast, a girl just needs to digest in the relaxing atmosphere of a warm, steamy heaven.* Before she got in, Carmen went to check on Sierra. She found her still talking with her friend. Unable to resist a growing temptation, Carmen stood before her and unrobed herself. She exposed her firm breast and irresistible, naked body, and after giving a seductive wink, Carmen walked away with an enticing swag, certain to distract her from the phone conversation.

Sierra was indeed distracted and was not confused by the message Carmen was sending. "Ah, hey, John, can I call you back in a little while? Um, my horse just got loose, and I need to catch her."

"Sure, I'll talk to you later."

"Okay, bye, and tell everyone I send my love."

Sierra tripped over her own jeans while she peeled them off herself. She bounced right back up, hoping Carmen hadn't witnessed her clumsiness. She then made a beeline for the hot tub that Carmen was elegantly occupying. Then, in an attempt to make her laugh, Sierra couldn't resist asking, "Did you see what happened to me a few minutes ago?"

"No, but I heard a crashing sound. What happened?" she giggled.

"Yeah, well, I about killed myself getting to you. My jeans fought me, and then tripped me to the floor. It was awful."

Carmen laughed. "Are you okay, silly?"

"Well, heck yes. Do you want to inspect me, Ms. Gadget?"

The splashing war was on, and the women squealed with laughter as they frolicked like young girls, behaving mischievously. "Wait, wait, I give!" Carmen pleaded while she laughed.

"Okay, I'm in; let's call a truce," Sierra replied, then made her way over to Carmen and sat directly in front of her. She touched her nose to Carmen's nose in a seductive way then began kissing her with gentle, teasing kisses to her mouth and neck. "Mmm, you taste so good. I love your sweet kisses," Sierra whispered.

"Mmm, I love yours, too," Carmen replied. "How do you feel about getting out of this hot bath and making our own heat?"

"I'd say your idea is ingenious." After they were out of the tub, Bear followed them back to the bedroom and plopped down on the floor. He made a slight grumbling sound, which attracted Sierra's attention. "Oh no, mister, you have to go in the living room while Mom has big-girl time. Come on, get up; I'll see you in a little while."

Carmen giggled. "That's funny. No canine viewers, huh?"

"He's like a kid to me, and it just feels weird to think that he's watching me, you know, do stuff," she shyly giggled, then added, "Hell, I can't even masturbate when I know he's around; it really kills the mood."

"Ah, well, in that case, I'm glad he's out of sight and mind."

"Right on, sister. Now come here."

Carmen kissed her quietly, and then gently coaxed her to lay back. She straddled Sierra and continued with a deep, passionate kiss as she ground her warm, wet pussy on her lover's knee. "Mmm, you make me so horny," Carmen whispered.

Sierra responded with a simple, "Mmm," while she suckled Carmen's erect nipples.

The room filled with sounds of pleasure echoing through the house. Moisture trickled from their skin as Carmen's body began to quiver. "Ah, ah, ah, oh babe, oh my God, right there, don't stop," she moaned then released a powerful and gratifying climax, breathless as she collapsed on top of Sierra's naked body. "Oh my goodness, thank you, you're amazing! Mmm, come here, it's your turn to experience the pleasure, pretty girl." Carmen began kissing Sierra's stomach with love bites that lingered with intensity. She traveled her way down to taste the sweetness of her girlfriend's warm, inviting kitty box. She savored the taste and sweet, succulent scent, as she fondled her lover's clit with vigor.

Sierra's senses were heightened as she took a tight grip on Carmen's hair. She pulled her in closer while she pressed against Carmen's face, then moaned, "Oh fuck yes, oh shit babe, right there, ah, ah, oh God bless America, woman, yes, you can drive anytime." They were no doubt pleased by the outcome, as they hugged each other close. They took advantage of that lazy Sunday and napped, nestled in each other's arms. The experience they shared would be one of many to come. Day by day they grew closer, building a bond that would be unbreakable.

Piper, on the other hand, made his repair job harder than it should have been; he griped and cursed throughout the project. "I know one thing for sure—now that this shit is done, I'm going down to the tavern and run up the boss's tab," he grumbled. Then he slung the tarred mop onto the ground and climbed down from the roof of the old camper. His pants slipped off his hips just as he made it to the ground. "Fucking bullshit there," he said as he grabbed a hold of his belt and struggled to get his dirty jeans pulled up over his protruding beer belly. "Yep, beer thirty," he said, not giving his appearance or hygiene a further care in the world.

After making his way to the local tavern in town, he helped himself to a seat at the bar as if it were an old-time friend. Piper then tapped the bar. "A double shot of house bourbon and a Bud. Hey, and make sure that shit's not watered down. I want my money's worth," he growled.

After placing the order in front of Piper, the bartender replied, "We don't water any of our liquor down. How are you paying for this?"

"Put it on the Hilltop tab; my boss owes me big. Hey, what's your name again?" Piper asked.

"Mitch," the bartender replied.

"So Mitch, you think you can turn on that television for me?"

"Yeah, I can do that."

A few shots and a couple of beers later, Piper ordered a burger and fries. He was eating his lunch when he overheard a patron say to another man, "I saw Sierra Wolfe at Jude's Café this morning, and I have to say, she's looking good as ever. She had a friend with her that was pretty hot, too; I wonder who she was? I haven't seen her in the area before."

"What did she look like?" his friend asked.

"Hmm, about five foot six, with a killer body and long, blonde, wavy hair. She was dressed in blue jeans that showed off her cute ass, too."

The bartender chuckled when he heard the men talking about Sierra and her friend. "I wouldn't spend a lot of time pining over either of those girls. If she was with Sierra, it was probably her girlfriend, as in 'girlfriend'; you get my drift," Mitch said. "And if it's the gal I am thinking of, I think she works for the EPA. She's been testing the water sources around here. When I was renewing my liquor license at the City Building a while back, I noticed Sierra greet her and introduce herself as her personal guide."

The patron chuckled. "Yeah, I bet it's personal. Lord, I'd love to be a fly on the wall when they got down and dirty. Hell, I'm getting a woody just thinking about it."

The other men laughed at his perverted comment, then ordered another round. Piper took all this in and was certain at this point that Carmen didn't die. *Unless I had the wrong woman all together,* he thought. Whichever way the cards fell, he was bound and determined to find out for sure. "What's the big deal for an EPA agent to be in these parts? I'd say it's a big waste of the government's money, if you ask me," Piper said, in hopes for more information.

"Pretty sure checking for contaminates in the water. There are plenty of organizations who are illegally fracking. They're not following proper code when they drill. Don't you ever watch the news, bro?" Mitch asked. "Those contaminates could cause us to get sick and even affect unborn babies with birth defects. Personally, I'm glad the government gives a flying fuck."

The other men agreed, but Piper wasn't satisfied; he wanted to know more. "So, where can I get in touch with this agent? I wouldn't mind her coming down to educate my crew. You know, to make sure everything at our drilling camp is up to par. I mean, we follow code, but it never hurts to be sure, right?"

"Like I said, I think she's staying at a cabin in the north Bold Creek area, probably not too far from Sierra. Just up north a couple of miles. I assume that's why Sierra picked her up that day; she's usually the one asked to act as a tour guide for greenhorns in that area."

"Okay, well, thanks for the food and spirits. I think I'll spend the rest of this day sleeping in a dry camper."

"You might consider taking a wet shower first," Mitch joked.

Piper sniffed his armpit through his soiled sweatshirt. "Yeah, you think, asshole? Unlike some of you, real men have to work like dogs for a living, you little prick." A burly Piper then got up and left, silently thinking, *I'm going to find that sweet ass today and make sure she's dead this time. I don't need some damn bitch standing in the way of my paycheck, and fuck that stupid boss of mine. If I run into her, I'm going to make her pay for humiliating me.*

Piper drove up the remote, twisting roads that led him into the north side area of Bold Creek. He kept his eyes peeled for any signs that might lead him to the agent's base camp. He saw a young man checking a mailbox alongside the road. "Hey, I'm looking for a cabin that the EPA agent is staying in. I need to drop her by a sample, but not sure if I'm heading in the right direction. Can you help me?"

The young fellow was Bryce, who helped Sierra with certain farm chores. "Well, I think that cabin is about three miles ahead and then left at Scouts Peak. You'll see a big green windmill; I'm pretty sure that's the place you're looking for."

"Thanks. You've been a big help, young man."

"No problem," Bryce replied.

After seeing the windmill Bryce had talked about, Piper was sure he had made it to his destination. Just before he pulled onto the property, he stopped and pissed in an empty Coke bottle, then capped it back up. "Yeah, that'll do," he chuckled. "Give her a real sample just before I choke the life out of that bitch."

He knocked on the door then tapped again. It was silent, like nobody was home. After checking the door handle that was locked, Piper went around the cabin, looking through the windows for any signs of life. He was disappointed to find nothing, then went back to the front porch and dumped his bottle of pee all over the welcome mat. "Ha ha, bitch, piss on you. I'll be back; I know where you live now." This wretched excuse of a man went back to the vehicle and drove back to his camp. He spent the drive calculating the best probable time he could find her there. "Surely she doesn't work through the night. I'll just hide my truck down the hill and show her an evening she'll never forget," he said aloud.

***

"Okay, up, up, up, sassy pants. We can't sleep this Monday away!"

"Carmen, no," Sierra replied in a lazy voice.

"Come on, babe. I made my all-time-famous French toast and even have coffee brewed."

"Okay, okay, I'll get up. Just don't look at my hair. It will scare you in the morning. That's why I'm always up first. Who in the heck lit a fire under your tail features this morning anyhow?" Sierra asked.

"Oh, that is not all truth. I was up one other time before you, and I saw your messy hair, so chew on that. Besides, I thought it was very sexy," she smiled. "And I'm only up before you because that damn chicken outside makes a lot of racket. I can't believe you sleep through it!"

"That's a rooster, not a chicken. You're cute, Carmen, like come here and give me a kiss cute."

"How can I resist that? You're cute, too," Carmen replied. "Now, come on, pokey, let's eat breakfast and discuss a plan. I'm ready to get this mission started."

"Yeah, I'm nervous about all this. What if something goes wrong?" Sierra asked.

"That's why we have to talk and devise a plan. We are two very smart women here. We can make this work, Sierra."

"Well, just keep telling me that, and I should be fine. I need to go to the City Hall and find out more about Hilltop Drilling Company. I'd like to know who owns it and how many laborers work there and what their names are," Sierra replied.

"That's a good idea, but I think I should be the one to do that. I would look less suspicious requesting the hard copies for all the drilling sites in the area."

"Yeah, that's probably true. We sure don't need questions raised," Sierra replied.

"If Piper is my attacker, and I'm sure he was his boss was there with him, coaching his every move. The pervert watched me go through that hell. However, I've decided I don't want the blood of two men on my hands. That could get messy and leave room for error."

"Yeah, no doubt, especially killing the boss would raise questions. I think we should somehow lure Piper to a remote place, bind him and force the truth out of him, a complete confession. I might even be able to get a hold of sodium pentothal; my cousin, Brittany, works at the crime lab. Maybe I could get my hands on some without anyone noticing. At the first of every month, she is busy taking inventory on drugs and other supplies. I could just bring her lunch on that day and offer to help her with inventory. I know how she hates doing that, and it would give me the perfect opportunity to get my hands on some," Sierra replied.

"That's not a bad idea at all, Sierra. I'll keep that in mind, but my first step today is to locate that business and snoop into their files. If I can prove they're not operating under proper code, I can bring the boss man down that way, you know, sink him for everything he has. But Piper is another story. I want to make that bastard pay for what he has done to me."

"You talk as if you're sure it was Piper who raped you and left you for dead," Sierra replied.

"Yeah, that day we ran into him by the river, when he spoke to us, his voice was a dead ringer, and the stench on his clothing was disgusting and familiar. I'm sure it's him, and I assure you, I will know beyond a shadow of a doubt before I act. Your sodium pentothal idea will come in handy, if you can make that happen."

"The first of the month is only a few days away. I'll be sure to do my best at obtaining some; I'm confident I can succeed. I'll call Brittany today and let her know I'll be coming by on Thursday to bring lunch."

"Sounds like a good plan, Sierra. I'm going to jump in for a quick shower, then head out for the City Hall."

"Okay. I have some chores around here to do then I need to run to town for some grocery items. If I'm not here when you get back, the spare key is under the rock by the backdoor patio entrance."

"Here's a hundred bucks to put towards grocery. If you see a bag of Dunkin' Donuts original blend house coffee, I'd sure love having it around. I've been missing that in the biggest way," Carmen replied.

Sierra giggled. "Sure will, and if you think of anything else, just text me."

"Cool. I could get used to this teamwork, Sierra."

"No doubt I could, too."

***

Piper's labor crew showed up one at a time Monday morning, and after a long weekend of heavy drinking in the local taverns, work was the last thing on their minds. This group of five men joined Piper around the campfire and drank coffee while discussing the task they would need to accomplish for the week ahead. "I talked to the boss yesterday, and he is riding us hard. He has a list of goals he wants us to reach and get done before payday. We either accomplish that or none of us will be getting a check on Friday," Piper advised his burly crew.

"No check, my ass! I have a family to send money home to," one man spouted.

"No shit, I do, too, and I spent way too much money between whores, drinking and the poker machines this weekend. I can't do without a paycheck. My old lady would sniff me out and hang me by my balls, if I go two weeks without sending her money," another replied.

Piper chuckled. "Well, then, I guess you pussies need to get off your ass and on your feet so we can get the shit done." Then Piper stood and walked over to the youngest fellow of the group, who was sitting on a stump by the fire. He took his hat off and smacked it on the man's head. "Hey, you little redheaded prick, why don't you run your sweet ass back to town and make sure you load up the coolers with some lunch and ice-cold beers for after work, and don't be jacking off—get there and get back."

With a smug face, the young man, Red, replied, "Yeah, I can do that," then took the one- hundred-dollar bill Piper passed him and went on his way.

"Bring back all my change, peckerhead, or I'll take it out of your ass, boy," Piper grumbled, then gestured by grabbing his crotch in a perverted manner.

A few of the guys laughed at Piper's crude taunt towards Red as he drove off, but Rodney felt inclined to speak out. "He's just a kid, man, give him a break."

"He'll think kid when I shove my dick up his ass. I'll show that boy how to be a man, real fast," Piper replied. "Now get the fuck up and let's get started; we're burning daylight."

The thunder rumbled throughout the day and forty-mile-an-hour winds whipped against the men's backs. The day was brutal, and the chilly afternoon had everyone feeling grumpy. They were all on edge. However, they were thankful the frozen rain that had been forecast held off for them. Around four o'clock, Piper climbed down from his tractor. "Hey, I'm going to put some meat on the grill and make sure my little buddy Red iced our beer down, good and proper." Then he pulled a flask out from his back pocket and took a long swig. His face cringed slightly as the stout moonshine washed down the back of his throat.

About an hour later, Piper's wind-beaten crew wrapped up their day. They were thankful for the large bonfire and the smell of meat grilling on the barbeque. Everyone was hungry and thankful they had plenty of beer to wash it down with. Piper praised his crew for a good day's work then opened a new mason jar of blueberry shine. "My brother sent me a case of this from West Virginia. It's the real shit and will stomp a mud hole in your ass, if you're not careful," he said, and then passed it around for everyone to share.

Red took a taste, and with a clenched jaw, commented, "Damn, that's some good stuff, strong but good."

Piper smiled. "You damn right; my brother lives in the hills and has been making moonshine since he was shitting green. It's been a highly favored recipe that's been passed down through my family for over one hundred years. It

85

doesn't get any better than this," Piper boasted. "Drink up, Red. I have plenty more where that came from. Hell, you might even grow some hair on your chest after a night of drinking like a real man."

Red was mystified by Piper's unusual good mood but was relieved he was being semi-nice to him. He had decided not to offend Piper, so he drank more than his share that night. Red became overly intoxicated by the end of the evening. Some of the other men laughed at his drunken state, while a few others decided to get back to their hotel room and get a good night's sleep. Piper noticed that Red probably wasn't going to make it much longer. He watched him stumble around and could barely make sense out of his slurring words. He knew the young man would fall out anytime then thought to himself, *I'm going to slip that boy a sleeping pill and get rid of everyone else.* Piper yelled out, "All right, guys, the fun is over. Let's wrap this up. We have a lot to do tomorrow, and we need an early start. Make sure you're all here by six on the dot."

"Do you want me to take Red and drop him off at his room?" one of the guys asked.

"No, just help him into his truck and bring me the keys. He can sleep it off there, unless you want him puking all over you on the bumpy road to town. This moonshine is much better going down than coming up," Piper chuckled.

"I am not drunk. I can make it," Red slurred.

"You won't make shit if you try to leave drunk like that, boy. Now man up and take your daisy ass to bed in your truck. That's an order!" Piper exclaimed. Then he provided him with an electric heater, saying, "Here, I plugged this bastard into an extension cord. That way you're not running all your gas out to stay warm."

Red could barely speak but managed to mumble, "Thanks, Piper."

"Yeah, whatever," Piper replied.

After the other men left, Piper went into his camper and retrieved a sedative from his hiding place. Then he went to the medicine cabinet and took out a regular aspirin that looked similar to the drug. He took both pills out to Red and opened the door to his truck and, like a snake, as if he were concerned about the young man's welfare, Piper said, "Hey, boy, take a couple of aspirins; it'll make waking up in the morning much easier. Trust me, I know." Without question, Red took the dose. "That a boy, you sleep tight now, and tomorrow you'll feel like a new man," Piper said.

He went back inside and peered out from his camper window, keeping his eyes locked on Red. Like a snake, he waited for him to pass out completely. He was unable to control his devious nature and grabbed a jar of Vaseline from his nightstand. "Mmm, I've been thinking about that tight little ass for months now," he said. The crazed beast proceeded outside and to Red's truck, where he found him passed out, just like he had hoped. Piper maneuvered the young man's limp body so he was face down and laying over the passenger seat. He made sure Red's legs dangled just outside of the open passenger door. Piper savagely pulled down the young man's jeans, then exposed himself. He made sure to lubricate himself, and then smeared a plentiful amount on Red's bottom. Just as Piper penetrated him with a thrust, he woke up, dazed and confused, moaning in pain. "Shut the fuck up, you little bitch, and go back to sleep before I knock you out!" He continued raping Red as he laid his weight heavy against him. He pressed in, harder and harder, until the helpless victim passed out completely. Piper spent the next two hours going back for more until he sexually exhausted himself. After he was done, he pulled Red's jeans back up and scooted him back into the truck. He closed the door then laughed. "Hell yeah, now that's what I'm talking about; I feel like a new man!" he shouted out, and then howled at the moon like the animal he was.

The next morning, the crew started to filter in, slow and sure. Like most mornings, the men sat around the campfire, drinking coffee and discussing what they'd be doing that day. "I see Red's still passed out. Poor little fucker should have known better than to throw back all that shine in one setting. He won't be worth shit today," one of the guys said.

"Yeah, I'm sure we'll be fine without him today. He wouldn't be worth a smelly crap to us anyways. We'll let the princess sleep it off. Let's get to work," Piper replied.

Shortly after the large machinery fired up, a foggy-minded Red woke up. He sat there, watching the men through the dirty windshield of his truck. He experienced vague flashbacks of the prior night. He could feel the sharp pains in his torn rectum and knew he had been raped by Piper. He was devastated with shame; tears ran down his face. He scrambled to find the gun that he kept under the seat. Without a single ounce of hesitation, the overwhelmed young man pulled the trigger and blasted his own brains out.

The loud shot rang over the sound of machinery running. "Hey, hey!" a crew member yelled, then jumped down from his tractor and ran to Red's truck. "Oh my God, the little fucker shot himself!"

They all gathered around the gruesome scene. Piper yelled, "What the fuck? Call nine-one-one!"

Not too much later the E.M.P. and investigating officers showed up. Red was pronounced dead, and his body was taken away to the coroner. The officer questioned the crew separately and determined his death was an obvious aggravated suicide. He took his hat off and spoke to the group. "You never know what some of these young guys might be thinking or even going through these days. I've seen some stuff in my years, and far too many young people take their own lives. Sorry you fella's had to witness this," the officer said. "I'll send a tow truck to bring his vehicle down."

"All his belongings are at the Mountain Peak Hotel in town, room number 712," Piper replied. The officer thanked him then left for headquarters to file his report. Then the heartless leader turned to his crew and gave his hands one solid clap. "Okay, let's get back to work. We have plenty of time to talk about this after hours."

The guys worked hard that day, but their minds were distant in thought, all except Piper. He didn't show an ounce of remorse and continued on, as if it were just an unfortunate turn of events. His biggest concern was he was short a laborer. By the end of the day, none of the crew stayed for a beer like usual. They all went back to the hotel and into their separate rooms. Each of them dealt with the tragic loss in his own way.

After getting a bite to eat, Piper made a call. "Hey, Boss, one of my men shot his brains out on the job. He did it in his truck, first thing this morning. The cop ruled it a suicide. The poor little bastard had more balls than I thought he did. The shitty part is I'm out a laborer. So you might want to send someone else up here to fill his position."

"Oh, that's fucking great, damn it to hell. That's all we need, is more attention pointing in our direction," his boss complained. "I'll see what I can do about getting another hand to take his place. Whatever you do, Piper, make sure you don't cause any trouble or draw any unnecessary attention!"

"I'm on top of that, Boss. No worries."

Later that evening, Sierra and Carmen were snuggled close together on the couch. They shared a bowl of salted, buttery popcorn. When the ten o'clock news came on, they were shocked to learn that a young Randy Rogan had taken his own life that day at the Hilltop Drilling site. Sierra grabbed her phone. "John, have you seen the news?"

"No, what's up?" he replied.

"Do you know a Randy Rogan, age twenty-one?"

"No. Why? What's going on?"

"He shot himself in the head this morning at the Hilltop Drilling site on the south end."

Carmen shushed her and whispered, "Don't make a big deal out of it; we don't need to draw attention to that particular site."

Sierra nodded and agreed. "Well, I just wanted to let you know, in case you knew him, that's all; the media said his nickname was Red."

"Nope, don't know him, but sorry to hear that he was young and couldn't find a better way to deal with his problems," John replied.

"When are you expected to be home, John?"

"I'm still on leave; I won't be back for awhile. It'll be a couple of weeks at least. I had more to handle than expected with wrapping up loose ends."

"Okay, well, take care, and call if you need anything."

"Will do, and talk soon, Sierra."

After she hung up the phone, Carmen squeezed Sierra's lips closed. "Looks like I'll just have to kiss you quiet, young lady."

Sierra giggled. "Oh yeah? Well then, kiss me, naughty girl."

"Me naughty? I don't think so. You know I'm an angel," Carmen teased.

Bear just laid his head down and gave a mournful groan. He knew what to expect next from these two girls, as they made their way to the bedroom. After a long day, they were thankful to be nestled in each other's arms, while the winds powerfully raged across the mountaintops, leaving a thick blanket of snow and ice across the land.

Carmen woke up to the succulent and familiar smell of Dunkin Donuts coffee roasting. After slipping into her robe, she made her way into the kitchen. She found Sierra sitting studiously and perfectly posed while reading the news on her laptop and drinking a cup of coffee. "Mmm, good morning, Sunshine."

Sierra glanced up over her reading glasses then smiled at the sight of her beloved Carmen. "Good morning, indeed, when it starts with the vision of your beautiful smile and this fine cup of coffee," she smiled.

Then Carmen looked over Sierra's shoulder to see what had her attention. "Ouch, looks like we can expect snow most of the day. I certainly hope this is the last of it, considering the first day of spring is this Saturday, I think."

"Yeah, it is, but Montana is a tricky state when it comes to the change of seasons. You never know what to expect. But the good thing is, it should clear off by this evening, and we can expect sunshine and higher temps tomorrow. It'll probably be melted off by noon," Sierra replied.

"Well, that's a positive note. So, I take it that we're stuck up here for the day?" Carmen asked.

"Yep," Sierra replied.

"Well, then, I'm going to find some crime shows on television and hope to learn a trick or two that I can put in my belt of justified vengeance. Would you like to join me, Sierra?"

"Sure, sounds good to me. So, you find us something educational, and I'll make us a quick breakfast."

"I'm not real hungry, so please don't get too extravagant," Carmen replied.

"Nope, I'm thinking light fruit and some whole-grain oat bread. I love that toasted with real butter melted all over it."

"That sounds perfect. Besides, on days like these, I like to munch on stuff all day long," Carmen giggled.

"No doubt I know what you mean and a girl after my own heart. I love that."

Unlike the girls, some people were not so fortunate and had to be outside working in the elements of the cold, blistery weather. Piper woke up in his usual angry mood, just mad at life in general. He barked out orders to his crew until he was interrupted by an incoming call. After Piper realized it was the boss, he grumbled, "Just get to work. We have a lot to get done." Then he walked up to his camper and took the call. "Yeah, Boss, what can I do for you?"

"I found some guy from Idaho. He'll be showing up there tomorrow afternoon to fill the vacant spot. Make sure you welcome him in and show him the ropes. He's supposed to have some experience fracking, but we'll see soon enough, I guess. His name is Mark Kisters; his résumé says he likes to be called Slim."

"All right, well, glad you found someone on such short notice. I'll have one of the guys meet him in town and show him to his room," Piper replied.

"No problem. I'll talk with you in a few days and check up on him."

"Okay, sounds good, Boss," Piper replied, then turned to his men. "Damn, looks like we have another greenhorn to break in, boys. I just hope he has more backbone than Red had. I don't need anyone else busting their brains out on my job." The men didn't know how to respond to Piper's callous opinion in regards to the situation; they just nodded their heads and were thankful to have a replacement sooner than later. "The boss said he's worked a fracking site up in Idaho. I just hope we don't have to spend a lot of time babysitting him. I'm sick of that shit."

"No doubt," one of the workers agreed, while the others kept on with their task at hand, still trying to absorb yesterday's tragic event.

Later that afternoon, the snow had slowed down as forecasted, and after Sierra had drawn the curtains back, the sunshine hit her face. Sierra smiled. "Look, babe, the sun is shining again." After sitting back down next to Carmen on the cozy, overstuffed loveseat, she gently tugged the quilt her lover was wrapped up in. "Share with me."

"Here, take some, silly, and yes, the sun is a welcoming gift indeed. We'll be able to get out and about tomorrow."

"Yep, that's the plan. You know, babe, I can't quit thinking about the guy who shot himself yesterday at Hilltop. It makes me wonder if there was something sinister going on. You know, like, what if Piper had something to do with it?"

"Maybe, and it wouldn't surprise me. I couldn't imagine working with Piper; he's a freaking creep. My main concern is finishing that bastard off. The thought of him hurting anyone else is repulsive. I can't stand him."

"I understand; that guy is creepy. I'm so proud of you for giving all this time, though, the time to think this through from all aspects."

"Yeah, seeing the months pass by on my calendar has shown me a lot about impatience and then the benefits of patience. Don't worry, we will get to the end of it, Sierra, and the world will be a better place because of it."

This wasn't exactly the response or perception Sierra had hoped for. She had somehow imagined the time would give her a change of heart. She had hoped time would provide the choice and opportunity to weigh out her options, the choice to just let it go and walk away. But Sierra knew it was ultimately her partner's decision, and she had chosen not to judge her. She reached out and took Carmen's hand. "You know, Carmen, this is about you and what you need to make this right. Like I've said before, whatever you decide, I will stand by your choices. But it's not about me. Any decision you make is for you and you alone."

"I know, Sierra. Thank you for understanding," Carmen replied. After watching back-to- back episodes of criminal-minded shows and enjoying each other's company that day, they were ready to stretch out for a good night rest and rise up to a new day ahead.

The next morning, during a brisk run through the misty mountaintops of her home territory, Sierra and Bear made it just in time to catch Millie, the local mail carrier, delivering mail into her rural mailbox. "Hey, Millie, nice to see you on this beautiful morning."

"Nice to see you, too, Sierra. Tell me, where in the world do you get the energy to run like that, especially in this cooler weather?"

Sierra blushed. "Well, in order for me to effectively act as a tour guide leading expeditions through the mountain trails up here, I need to stay fit; I'm just glad the work is more seasonal than not."

As Millie passed Sierra her mail, she smiled and said, "I imagine Frank and I will be seeing you this weekend at the preliminaries before the big Mud Dig event this coming summer."

Sierra looked shocked. "Oh shit, I've been so busy, I forgot all about that!"

"You still have time to sign up; the deadline is tomorrow by four p.m. at Jed's Auto Repair. The details are in the paper." Then she glanced at Sierra's handful of mail to verify she did get a copy of the *Times Local*. "Yep, all the information you need will be on page five."

"Okay, thanks for the buzz in my ear; I would hate to miss that."

"All right, well, I need to run and get this route over. I still have to go on the south side, and with all the snow melting off, the foggy roads have slowed me down. Oh, by the way, did you hear about that young fellow who shot himself up by the Hilltop Drilling site yesterday morning?"

"Yes, that was tragic. Makes a person wonder what could have possibly been that bad," she sighed. "Well, Millie, I'll be seeing you and Frank this weekend. Talk soon and drive safe."

"All right, hon, have a good day."

"You, too," she replied, then waved and jogged back up to the house.

After tossing her mail onto the table and making sure Bear had food, she went for a hot shower. Just a minute later, Carmen poked her head in. "Hey, gorgeous, want to conserve on hot water?"

"Sure. Dive in, sexy."

"How was your run this morning?"

"It was good, a little foggy, but temps were nice. I ran into Millie, she's our mail carrier, on the way back up to the house. She reminded me that I need to get into town and sign up for this Saturday's preliminary event. It will determine who participates in the Mud Digging contest this upcoming summer."

"Hmm, what is mud digging?"

"Ah, it's an event we have every summer that consists of mud and big, big trucks. The catch is whoever completes the course first without their truck breaking down or wimping out wins 10,000 bucks. I'm proud to say I've won the past two years."

"You're kidding me, right? Don't you need a special truck for that?"

"That would be Big Diggs, my Ford F-250. She's the boss and literally my pride and joy, next to Bear."

"Where is this beast?"

Sierra smiled. "Tucked away in the barn and waiting for a weekend like this one coming up. The spring preliminaries are always fun. It gets everyone stoked for the real thing."

"Oh my God, I want to see it!"

"You don't have to ask me twice. Come on, let's get out of this shower," Sierra replied.

After drying off and getting dressed, the girls walked out to the barn. "I'm so excited, and why haven't you mentioned this before now?" Carmen asked.

"Truth is, I haven't thought about much since I met you," Sierra replied. "Here, help me slide this big-ass door open; it can be a bitch." After a good struggle, they managed to get the heavy door slid back. "Stay here for a second, and I'll flip on the lights."

"This is exciting. I assume this huge mass covered in tarps is Big Betty."

"No, no, it's Big Diggs," she said as she unveiled the beast.

"Oh, pardon me, Big Diggs it is, then. Wow, what an enormous truck. She's purple and black!" Carmen exclaimed. "She's beautiful and powerful-looking."

"Yep, that's my baby. Her suspension is forty inches from the ground, the tires are forty-eight inches, and the pipes are glass packs that roar from here to high heaven. When I'm sitting inside, I'm about five feet up."

"This is like a Bigfoot truck that you see on television. I want to go for a ride; can we do that?"

"Yes, ma'am," Sierra smiled. "Grab that step ladder behind you and climb in."

Sierra started the motor and let it warm up. The sheer thunder of it vibrated the ground under their feet. "Good God, what size of a motor does this thing have?"

"She has an impressive 1,580 horsepower, mid-mounted, supercharged big-block. Okay, buckle up, buttercup; Big Diggs is about to rock your world."

"Oh God, I'm so excited!"

Sierra drove through the pasture and then down a steep hill, leading to more rugged terrain. Carmen screamed when all four tires left the ground after barreling over one hilltop. "Ah, ah, Lord have mercy, holy shit, oh God, you're crazy, Sierra," she frantically laughed. "Okay, okay, I give. I've had enough and am going piss all over myself if I don't get out of here!"

"Well, you did better than I expected," Sierra taunted. "Hold tight; we need to get back up the hill and put her away."

"Oh God, here we go, oh God!"

Sierra got tickled by Carmen's reaction to the whole experience. "Oh my, we'll make you a mud digger before this is all over," she laughed.

When Carmen climbed down from the truck, she kissed the ground. "I can barely stand; my legs are shaking so badly. That was much more exhilarating than any roller coaster I have ever been on. Oh my goodness, you're crazy, Sierra!"

"Breathe, just breathe, babe; it's all good."

"I know, and thankful I'm still breathing. I'm still in shock," she laughed. "Oh hell, and to think you're going to actually race this thing against others like it. Wow, crazy, just madness. You're all some thrill-seeking hillbillies around here, that's for sure."

"I know it's great!" Sierra replied with a grin stretching from ear to ear. "I need to get to Jed's and get my entry form filled out today; it's the last day I can do that. Can you roll with me?"

"Yeah, sure I can. So, how does all this work anyhow and how's the payoff work?"

"Awesome, babe, that's great. I love the thought of you going with me today. Oh, and regarding payoff, well, there will be about fifty contestants, give or take a few. We all pay three hundred bucks apiece to be in the preliminary trial race; that's about a fifteen grand jackpot. The first-place winner in this race will take home five-thousand bucks and second place gets two grand, and then third will win a thousand. The city village profits the remaining proceeds. Oh, and the first top-ten winning contestants move on to the Big Mud Dig Event. That will be held in the summer; it's a blast."

"That all sounds very exciting, Sierra. I look forward to it. I'm just thankful you're on board with me when it comes to Piper. I'm also grateful for the time we took yesterday to talk about it a little more. Just knowing you will support my decisions in the matter does mean very much to me, even though you choose not to participate."

"Thank you for understanding. Truth be known, I've had conflicting feelings, and the thought of killing another man would devastate me; I couldn't live with myself. I had a hard enough time . . .," she paused. "Well, you know."

"Yes, I know, and I appreciate your candor. I don't mind doing this on my own, and I will be certain before making any rash decisions concerning his verdict of guilty or innocent. I just need to know, however it turns out, that I can trust you not to share my business or thoughts with anybody, before, during or after," Carmen replied.

"Babe, you mean too much to me. I would never give away your secrets. I understand your reason behind this and the need to see a man like that eliminated from this life. The things he did to you and probably others before you are despicable and inhuman. I will help you research his background, but I prefer not being involved with anyone's death sentence."

"I completely understand how you feel, and I do appreciate any help you can offer." Carmen paused a brief moment. "Sierra, you mean an enormous amount to me, too. It's been years since I have felt this close to anyone. I'm scared. What if things play out with Piper the way I think they will—how will you feel about me then?"

Sierra had to clearly absorb the impact of the question, and before replying, she took Carmen's hand in hers. "Carmen, please understand me when I say I wish you would reconsider the premeditated outcome. We both know the impact of the decision I made and the outcome it had on me and even you; we've talked about it before. I was young and scared when I killed to save my mom. I was scared because if I didn't shoot when I had, there was a good chance he'd have done the same thing to me. I still remember what it was like to see the life drain from his eyes; it was awful. But in an odd way, I felt so bad for him, even after what he did. As for my personal feelings regarding the potential murder of a rapist, I can honestly say, had it been me, I'd want him dead, too. Just do me a favor, and think this through, and weigh the consequences of the aftermath; you might be doing yourself more harm than good."

Carmen lowered her head then sighed. "Yeah."

"Hey, I know, let's just take the rest of this week, and you can help me get Big Diggs ready for the competition. It'll be fun, I promise, and it will give your mind time to rest."

"Yes, that's probably a good idea. Besides, I am curious how all of this works, and I wouldn't miss it for the world. I'm especially excited that I can watch you from the stands and don't have to personally participate," Carmen replied.

"Um, who said you wouldn't be riding shotgun with me?" Sierra teased.

"Oh no, no, no, no, I won't be riding along with you. I about peed myself earlier. I'll be much better cheering you on from the sidelines, trust me."

"Okay, whatever you say, so our first step is to get that beasty girl into Jed's shop. He needs to give her the once-over, and I can sign up for the muddy fun, and better yet, I'll get to show off for this girl I have a crush on."

"'A crush on,' you better be talking about me, Miss Thang," Carmen teased. Then it hit her. "Oh geez, you mean we actually drive that oversized truck through town? Isn't that illegal in some way?"

"Generally, yes, it would be. But during the preliminaries, the township allows us to get our vehicle checked out and checked in; besides, everyone loves this event. It's actually a big deal around here, and the township profits, so it's a win-win situation."

"I can see that, and I must admit, it does sound intriguing."

"Hey, not to worry, our trip there and back will be a slow ride. I promise it won't be like your experience from earlier today."

"I'm glad to hear that. I'm not sure I can take any more adrenalin rushes," Carmen giggled.

Then Sierra looked at Bear. He could tell something was up, "Well, hell, come on, Bear, you can go on this trip to town with us."

After experiencing a more relaxed ride to Jed's, Carmen was happy to have ridden shotgun. Jed's eyes lit up when Sierra rolled up to his shop. "Hey there, girl, I was starting to wonder if you were going to sign up this year; glad to see you. Go ahead and pull Diggs around to the second bay, and I'll have the guys check her out. Come on into the office after you get it parked."

"Sure enough, and Jed, seriously, you know I could never resist a good mud event. I'll be up in a few minutes."

Jed chuckled. "All right, we'll talk more then."

Sierra turned to Carmen. "Okay, babe, if you and Bear want to wait up in the front office, I'll be there in a couple of minutes."

"Sounds good. Do I need a leash for him?"

"No, he'll be fine. Besides, he knows Jed keeps dog biscuits on hand."

"Ah, well then, come on, Bear; let's go get a biscuit, big boy."

After dropping the truck off for inspection, Sierra walked into the office. "Hey buddy, I see you've met Carmen, and, of course, you know Bear."

"Yep, we've met, and Bear is looking good. It looks like he's lost a few pounds since I've seen him last."

"Hmm, I hope so. We've been trying, huh, Bear?"

Jed passed Sierra the forms to fill out and then tapped the counter. "Hey, just for the record, we have some pretty mean trucks entering this year. I hope you're ready."

"Well, I'm glad we do. I'll actually have some competition then," Sierra replied with a cocky grin, then turned to Carmen. "Okay, we can take a walk out back while they're looking over my truck. There's a nice pond just down the path."

"Sounds good," Carmen replied.

Bear trotted ahead of the girls, sniffing out all the new smells. Carmen zipped up her coat. "Burr, it's chilly out here this afternoon." Just about that time, Bear found the pond and jumped in, full force. "Oh my God; he's swimming in that cold water!"

Sierra giggled. "He's okay, and he's made for this climate. That's what Newfoundland dog breeds do best. They've saved sailors by water rescue on several occasions, even when the water was ice cold." About that time, a soaking-wet Bear pounced back onto the shore and ran straight towards the girls. "No, Bear!" Sierra warned, as she prepared for his wet shake all over her.

Then he went to Carmen. "No, Bear, oh my God, that's cold!" she exclaimed. "You big Moo, that was rude."

Sierra laughed. "Oh gracious, buddy, you are rude. That's enough water for you today, mister, gee whiz. Come on, let's head back and see how Diggs is doing."

After making it back into the shop, Jed passed her the keys. "She checked out fine. I'm looking forward to seeing you run this weekend."

"Thanks, Jed. I'll make sure to impress you once again," Sierra boasted.

"Yeah, I'm sure you will. Good luck, girl."

Sierra walked over to the passenger side of her truck and opened the door. "Hey, cutie, do you want to drive her home?"

Carmen giggled. "Have you lost your mind? You can't be serious."

"Sure I am. It's just like driving anything else, but much bigger."

"How about you get us out of town, and then I'll try."

"Okay, I'm holding you to it." After Sierra made it to the back roads home, Carmen took over. "Now just relax, take it slow, and stay in the middle of the road."

"Oh, you make it sound so simple. Hold on, here we go," she nervously whimpered, then with an exhale of breath and an obvious adrenalin rush, Carmen squealed, "Whew, this thing does have power," as she felt the truck pull forward at takeoff.

Sierra remained calm but alert when she saw a normal, full-sized truck coming towards them on the narrow mountain road. "Okay, just stay calm and stop the truck. The other guy should know the rules of these roads, and he'll probably back up to an area he can pull over at."

"Okay, if you say so," Carmen replied and then stopped.

The oncoming traveler kept driving towards them. He yelled something, but they couldn't hear what he was saying, due to the loud motor in Sierra's truck. He rudely honked and waved his arms. They didn't recognize the vehicle, but after it approached closer, in a second glance, the girls said in unison, "That looks like Piper!" They couldn't have been more right. Carmen got almost a nauseous feeling and said, "Okay, what do I do?"

"Just stay stopped. I'm going to get out and talk to him. Look, I have a handgun loaded in the glove box, if you feel we need it. But I'm sure everything will be fine," Sierra replied.

"Can't we just drive over his ass, like you see on television?"

"Ah, no. Just hold tight and I'll be right back."

Sierra walked up to his truck, and, sure enough, it was Piper. He rolled his window down before she got there and shouted, "What the fuck is going on? Move that piece of shit! I don't have time for this."

His comment and attitude didn't set well with Sierra. "Hey, listen here, buddy. I'm not even sure why you are in this area. I have a permit to drive this truck in these parts. So back your truck up off the road so we can pass. I don't want any trouble."

105

Piper rolled up his window, not bothering to comment back, and grumbled aloud to himself, "Fucking bitches, I'd like to show them both a lesson," then backed up. After the girls passed him, Piper gave them the finger. "Fuck off," he yelled. He continued to watch the direction they were headed. When they went around a curve and just out of sight, he followed them. He stayed just far enough behind so they couldn't see him. Eventually, Carmen turned the truck into Sierra's driveway and drove down the path towards the cabin. Piper parked his truck in a secluded area, then boldly worked his way through the heavy forest and around to the backside of her home. He spied on the two women while they were putting the truck inside the barn. They were unaware they were being watched by this spineless bastard. They shared an intimate kiss before walking into the house together. "Oh, I see now, they really are filthy, dike bitches. I'm sure I'll have some fun with this when the timing is right." Piper was pleased to know where Carmen was staying and looked forward to showing them a lesson.

"That was so cool, and I did really well for being a first-timer, driving a truck that massive!" Carmen exclaimed.

"You did an awesome job, babe. I had no doubt that you could indeed handle Big Diggs; you just have the right touch," then kissed Carmen another time while she squeezed her butt firmly, and then gave it a playful smack. "Okay, how about some food? I'm starving. Afterwards, maybe you will help me give Diggs a good bath; she has to sparkle before any big run."

"Well, of course she does. I just wish we could have run her over the top of Piper's shitty pickup. One thing for sure, I'm glad to know what he drives now."

"Yeah, that's good to know, and, seriously, that guy is a real dick, for sure; he gives me the creeps, too," Sierra replied.

"Yes, a very creepy guy. I feel so much safer being here with you."

"I'm glad you feel that way because I wouldn't want it any different, Carmen."

Piper headed back to his camp and was even more determined to punish his adversary. "Ha ha, stupid bitch, I know where you are now. I'll be back. I'll be back to show you how a real woman should behave. She'll be sorry she was ever born. Driving a big truck, who does that bitch think she is and her nasty cunt of a girlfriend. She'd like to think she owns everything up here. I have news for her—I'll own her ass," he talked aloud to himself, as he often did. After smacking his fist on the dash of his truck, he worked himself into a rage of his own, repeatedly hitting it. "Oh man, I want her now; she needs to pay for making me look like a fool with my boss. I want to beat her face in!" he shouted aloud.

Just about the time he was going to turn around, he received a call from one of the crew on his job. "Hey, Piper it's about quitting time; if you're still near town, can you grab us some beer and ice? I'll pitch in, and so will the others."

"Yeah, I'll grab some, and you're damn right you'll pitch in. I'm getting sick of flipping the bill on you bastards. Fucking pantywaists cry about sending your paycheck home— I'd tell my bitches to fuck off, that I have a life, too. I mean, what kind of man does that shit?"

The man replied, "Speaking for myself, I don't send home everything. I keep some for my own needs."

"Oh, fuck off. I'll be there in a few minutes, and I hope you guys made some good headway today and didn't dick around while I was gone," Piper replied.

"You'll be surprised; we had a busy and progressive day," he replied.

"We'll see." Piper remained in another of his moods throughout the evening. He took out all his frustrations on his crew until they couldn't handle it anymore. They all knew better than to argue any point with him when he acted this way. It didn't take long before the party was over and the boys went back to their hotel rooms, where they finished up their evenings in peace and quiet, away from his relentless raging. Piper watched them drive off, and then yelled out, "Yeah, you all run, but you better be here on time in the morning, or I'll have you by the balls, you hear?" He spent the rest of evening drinking his bottle of cheap whiskey and chasing it down with beers. He bitched aloud to nobody but himself and was still worked up by the passing of the girls today. The mere thought of backing up his truck by a woman's request had him in a real tizzy.

CHAPTER FOUR

The rooster's crow echoed throughout the early morning. A lazy Sierra groaned. "Oh geez, that rooster's lucky that I like him more than fried chicken," Sierra grumbled, as she glanced at the clock through squinting eyes. "What, oh my God, five-thirty! Carmen, quick, babe, we have to get up and get ready! Shit!"

"Sierra, no! Geez, woman!"

"Sorry, babe, but it's Saturday, you know, the big day."

"I know, just relax, we'll be there on time."

"Do you want to take a shower with me to save time?" Sierra asked.

Carmen smiled with that look in her eye. "Sure do."

Sierra noticed that sparkle in her lover's eyes. "Babe, we really need to make it a fast one. That means no sex this time, strictly cleansing ourselves, deal?"

Carmen giggled. "You are so serious this morning, and if I have to make that kind of deal so you can be calm, then consider it hands off."

After the shower, Sierra picked out her favorite and well-worn pair of faded Levis that fit just right. She slipped on her tattered cowboy boots and favorite hooded sweatshirt. It was light gray and oversized, just enough to wear a T-shirt under it.

Carmen took one look at her lover. "Damn, you're sexy, girl. You look so hot today. Are you sure we don't have time . . ."

Before she could finish, Sierra interrupted. "No, babe, but come here and kiss me."

"Oh, you're a tough cookie when you have on your serious face. However, I do want that kiss," Carmen teased.

After engaging in a passionate kiss, Sierra popped Carmen's butt. "Okay, babe, while you get dressed, I'm going to get Big Diggs ready."

"Okay, see you out there in twenty minutes."

"Twenty minutes, babe?"

"Yes, twenty. We have plenty of time," Carmen replied.

Just as Sierra was ready to walk out the door, Bear looked for her approval to come along. "I'm sorry, Bear, but not today; Mom's got a lot going on. But I promise to take you another day." Bear looked downhearted as she walked out. He grumbled a mournful sigh, then plopped down onto the floor. Sierra loaded the cooler into the SUV and then started Diggs up.

After pulling the oversized machine out and into the driveway, she noticed Carmen standing on the porch, waving her arms. "Hey, Sierra," she yelled. "Where are the keys for the SUV? I think I should drive that, in case Big Betty breaks down out there today."

"Babe, her name is Big Diggs, not Betty, geez. And yes, we're taking the SUV, too. I already have it loaded. The keys should be on my nightstand or in the jeans I took off last night," Sierra replied.

After retrieving the keys, she yelled loudly over the sound of the massive motor running, then raised her hand and jangled them. "Okay, got them. I'll follow you there!"

In a boastful gesture to show off, Sierra gave one final step on the gas while it was still in park. The glass packs rumbled with a mighty roar, then she threw it in granny low and popped a wheelie. "See you there, babe! I love you!" she hollered while she waved her hat and then headed down the mountain for the Mud Digging event.

Carmen looked puzzled. "Oh my God, she's a crazy mess. Wait, did she just say, 'I love you?'" she questioned herself. "Could have sworn she said it. Geez Louise. What a way to tell a girl something like that for the first time."

While approaching the gates into the event, Carmen stayed close behind Sierra's truck. She followed her every inch of the way through the crowded maze of participants and patrons. After they found spaces to park in the contestant area, Sierra climbed out of her truck and walked over to the SUV. Carmen rolled the window down and sported a big smile. "Uh, what was the last thing you said to me, just before you popped a wheelie, then drove off down the mountain? I couldn't quite make it out."

"Um . . . mm, maybe 'see you there?'" she replied.

"Oh okay, I was sure you said 'I love you' at the end of that. But it was probably my mind playing tricks on me; the truck was very loud and made it hard to hear."

"I see, and I do recall that now," Sierra replied. "It was a natural reaction because I do love you. I hope that's okay."

Carmen got out of the vehicle and smiled. "Oh, just kiss me, pie face, so we can get this party started." After a playful embrace of affection, Sierra took Carmen's hand. "Come on, we need an event calendar, and I want to show you around before the games begin."

"Whew, all this dust and exhaust can't be good for anyone," Carmen winced.

"Wow, now that was spoken like a true-blooded EPA agent, babe. But trust me, we'll be fine."

While checking in at the competitors' booth, the girls were standing side by side. Carmen reached around her beautiful lover's waist and rested her hand in Sierra's back pocket. Both women looked very sexy in their faded, worn Levis and cowboy boots. Carmen had golden locks of blonde hair waving down her back, while Sierra wore her long, dark hair up and under a ball cap. The sight of the two women would complement any scenery. "Hey, Sierra, I figured I'd be seeing you early today. How have you been, girl?" the gentleman at the booth asked.

"Hey, Nathan, I've been fine, thanks. I need to sign in and get my lucky number seven for my truck."

"Oh, the next number in line is eight; you just missed the seven spot," Nathan replied.

"Oh no, I have had seven forever. That's always been my number, Nate," she pouted until Nathan felt bad enough to do something about it.

"Well hell, hang on, girl, I'll see if I can work something out. Good Lord, you're a pain in the ass."

Nathan texted the man who had the number seven and insisted he bring it back to the front and pick up a new one. Then he warned Sierra, "Now when he gets here with that number, don't say shit. Just let me handle it."

"Fine, no problem. I can do that," Sierra grinned.

Carmen gave a little smack to Sierra's butt. "You're rotten, woman. Do you always get your way?"

"I've got you," Sierra replied.

After a few minutes of finagling with the other contestant, Nathan got it squared away. "Okay, hello." He snapped his fingers as he tried to distract the two women from flirting with each other. He pushed a clipboard towards her. "Sign here," he said as he pointed at the dotted line. "And here's your number, with the events schedule. Give 'em hell, girl."

"Awesome. You rock, Nate! And trust me, I'm going to give it hell, buddy," Sierra boasted.

Sierra passed Carmen the schedule. "Here, babe, check this out for us. I need to get the number on Diggs." After she attached the number seven flag to Big Diggs antenna, she jumped down and admired her truck. "Yep, you always look good with that lucky number attached to you, girl."

Carmen admired her lover. "Hey, babe, I want a picture with you standing next to Betty."

Sierra sighed, then stood next to her truck and smiled as she spoke through clenched teeth. "Diggs, babe, Diggs."

"Oh shoot, I'm always messing that up. You should have named her Betty; she looks like a Betty," Carmen tauntingly replied.

"Okay, you can call her whatever you want to. But just so you know, Betty sounds like a sissy name. I'm just saying."

"Okay, I will keep that in mind. So, wow, look here, babe. We have mud wrestling tonight at eight o'clock; that looks fun. The quads will be competing soon, and we still have three hours before the big truck event. I'm starving. We have time to grab something to eat from one of the concessions." Then Carmen saw her all-time-favorite carnival ride and pointed. "I want to go on that Ferris wheel with you."

"Aw, you're a kid at heart. I didn't know that about you. I can't wait to ride that with you. Come on, let's try Chicago Dawgs. I heard they have some excellent menu choices."

While standing in line, Sierra felt a tap on her shoulder. "Sierra Wolfe, is that you?"

Before turning around, Sierra's heart dropped to the ground. She hauntingly remembered the sound of her ex-lover's voice saying her name. "Sadie, wow, when did you get back into town?" Sierra asked

"Yesterday morning. I wouldn't dare miss this event. Besides, my youngest brother, Mathew, is running his truck this year," Sadie replied.

Carmen gently squeezed Sierra's hand. "Oh hey, this is my girlfriend, Carmen. Babe, this is Sadie, an old friend from my past."

"Nice to meet you, Carmen; I hope you're keeping this cowgirl in line," Sadie replied.

"Oh, she's a handful for sure, but I'd rather not tame her wild side, if you know what I mean. I know this might sound silly, but has anyone ever told you that you look so much like Demi Moore?"

Sadie giggled. "Yes, I have been told that a time or two, and thank you, I take that as a compliment."

Sierra's face shone with a pink blush, then she squeezed Carmen's hand. "Well, it was nice seeing you, Sadie, and best of luck to your brother."

"Thanks, and it was a thrill seeing you, Sierra; it's been way too long. Maybe we can catch up sometime soon. I'll be in town for a little while and staying at Mom's house, which is still on Railroad Street. I'm certain you remember the way."

"Sounds good; we'll try to do that," Sierra replied, with a half-cocked grin.

After getting their food selections from the vendor, the girls headed towards the Ferris wheel. "So this Sadie girl, she wouldn't happen to be the ex-girlfriend Sadie, would she? I sensed some kind of connection when she looked at you. Am I right?"

"Yes, we had a little something years ago, but I told you about that. It was nothing that would have ever lasted. She was the girl I went into the Army with. Then she took off for college and never looked back."

"Oh, I see, the reporter, right?"

"Yeah, I've been told she's an investigative reporter now. I heard she works for some big newspaper in Idaho. She always loved that stuff and has always been one to keep her nose in everyone's business," Sierra replied.

"Oh well, that's sweet," Carmen smirked. Sierra was flattered by Carmen's inquisitive questions and found the tinge of jealousy flattering.

The echoes of the event bellowed throughout the mountains, and Piper was curious about the ruckus going on near town. After he finished his morning routine, he couldn't resist and decided to take a drive there for a better look. "Oh yeah," he said to himself. "I remember the boys saying something about this." After parking at the event, he walked up to the entry booth. While purchasing his ticket, he was surprised it cost twenty dollars. "Geez, this better be good because the price is steep. Hell, I'm surprised you didn't ask for my left nut," Piper growled.

The ticket master replied, "It's always better than good, mister. I can assure you that." He smiled.

"Yeah, we'll see," Piper replied, then moseyed on in. After he walked around the event and admired all the enormous monster trucks, Piper caught sight of Carmen. She was just coming off the Ferris wheel and arm in arm with Sierra. His eyes followed them surreptitiously as they walked back to their truck. Piper smirked. "Oh God, don't tell me those dike bitches are participating in this event," he mumbled. He could barely stomach the obvious fact that they were having a good time. The smiles and laughter that he witnessed were more than he could handle. He made a beeline for the nearest beer tent. His homophobic perspectives seemed quite contrary, considering his brutal attack on Red. Perhaps he didn't consider that wrong. He sure didn't seem to show any signs of remorse, nor did he see any relation between that and a lesbian couple. After he made his way up to the bar, Piper, being Piper, grumbled, "Hey, boy, what's your name?"

The beer tent server took a hard look at Piper. "Jason. Jason Zachariah. What can I help you with?"

"What does a beer cost in this joint?"

"That'll be two-fifty for drafts and three-fifty for cans," the bartender replied.

"Are you fucking serious? I just paid twenty bucks to get into this parade of bullshit. Then I find out some stupid dike bitches are participating in the event." He pitched his money down on the counter and grumbled, "It better be cold, is all I can say."

Jason had a hard time swallowing Piper's abusive comment regarding dike bitches and replied with a low, steady tone, "The beer is cold, mister," then took Piper's money.

"But I suggest you watch your language around here. Talk like that could get you into a world of hurt."

Piper scoffed, "Whatever."

Sitting in a quiet corner, Sadie overheard his sarcastic remark regarding dike bitches and glanced over her newspaper and glared at his outrageous personality. It was all she could do to just bite her tongue and keep her remarks to herself, thinking, *Ugh, the nerve of some people.* She made eye contact with Jason and then gently shook her head, as if she were apologizing for Piper's bad behavior.

Piper plopped down at a table, and while he drank his beer, he dribbled some onto his long, dirty beard. He looked up to make sure nobody noticed, then took his sweatshirt and dried it off. He saw Sadie sitting intellectually and was unable to resist his animalistic side, thinking, *Damn, she's a fine piece of ass.* After he gulped his beer down, he ordered another, then went over to her table. He rudely flicked the paper she was reading to capture her attention. "Hey, I'm Piper. Why don't you put that paper down and read me? I'm much more interesting, wouldn't yah say?"

"The only thing I read about you is you're an apparent asshole, and I don't want to be bothered by your disturbing presence. Besides, I lick pussy, and I love it," Sadie replied.

Piper was humiliated by her response and embarrassed when Jason chuckled at her reply. After chugging his beer down, he crumpled his cup, then tossed it on the ground. He looked at Jason. "This shit is warm, more like hot. What the fuck?" then walked out.

After Piper was gone, Sadie looked at the server. "I'm sorry if I caused any trouble, Jason, but that guy had 'creep' all over him."

"Yeah, tell me about it. He was a real work of art," he chuckled. "No harm, no foul. I'm just sorry he bothered you."

Sadie giggled. "I'm sorry he bothered you, too."

"No problem. I don't let jokers like that get to me," he replied.

After folding up her paper, she gave it to Jason. "Here, you're welcome to have it. Maybe this will help pass time, at least until your tent gets filled up with happy drunks," Sadie smiled. "I'm going to try and find a place in the bleachers before it gets overly packed."

"Thanks, and yes, that's a good idea. Wish I could watch from the stands—this T.V. doesn't do it justice. I heard it's going to be especially good this year," he replied.

"Yeah, I believe it will be. My youngest brother is participating this year, along with a friend of mine, who is an all-time-favorite of the people—Sierra Wolfe."

"Yes, I always enjoy watching her drive that big beast; she is fearless," he chuckled. "Good luck to your brother, though. I hope he has a good run."

"Thanks, and yes, she is fearless. Have a good one, and I'll probably be back later," she replied.

On her way to find a seat, Sierra noticed Sadie. "Hey, Carmen, do you mind if I invite Sadie to sit with you while I make my runs?"

"Sure, babe, I don't have a problem with that," Carmen replied.

"Cool. You're awesome, hon," then waved Sadie over. "Hey lady, Carmen has an extra spot next to her, if you'd like to join."

"That would be great, thanks," Sadie smiled.

Carmen returned the smile. "No problem. Hopefully you can educate me during the run. This is my first Mud Digging event ever."

"Well, you're in for a treat. It's quite exhilarating and self-explanatory," Sadie replied.

Sierra listened to them converse and was glad they were getting along. But the bell sounded, calling all drivers to get ready. "Okay, ladies, I need to go and get posted on the start line. Give me good-luck kisses, babe."

"Kisses, baby, with lots of good luck! Please be careful. I love you," Carmen replied.

"Love you too, babe, and it's all good, I promise. Just yell real loud for me," she giggled.

"I will, I can do that. Now get out of here, tiger, and shake up some dust," Carmen replied, then blew exaggerated kisses to her lover. Afterwards, she turned to Sadie. "This is exciting, and did I recall you saying your brother was participating, too?"

"Yes, Mathew is running this year. It's actually his first go at it and very excited, might I add. He's been waiting to turn twenty-one since he was six years old. It's been one of his lifelong dreams to participate in this event. He's always been fascinated with big trucks, and my folks bought him his first truck when he was sixteen. Lo and behold, it didn't run at the time but gave him something to work on over all these years. It kept him out of trouble, at least ninety-nine point nine percent of the time," Sadie replied.

"That's awesome. I hope he does well and is safe," Carmen replied.

"He has had plenty of practice running the farm in his truck. I'm sure he'll be able to hang with the best of them. He's quite the truck monkey."

"Yeah, Sierra gave me a run on her farm, too. I about shit myself, excuse the French," Carmen giggled.

"No problem, I understand. I'm certainly more of an observer to this sport myself," Sadie replied.

Piper was on a mission to find a seat. He grumbled his way through the crowd and up into the bleachers. After he found a seat in the stadium, he flagged down the beer maiden. "I'll take two drafts, and make sure you come back and check on me often." He didn't seem concerned at that time whether his beer was warm or even costly. He was just ready for the show to begin. He was unaware at the time that, just two rows below and almost directly in front of him, sat Carmen and Sadie. As the girls continued their conversation, they both froze in silence when they heard Piper's rude insults to other patrons who were sitting next to him. "Come on, scoot over, for fuck sake. I don't need you fat fuckers squishing me on both sides."

Sadie looked over her shoulder and realized it was the same guy who had made such an ass out of himself. With disgust, she whispered, "Oh my God, it's that belligerent asshole from earlier. He was a real dick in the beer tent."

"Do you know him?" Carmen asked

"No, but had a bit of an encounter with him earlier. He's a real piece of work, to put it politely."

"Yeah, he sure is; his name is Piper. I am an EPA agent and have run into him a couple of times. Each occasion has been dreadful, to say the least. He works for a fracking site in the area that I've been investigating. I'm almost certain his company isn't following proper mandated codes and regulations for drilling. If that's the case, they're contaminating the water source with life-threatening chemicals that seep into the river," Carmen replied.

"Good Lord, I didn't realize it was that serious. Listen, I'm not sure I can be of any help, but I am an investigative reporter. Maybe I could assist in some way; I am very resourceful."

"Thank you, that's very generous of you and would accept any help you could offer me. I've had all I can take of this creep. I'd be thrilled to end the livelihood of this particular organization, but I warn you, this has to stay quiet. If they get word their site is under investigation, it could blow any chance I have at sending them down river," Carmen replied.

"Trust me, in my line of business, discretion is the name of the game, Carmen. I fully understand how important silence can be."

Interrupted by the loud speaker announcing the lineup of Mud Diggers, the crowd exploded with excitement when their favorite contestant was introduced. Carmen waved her arms and cheered loudly for Sierra. "Yeah, that's my girl. You got this, honey. Show them what you're made of!" Sierra saw Carmen and waved her hat back and blew a kiss to her supportive partner. Then a young man stepped forward with a microphone in hand and sang the national anthem. The crowd stood proudly as they listened. Piper was appalled when he realized that was Carmen just a couple of rows below him and then saw the girl he met in the beer tent next to her. He thought to himself, *No wonder she was a bitch—she's friends with those nasty dike whores. I'd like to be a fly on the wall when they're all packing each other with a strap-on. The worthless cunts want to be men and don't have what it takes to get the job done.*

At the sound of the starter gun, all trucks revved their engines. The earth rumbled from the loud and powerful vibration. The crowd stood and cheered as they proceeded through the obstacles of slick, mud-covered hills and pits. It wasn't long before Carmen could barely identify Sierra's truck. After coming back around the course, three trucks that were almost side by side made an impression as they fought each other for the front lead. They barreled over obstacles and each other; their performance had the crowd roaring with excitement. A few minutes later, Sierra flew over the same turn and popped a wheelie as she topped the large hill. Carmen screamed out, "Be careful, baby, oh my God, be careful," then turned to Sadie. "How long does this go on?"

"Until the last man stands, or woman, in your case," she replied. "Looks like some of the competitors have already fallen out. If you look over there to your right, you can see three who have already stalled out in the sand pit. That makes it harder for others to get around them. They just have too much mud on their axles and bogged out when they hit the pit. I'm sure they're newcomers to the game because seasoned diggers make sure to grease the axles well so the mud slides off easier."

"Oh look, there's my girl again. She's going through the sand trap now. COME ON, BABY, KICK ASS, YOU CAN DO IT!" Carmen yelled loudly. Amazed by Sierra's skill, she actually had to climb over the top of a buried truck and plowed through the sand like it was nothing. "Yeah, go, baby, go!" Carmen jumped and cheered for her partner's success. After four laps, Sierra finally took the lead. She pushed her way over and around others in her path. She certainly was a crowd favorite by the way her supporters cheered her on.

Piper was personally disgusted and yelled out, "It's all rigged! She's only ahead because it's been planned that way!" One spectator who was near Piper yelled, "Shut the fuck up, Zero!" And others made their feelings known as well, in regards to his opinionated remarks. Sadie and Carmen were delighted that Piper had been shaken by Sierra's lifelong fans and hoped it would shut him up for a while.

In what seemed like a split second, Sierra once again topped the highest mud hill. The front end of her truck reared up on the back two wheels, and with a blast of the packs, it threw Big Diggs over backwards. Sierra toppled several times down the steep hill. Carmen was beside herself when she witnessed her lover tumbling. "Sierra, oh my God, Sierra!" Carmen yelled out. Just as she jumped up from her seat to race after Sierra, Sadie grabbed her around the waist. "No, Carmen. She'll be fine. She's safe inside and knows what to do. She has safety gear on, and she's strapped in tight. Trust me, her truck is built to handle this and keep her safe at the same time."

Piper broke out in a bellowing laughter. "Silly bitch done got herself in a pickle!" Two brawny spectators sitting directly behind Piper grabbed him from behind and commenced to beat him down to the ground. Security arrived to break it up and drag Piper out of there.

Meanwhile, a tow truck winched onto Big Diggs and flipped her back over with Sierra still strapped inside and mostly unharmed. Sierra gave thumbs up, indicating that she was okay, and threw a kiss out to Carmen. "I love you, Sierra!" Carmen yelled out. The crowd wailed with praise for her good recovery and what could have been a hopeless end to her run. Back on course and plowing over all obstacles, Sierra had lost vital time and was behind by two laps on the top runner. Grinding hard to make the catch, the final horn went off, and she sadly came in fourth place. Sadie was happy that Mathew came in at third. After parking her truck off the field, Carmen ran to her and helped her out. "Are you okay, baby?"

"Yeah, I'm fine, just my ego that's bruised," Sierra replied.

"But you did a great job, and wow, I was totally impressed. Seriously, did you get hurt when you rolled like that?"

"No, at least I don't think so. I may be singing a different tune later tonight, but nothing an ole' hot tub and a little loving won't fix." Sierra smiled, then hugged her lover close, wincing out an "ouch, oh."

"Oh baby, I knew you hurt yourself. Do you think you need to see a doctor? I'd feel better knowing you didn't have any internal injuries."

"No, seriously, just a little bruised," Sierra replied.

"Well, can we go home now?" Carmen asked

"Yeah, I don't see why not, babe. Hey, wait, didn't you want to see the mud wrestlers later?"

"No, not now, I'd rather get you home. My mighty tomboy, you were so brave out there."

Sierra smirked. "Yeah, well, my pride is saying otherwise. I'm just pissed that I hit that hill so hard; I knew better than that."

"You did an awesome job, and I'm proud of you." After saying goodbye to Sadie and congratulating Mathew on his third-place win, the girls headed back home.

The night of fun went on for many, as they enjoyed the springtime event into the wee hours of the morning. As the girls nestled close in bed that evening, they could hear the echoes of celebration still taking place in town. But for these two lovers, there was nothing like the serenity of a peaceful Sunday morning. They had counted on sleeping in after an eventful weekend. That is, until they heard the rooster crow at five-thirty a.m., with his screechy "cock-a-doodle-doo." "Oh my God, I'm going to kill that chicken fucker!" Carmen exclaimed.

Sierra groaned, "Babe, it's a rooster, a *rooster*, as in cock, like 'cock-a-doodle-doo,' cock," then placed a pillow over her head.

"Oh well, that makes all the difference, babe. It's a cock, so it has the right to cock, eh? I still want to choke his chicken cocker. He's such a noisy bastard."

"Honey, I'm trying to sleep. Ouch, Lord, ah," Sierra winced.

"What's wrong? Are you okay, babe?" Carmen asked.

"Yeah, fine, just stiff and a little sore after yesterday's tumble in Big Diggs."

"Oh geez, babe, I think we should go to the hospital. You could be hurt worse than you think you are," Carmen replied with genuine concern.

"No, no I'm fine, seriously. Maybe you could rub some mineral ice on my back; I'd appreciate it a lot, babe. It's in your nightstand, top drawer."

After rustling through the drawer and finding everything but mineral ice, Carmen touched Sierra's shoulder. "Well, maybe you put it somewhere else, hon. However, I did find some Tylenol Arthritis pain medicine. Would you want some of that?"

"Yeah, that'll be good, thanks. I'll look for the other stuff later; it has to be here somewhere," Sierra replied.

"I did find some of that warming massage oil. It's the stuff we used awhile back. Maybe that will help some. Want to try?" Carmen asked.

"Yeah, sure, anything would be helpful, babe."

"Okay, on your tummy if you want me to massage this oil in, Ms. Thang."

"Mmm, ouch, just take it easy on me, babe," she moaned, as she rolled over to her tummy.

"Okay now, slide over in the middle just a little more. I need to straddle your legs, sweetie." Certain to get positioned just below Sierra's buttocks, Carmen squeezed a large amount of oil in the palm of her hands and played it back and forth, until she felt it warming up. She gently massaged it into Sierra's back and hips. "How's that feeling, babe? Let me know if I'm too rough."

"Mmm, that feels better already, Carmen. I love your hands on me, no matter what you're doing."

"Oh yeah," she giggled. "I think you're just horny, although I must say, I'm glad you sleep naked; it's so much easier to get to you," Carmen replied. Unable to resist her control over the situation, Carmen stretched her bare body out on top of Sierra's back and moved gently in a flowing, easy motion of seductive power. She whispered in her lover's ear.

"Can you feel it?" she asked. "The universe—it's moving just for us." Then she placed an alluring kiss on the back of Sierra's neck. "I need you," she whispered again. "I feel the energy pulsing through my veins," as she continued taunting her woman with enticing kisses.

Sierra tried to roll over to her back, but Carmen restrained her attempt. "No, not yet," Carmen whispered. "I'm not done with you in this position," then began biting her back with the slightest nibbles. She straddled her wet and pulsing pussy over one of Sierra's thighs, then ground for her own pleasure. With her hands full of Sierra's long, black hair, she tugged firmly as she climaxed, filling the room with her echo of pleasure.

In the aftermath, as Sierra felt Carmen's grip loosen, she turned over and sat up in bed. "Come here and sit on my lap facing me, babe." Glad to oblige, Carmen submitted to her lover's request. Sierra had her hands wrapped full of her partner's hair. She pulled her head back, while she kissed her neck and just under her chin. "Yeah, I feel it," she whispered. "I feel the universe moving just for us, Carmen." After releasing the hands full of hair, Sierra embraced Carmen's breast. She suckled the sweetness from her erected nipples, as if she were a starving baby. After laying her lover down on her back, she took complete control and positioned herself in the sixty-nine position. They used their tongues to pleasure each other with an insatiable desire of passion. After experiencing electrifying orgasms and exhausted from the early wakeup call, they both fell back asleep, while coddled in each other's embrace. They spent most of their time enjoying the closeness of this newfound lovers' relationship. Together they grew stronger and welcomed in the new season that brought warmth and sunshine to their days.

With a pounding force, the spring rain poured down, and thunder roared through the heavens. John was glad to be off the road from a long drive home, but the heavy rain made it hard for him to see. He was thankful to have had time with his siblings that past winter, enjoying Cancun. It had helped them accept the death of their mother as a family unit. But his eyes lit up when he saw Jude's Diner. He was ready for some good ole, down-home cooking. As he walked through the door, his hat and trench coat dripping with wetness, Jude noticed him immediately. "Hey stranger, glad to see you found your way home, after all this time." She passed him a towel to dry off with, then took his coat and hat. "I'm sorry to hear your mother passed away. How have you and your family been dealing with that?"

"Oh, I could be better, Jude. The family vacation really helped us all to deal with and accept our loss. I'm just glad I could be there for her. Right now, though, I'm especially glad to be home," John replied after giving her a warm hug.

"Sit at this table near me; that way I can enjoy you while I fold napkins. I think we probably have some catching up to do, eh? I bet you enjoyed the family vacation; I'm sure it was nice getting away from it all." She then passed John a menu.

"Yes, it was nice." After glancing at the menu, John slid it aside. "I don't even know why I bothered to look at the menu. I've been craving your biscuits and bacon gravy with three eggs over easy and hash browns. Then, of course, a cup of coffee and orange juice; that would set it off. I'm starving."

"That a boy, I love feeding someone who eats good, especially my cooking."

John smiled. "So what's been new around here? I hate I missed the Mud Dig event, but I'll be sure to catch the big summer blow-out. So give me the dirty, who won?"

"Some new contestant, I think his name was Marc Duitsman. Poor Sierra took a hard knock around when her truck reached the peak of a steep hill and then toppled back down; she rolled several times but came out okay. She took fourth place, and I know it bruised her ego and probably herself, but lucky for her, she made the preliminaries. I'm sure she'll come back with a vengeance this summer, though. She is one stubborn girl," Jude giggled.

"Glad she was okay, and I'm sure she'll come back for another go at it, next run. I need to go see her," John replied.

"She'd like that, John. She and that Carmen gal seem to be quite the item lately; she seems very nice."

"Oh really? She didn't bother mentioning that to me," John chuckled. "Imagine that."

"Oh yeah, before I forget, I didn't see it but heard about it. Some guy who was in the stadium during the event began yelling out hate speech towards Sierra while she competed. I heard the crowd turned on him, beating him ragged; I think they said his name was Piper, some fellow that's been working a drilling site around here. From what I heard, nobody has much good to say about the dude."

"Oh really? That's interesting, Jude. I'll have to look this guy up." After eating his breakfast, John gave Jude a hug. "That was delicious as always. Thank you. You know, before I leave, can I have three cups of coffee to go and two toasted bagels, heavy on the cream cheese. I think I'll go drag Sierra and her friend out of bed and do some catching up."

Just as John walked back out into the rain, a sight for sore eyes appeared. John gladly held the door open for her, as she collapsed her umbrella closed. "Hey there, lady, long time no see!"

"John!"

"Sadie!"

She laughed. "Wow, I was just thinking about you yesterday and was wondering how you've been. What an awesome pleasure; can I buy you a cup of coffee?"

"Yes, but let's take a rain check for another time, very soon. I was just on my way out to bring Sierra some coffee and a bagel. Do you still have the same number?" John asked.

"Yes, I sure do, and John, I'm very sorry to hear about your mom passing away. She was such a great influence in my life when I was growing up. She'll be missed by many, I'm sure."

"Thank you, she thought a lot about you, too. Okay, hon, I'll see you soon. Enjoy your breakfast."

"I will, and I look forward to it," Sadie replied.

Shortly thereafter, Sierra woke to the familiar sound of John's truck pulling into her driveway. "Sounds like John's here, babe," then scurried to the bathroom for a quick once-over and anxiously opened the door to a very big hug from her old-time friend. She laughed, "How was Cancun, buddy?"

"It was great, better than winter here. Jude updated me on the Mud Dig event, told me about your spill; sorry it worked out for you like that. Hey, but looks like you made it through just fine. I heard you took fourth and will be competing this summer."

"Well, hell yes, and will blow their socks off this time. I'm so glad to see you; are you home for good now?" Sierra asked.

"Yes indeed, and I hear you've been holding out on me, young lady."

"About?"

"Uh, about your new love interest," he smiled.

"Oh right, that. Well, it's not that complicated. After Carmen moved in with me on a temporary basis, we decided we liked it and made it a more permanent thing," she grinned.

"How's she been doing since the attack?" John asked.

Before Sierra could reply, she heard Carmen stirring. "Can you hang tight for a minute? I'm going to tell her we have company."

"Sure, no problem. Hurry, though, your coffee and breakfast will get cold."

"Hey, baby, that was John I heard pull into the drive. He brought coffee and bagels for breakfast; are you okay with that?" Sierra asked.

"Sure, babe, just give me a second to get dressed, and I'll be out."

"Okay, see you in a few, and just so you know, our early-morning love making was especially good," Sierra whispered.

"Especially," Carmen smiled. Just as she took a good long stretch, Carmen realized the rain was pounding down and thought, *Hmm, no wonder that chicken's not cocking now. That's right, let the rain pour down, drown your cock-a-doodle-doo, feathered, noise-making ass.* After pulling herself together, she joined the others. "Hey, what a surprise, John. I'm glad you could make it by. It's very nice to finally meet you in person. I've heard so many good things."

"Yes, I have been gone too long and have missed home. The pleasure is mine; I've heard good things about you, too. Here, I got you both a coffee and bagel. I hope it's the way you like it."

"I'm sure it's perfect. Sierra told me about your mother, I'm sorry to hear about that, John."

"Yes, thanks," he replied. "So how have you been? Are you doing okay after your attack?"

"Yes, thanks to Sierra. She has given me new reason to live and push on."

"Aw, babe, I feel the same way," Sierra replied, then gently took Carmen's hand in hers.

"Well, I'm happy for you both," John replied. "I heard about some Piper guy getting his ass beat for mouthing off during the event?"

"Oh that," Sierra replied.

Before she could answer, Carmen stepped in. "Oh, he was an asshole from hell who deserved every hard lick he took and plus some, if you ask me. He is beyond rude and so obnoxious, to say the least."

"Hmm, sounds like trouble," then John shook his head. "Well, it's probably a good thing he got a good old-fashioned welcoming in our parts. Just glad you're both doing well. I hate to cut this short, but I need to get back to town and look up Sadie. I saw her at Jude's just as I was leaving and promised to get with her and catch up on current events."

"Yeah, she's been back in town since the mud event; I'm surprised she's still around. I figured work in Idaho would be keeping her busy," Sierra replied.

"I really enjoyed meeting her, too; she seemed very nice. She mentioned to me that day of the event that the company she works for was in transition and she was on temporary lay- off," Carmen replied, then added, "Hey, thanks for coffee and breakfast; that was very thoughtful of you."

"Yeah, thanks, John. I hope you can come by when you can visit longer. Carmen and I would love to spend more time with you."

"Same here, girls. Take it easy, and enjoy the rest of your day." While walking out to his truck, he called Sadie. "Hey girl, are you still at Jude's?"

"Yes, I'm doing some research since there is Wi-Fi here; Mom is still the old-fashioned type," she giggled.

"Good. Do you mind if I come by and have a cup of coffee with you, or would I be interfering?"

"No, come and join me; I'd love to catch up. I need a break, and this is nothing that can't wait," Sadie replied.

"Good deal. I'll see you in a few minutes."

"Okay."

Just as John was coming around the mountain pass, some burly guy driving an old truck swerved and about ran him off the road. "Hey, dumbass, what the hell!" John yelled out his window, hoping the guy heard him, but he just drove on, acting as if nothing happened. A bit flustered after walking into the diner, John smiled. "Hey girl, hope I didn't keep you waiting too long. Some joker about ran me off the road as I was coming around the pass."

"No kidding! Did you get the license plate number?" Sadie asked.

"No, I didn't have time; I had to regain control of my own truck. I did get a good look at the person driving, though. Trust me, I'll catch up with him."

"Did you recognize him?"

"Maybe, but I can't be sure. Like I said, I'll catch up with him sooner or later."

"Well, I'm just glad you're safe. That pass can be rather treacherous, if I remember right," Sadie replied.

"Yeah, that hasn't changed any." A few minutes later, John glanced up and saw that same truck pull into the liquor store parking lot just across the street. "Hey, that's the truck—it just pulled into Benson Beverage. I'll be right back. I'm going to confront this asshole."

Sadie followed John outside the restaurant. "That looks like . . ."

Before she could finish her thought, John said in a firm tone, "Stay right here; I'll be back in a few minutes."

The man tugged on the door of the liquor store and became aggravated that the business was not open yet. "Well, isn't that just fucking dandy!" he grumbled.

John made it across the street and stood directly behind the patron. "Yeah, it's Sunday. No alcohol is served around here until noon. Besides, you reek like a bottle of bourbon already," John said in a low, deep tone.

"Is that right? Who the hell are . . . " Before Piper could finish his sentence, he turned around and was surprised to see who was behind him. "Oh, hey, I wasn't expecting you back so soon."

"I'm back, dumbass. You about ran me off the road about five minutes ago. What the fuck were you thinking? You didn't even see me."

"I'm sorry, Boss. I dropped a cigarette on my lap, and it was burning me. When I tried to knock it off my lap, I lost control."

"You smell like a fucking rotten egg and reek of alcohol," John spouted, as he shoved his finger onto the man's chest. "And don't be calling me 'Boss' around here, moron. I've warned you about that before, you fucking slob." John paused for a moment. "Shit, you are ate up with the dumbasses, I swear. So here's the deal: Give me your keys. I'm going to walk you across the street to the diner. You can have some coffee and breakfast. Then you'll take a nap in your truck until you are sobered up. I warn you to mind your manners while there, too, or I will make you pay a very harsh price. Don't even act like you know me, you drunk fucker. I'll be watching you," John sternly warned him.

Piper complied with John's request but mumbled under his breath his complete distaste with this whole matter. "When will I get my keys back?" he asked.

"I'll be around," John vaguely replied. "Now, follow me to the diner."

Sadie noticed John coming back with Piper and went back inside to her seat. She hoped to avoid any chance of confrontation with this belligerent character. Then she spoke in a low tone. "Hey, Jude, be prepared for this guy coming in. He can be a real ass," Sadie warned.

"Oh, I've dealt with some pretty foul sorts in all my years. I just make sure to add my special spice to their orders," Jude giggled. Sadie looked surprised by her reply and didn't bother to encourage the spiteful notion.

As the two men walked in, John took Piper by the arm. "Sit down over here, and I'll order for you," John said.

"Can I get pancakes covered in bourbon?" Piper replied.

John scowled at him, then nodded his head as he leaned in close to Piper. "Do yourself a real favor and keep that smart mouth of yours shut while you're in here." Then he walked up to the counter and approached Jude. "I need three pancakes, hash browns, sausage and black coffee for that guy over there. When his order is up, I'll bring it to him."

"No problem, hon," Jude replied.

John returned to his seat with Sadie, then spoke quietly. "Yeah, he was the guy who about ran me off the road. He's already half drunk and seems like real piece of work, to say the least; I don't trust him."

"Well, I'm sure half the township would agree with you. That was the guy at the stadium, yelling out absurd hate comments towards Sierra's performance and sexual preference. His name is Piper," Sadie replied. "I had my first encounter with him in the beer tent that Jason Zachariah was working in. Take my word for it, this guy is a real creep."

"Yeah, that's what I heard. I just wish I could have been there. I would have plowed that dude, too," John replied, then paused for a brief second. "Not to change the subject, but how well do you know Carmen?"

"I just met her once at the mud fest; she seems very nice. Why ask?"

"Oh, it's nothing. I was just curious."

"Oh, come on now, you can't just ask me a question like that and not have a reason," Sadie replied.

"Order's up," Jude informed John.

"Thanks." After John gave Piper his plate, he returned back to his table. "Well, speaking confidentially, Carmen was viciously attacked, shortly after arriving in the area this past autumn. For her own reasons, she chose not to press charges; Sierra was the one to find her and rescue her that day."

"That's awful. Was she attacked, as in raped?"

"The lab results came back positive for semen, but she denies being raped," John replied.

"So why are you bringing this up now, John? Do you think Piper was involved?"

"I don't know, Sadie, but I sure don't have a good feeling about this dude. The bad part is, if he had anything to do with it, he'll sail free, unless she decides to open up about what happened that day or she can identify the man who did this. If you hear anything, do me a favor and keep it under your hat and let me know first. I want to bury the guy, and for my sake, don't tell Sierra or Carmen that we spoke of this today."

"I give you my word, John. But seriously, with his attitude, I'm sure it won't take long for him to show his ass again, and he'll eventually wind up in the clink for something or another," Sadie replied.

"Yeah, you're right, girl, and I intend to keep a close eye on him for everyone's sake; he seems like a loose cannon. I suggest you stay clear of him."

Just about that time, Piper grumbled from across the restaurant, "I'm finished, I'm going to my truck, and make sure my keys are around when I wake up." Just before he walked out the door, he looked at Sadie and huffed, "Seriously, man, why in the hell would you spend your time with the likes of this dike?"

John was out of his chair in a second flat and plowed Piper with a left hook, knocking him to the floor. Then he yanked him up by the scruff. "You filthy piece of shit, don't ever come back in this diner again, and don't ever talk about my friends like that again. This will be your last warning. Next time, I will tar and feather you, then drag your sorry ass out of my town, personally." Then he shoved him out the door.

Sadie stood up from her seat. "John, you didn't have to do that. His words don't bother me. He is more harm to himself than to me. Are you okay?"

"I'm fine. That guy is a real trick, and I will see him to hell and back before he ever harasses anyone here again."

Just about that time, Sadie received a text from Carmen. "Hmm, excuse me for just a second, John."

Carmen: *Hi, it's Carmen. Hope I'm not bothering you too early, but Sierra is going to the township hall tomorrow morning and meeting with a group of people from Mountain Life Magazine she'll be leading as a tour guide for the next couple of weeks. I was wondering if you had time see me in regards to Hilltop Drilling; I have a couple of ideas I'd like to run past you.*

"Well, that's kind of odd. Hold on just another minute, John; I need to reply to this comment."

Sadie: *Sure Carmen, you can meet me at Jude's Diner in the morning if you'd like or I can run out to Sierra's farm. Just need a time that'll work for you.*

Carmen: *Yes, the farm would be great, say around ten o'clock, and thank you so much.*

Sadie: *No problem, I'll see you then.*

"Wow, Carmen wants to meet with me tomorrow regarding some ideas she would like to throw around. I feel honored she asked for my assistance. You know me, I can't resist a good investigation; this could be interesting."

"Right. Did she say what it was about?" John asked.

"Not really. She was brief and not sure I should say anything more until I have talked to her. It might be a confidential matter, but certain I'll know more tomorrow," Sadie replied.

"Just do me a favor, Sadie. Keep me informed if it's anything remotely dangerous, especially if it involves Piper; I don't trust him."

"I don't know but will certainly tell you if it concerns him," Sadie replied.

"Good, I'm glad to hear that. Well, hon, it was nice chatting with you, but I really need to head home and get some things done. Do me a favor—stay clear of Piper. I mean it, Sadie. I don't want to hear that you girls have been investigating him; that guy is bad news."

"Don't worry. I have no intentions of getting around him, John, and yes, I enjoyed our visit—was anything but dull, to say the least." Sadie smiled, then gave her friend a hug bye.

Bang, bang, bang. John pounded his fist on Piper's truck window. "Hey, get up!" he shouted. "Here are your keys, and do yourself a favor, get yourself back to camp. I don't want to hear a single word of you causing any more trouble in this town, you hear! I'll be by there tomorrow afternoon. We have to talk, and just make sure your dumb ass is sober."

Piper took his keys and watched John drive away, then looked at his watch. "Uh huh, about time it's noon. I need some damn whiskey." Then he went inside the liquor store and stocked up. "Give me a case of bourbon," he told the counter help.

"What happened to you?" the help asked.

"What the hell are you talking about?" Piper snarled.

"The dried blood on your face and nose. Are you okay?"

"Mind your own fucking business, taco, and get me my damn whiskey."

After climbing back in his truck, he looked into the mirror. "Oh well, isn't that fucking beautiful. Fucking prick and his swarm of dikes, I'll show them all." He didn't have to try hard to work himself into a rage; it just seemed to come natural for Piper. He spent his drive home planning a way to avenge his dislike for the three women he referred to as dikes, saying aloud to himself, "I'll start by burning that bitch's barn down and blowing up that truck of hers. I don't know who she thinks she is anyways, driving a man's truck like that! Wish she would have broke her fucking neck that day she rolled it;

could have saved me the headache of fucking with her! And that EPA slut, she's going to get hers, and I'll enjoy doing it." He bellowed a loud and evil laugh.

That night Piper drank himself to sleep while his mind wandered into a past of childhood torture. He whimpered through his nightmares, mumbling the words, "no, no," then screeched out a chilling scream that woke him up. He jumped from the bed and ripped his shirt off. He stood before a dirty, cracked mirror and touched a scar that his father had burned onto his chest with a hot branding iron. "Hmm, I'm still alive, you fucking bastard!" he laughed, "You didn't hurt me, and you never did. I am fucking King Kong, and you're six feet under, so take your dick and shove it up your own ass, you worthless prick!" Then he threw an empty whiskey bottle at the mirror and watched as it shattered to the floor.

Just north of Piper about four miles, there was a peace and blissful chill taking place, as Sierra and Carmen had turns rubbing one another's backs and sharing dreams of a beautiful future together. "I love you, Carmen, and promise to always be good to you."

"I feel the same, Sierra. We will live a wonderful life in love." Then she wrapped her arms around her lover and snuggled close. "I do love you," she whispered, "but we should get some sleep. You have a busy day tomorrow. If there's anything I can help you prepare for during your big tour guide expedition this week, just let me know."

"That's nice, thank you. Ugh, you had to remind me. I was enjoying the time off," she sighed.

"Oh, it might be fun," Carmen replied.

"Ha, I can't see taking a bunch of greenhorns traipsing through the mountains as fun. Although I must say, the money is good and needed. I have enjoyed the winter off and sharing it with you, though; I wouldn't have changed a thing."

"See, there you go, a positive attitude will go a long way. Money is always a good form of motivation, although I have loved this lazy winter with you, too," Carmen giggled. "Hell, I wouldn't want to do my job, either, if it wasn't for the large bonus they offered. Hey, speaking of job, I hope you don't mind, but I asked Sadie to meet me here at the house tomorrow. I think she can help me find out more about the owner of Hilltop Drilling; I hope that's okay with you."

"Sure, babe, I think it's a good idea. She is very resourceful; just don't let her charm you," Sierra replied.

"Ah, do I detect a hint of jealousy?" Carmen asked.

"Of course not. I'm just saying she can be very charming at times."

"Oh my goodness, you are a little jealous, babe. I won't have her over then, it's okay, and I can figure this out on my own. Just thought her investigating background could save me a lot of work. Besides, I don't even think she's pretty, and you're the only woman I have eyes for."

"Good, because I feel the same about you, Carmen. Hey, don't change your plans. Your work is as important as mine, and if it's going to help you gain information on this company, by all means, then please follow through."

"Okay, I'll think about it. We should get some sleep. I know we both have a busy day ahead," Carmen replied.

However, Piper was unable to sleep and decided to make a late-night call doing the devil's deed. "I'll show those bitches who they're dealing with," he grumbled, then grabbed a gas can and pitched it in the back of his truck and drove north. He stopped about a quarter mile before Sierra's property and hid his truck in a thick picket of trees and tall brush. He snuck quietly and unnoticed up to Sierra's barn and poured gas all around the perimeter of it, then struck a match and watched until it took a good flame. He hurried his way back to his truck before anyone noticed the blazing inferno. He drove like a bat out of hell back to camp, then took a hose and sprayed his engine down to cool the motor, just in case anyone suspected him of this dreadful action. "Ha, that should do it. If anyone comes looking at me, well hell, I've been sleeping, and my truck hasn't moved all night. I can outsmart them anytime. They think I'm a dumbass; those sorry fucks haven't seen shit yet," he laughed.

Stirred awake by a light flickering through their window, Sierra glanced outside to see the barn engulfed in flames. "Hurry, babe, call fire dispatch!" she yelled out. "I need to check on my horse!" Sierra grabbed on her boots and ran outside. She was thankful to see Jess running through the pasture, spooked but unharmed. She backed up from the heat and ran into the house. "Did you get a hold of the fire department?"

"Yes, baby, they're on the way now. What do you think happened? How did it start? Did you find your horse?" Carmen asked.

"Yes, she's fine, and I don't know what happened. I never keep any flammable liquids in there; I keep all that in the metal shed out back!" she exclaimed. "Fuck, my truck, I need to try and save it!"

Carmen grabbed Sierra by the arm. "No, baby it's too dangerous. Please, calm down some. You have insurance, right, on both barn and truck; it will all be replaceable. Baby, please just be thankful your horse is okay."

"Yes, I'm thankful for Jess, and I do have insurance. This all just sucks really bad. My grandfather had some old antique farming and mining tools in there. Memories like that don't just get replaced. And my fucking truck, oh my God! I feel sick," Sierra replied.

Shortly after the fire truck barreled in and began working quickly to drown the blazing inferno out, Sierra and Carmen stood by watching. Shortly after, John came rushing up her lane. "What the hell, Sierra, what happened?"

"I don't know, John, everything was calm one minute, and then my barn is flaming up in smoke," Sierra explained, and then, overwhelmed by the sight, she bent over and hurled up the dinner she had eaten earlier that evening.

"Easy, baby," Carmen said as she rubbed Sierra's back gently. "Everything is going to be okay, hon. Just breathe, babe."

John noticed her anguish and spoke with loving intent. "Why don't you girls go inside and try to get some rest? There's nothing we can do until the smoldering heat cools down. The fire marshal will be here tomorrow morning to assess the cause, and the fire department has it under control now." John paused for a moment, then placed his hand on Sierra's back. "It'll be okay, Sierra. The damage has been done, and it's all replaceable."

"Not all of it, but thanks for coming, John. Can you see the fire department off the property when they are done?"

"Yes, no problem, Sierra."

The night lingered on, and sleep was not easy to come by for Sierra. She kept her eyes glued to the window until everyone left. Amazing how some people can find such joy in inflicting their hateful deeds on others who are innocent of their convictions or simply being just who they are. Perhaps these types of offenders are just afraid of things they are not familiar with. Or maybe they were raised in a tormented upbringing that left them tainted. Whatever the reason, this person found comfort in witnessing the pain he could inflict on others.

CHAPTER FIVE

Piper woke early that morning to the sound of his laborers arriving to work and on time as usual. He came out from his camper all smiles and greeted his men. "Good morning, guys, or should I say, my happy helpers," he chuckled. A silence from the men was a contagious reaction, due to his unusual good mood. They were afraid to reply with any more than a half-cocked grin or a nod of the head. They were fearful if they said anything, he might just snap back into his normal, hateful antics, raging about anything and everything under the sun. "So, boys, anything eventful happen this weekend?" Piper asked his crew.

One man replied, "Over coffee this morning, I was watching the local news. There was a late-night barn fire that had the township on their toes. Lucky for the property owner, nobody was hurt or killed. But it looked bad. I'd say it was probably a total loss, by the looks of the media clips. Oh yeah, and it was that lady who drove in the Mud Digging contest, the one who rolled her truck. Showed pictures of that truck burnt to a crisp. I imagine that was heartbreaking, and pretty sure her name was Sierra Wolfe."

Piper bellowed out a laugh. "You don't say. Well, after her failing performance from tumbling that truck, she doesn't have any business acting like a man. Waste of good pussy, if you ask me." Some of the guys laughed along with Piper, just to amuse him. They hoped his mood would stay on the unusual upswing of good. Then he remembered. "Oh yeah, the boss might be coming by sometime today, so be on your toes. He is nobody to fuck with."

Surprised by Piper's last comment, one of the laborers spoke up. "No shit, so we are finally going to meet the big guy, huh? I've been with Hilltop for almost three years and have yet to meet him and still don't know his name."

"Yeah, well, he's not the real social type, if you know what I mean. As long as that bastard pays me, I don't give a fuck what his name is!" Piper exclaimed. "Speaking of money, we're burning daylight. Let's get fracking, all you fracker's," then laughed like a fool at his own sense of humor.

Unlike Piper, Sierra barely slept and worried about ordering more hay and feed for her horse. "Carmen, I have two hours before I need to be at the township hall. I've written a list of things I need to accomplish before I leave. Do you think there is any way you can cancel your appointment with Sadie, at least until tomorrow? I could really use your help."

"I'm ahead of you. I've already texted her and asked if we could make it another day. I'm all yours. So what can I do to help out, babe?"

"I called my insurance company, and they'll be here this afternoon, after the fire marshal makes his report. I ordered hay and feed that will be delivered in a few hours. Can you make sure they stack it on the pallets near the metal shed, and then cover it with a big tarp? The feed can be put inside the shed. I'll also need you to do some research on local excavators and organize appointment times that they'll be able to bid the job. As soon as possible would be best, and make sure they know I want the whole area cleaned spotless. I would also prefer they dig a large pit on my land, just out back. I want them to dump all the debris in it, and I'll cover it over after they're done; that is, if I can get that old backhoe started up. I don't want to pay for landfill; that can get outrageous. When I get back from my appointment, I'll start an inventory list of all damaged items that were in the barn."

"No problem, Sierra. I'm sorry you have to deal with any of this and am glad I can be of help. I don't want you to worry about all this; you should focus on the expedition."

"I am a little concerned. I was going to set up camp on the reservation, but that's a few miles away, and I'd feel better being near home. I was wondering, as long as you're good with it, if I could set camp for them at the cabin you were staying in?"

"That would be fine, babe. We just need to keep it quiet; I wouldn't want to alarm the agency. Besides, they think I'm still staying there. But I don't see any problems with it; sounds like a great idea. Just make sure they keep any messes cleaned up," Carmen replied.

"Thank you, Carmen. I can't tell you how much this takes off my shoulders. I love you so much."

"That's what partners are for, and I'm thankful I can help," she said, then hugged Sierra. "I love you, too, and everything is going to be okay. Just breathe."

"I need to get in the shower and be at the appointment on time. I'll be sure to call you after I'm done, so I can let you know what's happening."

"No problem, babe, do your thing, and I'll start looking up excavators now," Carmen replied.

After her shower and her way out of the driveway, John drove up beside Sierra. "Hey, lady, how are you holding up?"

"I'm fine, John. I have to get down to the Village Hall and meet with a group of people that I'll be leading on an expedition. Sorry I can't chat long, but we'll catch up later after the fire marshal has been here."

"No problem. If you don't mind, I would like to take a look around the scene of the fire before he gets here," John replied.

"Sure, no problem. Carmen is home; she's looking up some excavators who can help clean up this mess, and there will be a delivery of feed and hay for my horse sometime soon."

"I won't be in the way and will probably stop in and say hi to Carmen. I need to give her the number of a good excavating company—a friend of mine. Are you cool with that?" John asked.

"Yeah, no problem, just knock before you go in. And do me a favor—don't ask or probe about her past incident. She wants that left behind her," Sierra replied.

"No worries." Then he waved bye as she drove off.

John spent about twenty minutes walking around the burn site and was feeling anxious about the fire marshal's report that would determine the cause. He had his suspicions. A few minutes later, he tapped on the front door, and Carmen cracked open the screen. "Hey, John, come on in. How can I help you?" she asked.

"I wanted to drop by a number for Dwayne Darling; he's a friend of mine who has an excavating company. I'm sure he'll give you a good deal on cleanup."

"That's awesome. I was just getting ready to make some calls regarding that," Carmen replied. "Do you think they could dig a big pit to put it all in? Sierra prefers that over paying for landfill services."

"I'm sure that wouldn't be a problem. He lives a county away, and I'm certain that he wouldn't mind helping out. Just tell him I referred you and that you're a close friend of the family."

"Thanks, John!"

"No problem. I'd do anything for Sierra; she's like a sister to me. Oh yeah, one more thing. I was talking to Sadie yesterday after I left here. She said you were interested in having her help regarding some type of investigation. Do you mind if I ask what that's about?" he asked.

"Well, I prefer to keep my business quiet. I hope that doesn't offend you."

"Sure, no problem. I understand. However, if it has anything to do with the Hilltop drilling site, I strongly suggest that you stay clear of that place altogether. That particular business is already under suspicion for various reasons, and I would hate to see you fined or, even worse, arrested, for interfering with a federal investigation."

"Oh wow, thanks for the heads up. I didn't know. Just glad to hear someone is taking action; saves me the trouble," she giggled.

"Yeah, I would hate to see any more trouble come to you or Sierra," he replied. Then Bear bellowed a loud bark at a vehicle coming down the drive. John glanced out the front door. "The fire marshal is here; I'll let you know what he has to say."

"Thanks, John. I didn't want to deal with that."

"No problem." Then he walked out to welcome him. "Hey, Mike, good to see you. It's a shame it had to be over something like this and not a cold beer in the tavern," he chuckled.

"Yeah right, so how have you been, John? I heard your mom passed away; I was real sorry to hear that. How's the family holding up?" he asked.

"We're all doing fine; just takes time. Thanks for asking."

"So, let's see what happened here," Mike said as they walked over to the remains of the burned barn. After probing around awhile, Mike looked concerned. "Hmm, I hate to say this, but everything indicates that it was started by an accelerant—gas would be my guess. Do you know if Sierra was having any financial problems?"

John looked confused. "No, no, I'm sure she's been fine. Besides, she would never do something like this."

"Fact is, you can never predict someone's actions when things get tough," Mike replied.

"She didn't do this, Mike. If the fire was set, then it was someone else. I know Sierra, and I'll get to the bottom of it. Do me a favor, and mark it up as faulty wiring. I give you my word, I'll find out what happened here, but in the meantime, she needs her barn rebuilt."

"Geez, you put me in a tough spot, John." After scratching his head, he said, "Okay, I'll do this one for you. But let me know when you find anything out, and hey, buddy, you owe me one."

"I got your back, man, and thank you," John replied.

After Mike wrote up his assessment, he passed it to John. "Can you see Sierra gets this?"

"Sure, no problem, and thanks again, man."

"Yep, be seeing you around, and hopefully you buy me that beer," Mike chuckled.

"You can count on it, buddy."

After Mike left, John looked over the assessment, then went inside and laid it on Sierra's table. He glanced around for Carmen, then called out, "Carmen, if you're not busy, I'd like to go over a couple of things with you before I take off."

Carmen appeared around the corner. "Hey, John, what's up?"

"Mike, the fire marshal, just left and said it was due to faulty wiring; Sierra will need to give this to her insurance company if they ask."

"I'll see she gets this, and thank you so much, John."

"You're welcome, and remember what I told you— stay away from Hilltop. We don't need any problems with the feds. Also, keep this quiet; we wouldn't want to jeopardize their investigation."

"I promise, John," Carmen replied. Just seconds after he left, she watched him get in his truck from the kitchen window, then thought, *Piper still needs to pay for what he did to me, and he will.*

John had a lot on his mind, knowing the fire had been set by accelerants; it made him wonder who would have done something like this. Piper was his first thought, and he decided to call him, but there was no answer, so he left a voicemail. "Hey, call me as soon as you get this message. I need to talk to you." The more he thought about it, and against his better judgment of showing his face to the other laborers, he decided to take a drive up to Hilltop and confront Piper head on, thinking, *I'm in my patrol truck; they won't know who I am anyways, as long as that dumb fuck Piper doesn't call me "Boss" in front of them.*

After the men were busy into their day, Piper was sitting on his tractor and saw a fast-approaching SUV. The closer it got, he realized it was John in his police vehicle. He had a bad feeling this was not going to be a good encounter by the way he was driving. Piper jumped down off his tractor to meet him and was almost choked by all the dust created when John skidded on his brakes. The other men noticed the police vehicle and shut down their equipment, but Piper yelled out, "Get those tractors moving! This is no concern of yours!"

As Piper walked up to the truck, John rolled down the window and said in a firm tone, "Get in."

In a matter of seconds, a million thoughts were going through Piper's little mind. He walked around to get in the truck and hoped nobody had seen him near the fire last night. Before Piper could even say "hi," John grasped him up by the collar. "Where the hell were you last night?"

"Here, I was here all night, Boss. What's going on?" Piper replied with a certain fear on his face.

"And I call bullshit!" John exclaimed. "You burned down my best friend's barn. Sierra is my family, like a sister to me, you worthless piece of shit!"

"No, Boss, I swear I don't know what you're talking about! I was here all night, sleeping off my drunk."

John wasn't buying a second of his explanation, then took his gun from his holster and pointed it at Piper's head. "Tell me what you did, or I'll kill you right here!"

Piper felt the cold, hard steel pressing into his temple, and beads of sweat dripped from his forehead. "Boss, please, I didn't go near her place. I didn't have anything to do with it."

"What do you mean, you didn't go near her place? That tells me you know where she lives, and you're the only one stupid enough to pull some shit like this! Do I look stupid to you? I know how you feel about her and Carmen being lesbians and the fact that you failed as a man to kill Carmen, when you had the chance to. I also know you had your ass kicked at the Mud Dig event. You spewed profanities regarding their sexual preference. You wanted to teach them a lesson, didn't you?"

"Boss, you're right, I don't like lesbians. I especially don't like these two women or even their friend you were with at the restaurant yesterday, but I didn't do this. I didn't burn down her barn, I swear to that," Piper replied with a deep sigh, then continued, "Boss, why in the world would we not complete our mission killing Carmen? What makes her less dangerous to our business now?"

"I have taken care of her. She won't be nosing around Hilltop anymore. The best thing you can do for yourself is to keep your lousy, drunk ass right here, on site, and forget about anything but work. If you want that two point five million bonus payoff, then you'll take what I'm saying seriously."

"That's all I want, Boss, just want to make sure our business pays off," Piper replied.

"Not 'ours.' moron, 'mine,' and as long as you keep your ass out of trouble, you'll get your money. Now get your ass back to work and make me some money. I'll have a buyer by next month, and all this shit will be over." John lowered the gun from Piper's head and said in a low deep tone, "Stay away from Sierra and Carmen. Last warning, or I will kill you."

Piper exited the vehicle and watched John drive away. As he walked back up to his tractor, one of the guys yelled out, "Hey, is everything okay? What did the cop want?"

"Everything is fine. Now get back to work!" Piper growled.

Later that afternoon, Sierra escorted her team of tourists up to Carmen's cabin. "This is where you'll be staying. I know the accommodations are cramped, but consider yourself lucky that you won't be camping outside; the sow bears can be very territorial this time of the year with their new cubs. Please be ready at seven a.m. sharp. That means make sure you have eaten a healthy breakfast and have your backpacks loaded with everything you think you'll need to survive a fifteen-mile hike. If there aren't any questions, I'll be heading back home. Please feel free to call me if you need anything between now and seven o'clock tomorrow morning."

"I have a question. Can we make a campfire?" one of the tourists asked.

After glancing around outside, Sierra saw a fire ring where other fires had been. "Certainly, I don't see why not. Just make sure you keep it in this ring, and you'll have to forage for firewood. I suggest that you do that before sundown. And one more thing—please be responsible with it; we don't need any forest fires."

Carmen was busy in the kitchen preparing a nice meal for them, when she noticed her lover coming up the driveway through the kitchen window. *Shit, what did I do with that lighter? I want these dinner candles lit before she gets in here,* she thought. At the sound of the door opening, Carmen used her body to block the kitchen area from Sierra. "Hey, babe." Carmen smiled a mousy grin. "I'm glad you're home. Do you have a lighter?"

"Um, yes I do. Is everything okay?" Sierra asked hesitantly.

"Yes, of course it is; well, it is now that I have a lighter. Can you just go wait in the living room or something? I need a moment to finish up here."

"Sure."

After lighting the candles on a beautifully set table, Carmen was ready to share a romantic dinner with her partner. "Okay, babe, you can come in the kitchen now."

"Wow, this is nice, Carmen. The setting is beautiful. You never fail to amaze me with your thoughtfulness, babe. I'm starving."

"I thought you would be, and hope you like your prime rib medium rare; I had them special cut for us today when I was at the market," Carmen replied.

When Sierra washed her hands at the kitchen sink, Carmen stood close behind her. She wrapped loving arms around Sierra's waist, then kissed her on the back of the neck. "Mmm, I missed you today, Sierra Wolfe."

"Mmm, how do you that? Every time you touch me, you take my breath away." Then she turned around to greet her lover with an insatiable kiss. "And I love my prime rib medium rare, Carmen Storm."

While enjoying a nice dinner together, Carmen presented the fire marshal's assessment. "John was kind enough to bring this in, and it appears to have been started by faulty wiring. He said you'll probably need this for insurance purposes."

"Ah well, that's good. I guess that takes away the mystery of it all. Now to get the insurance company to build a new barn and replace my truck without any issues will be the next step. I'm just thankful that I have a reliable company to deal with," Sierra replied. "So how did everything else go today, babe?"

"It went very well. The feed and hay were delivered shortly after you left, and John showed them where to unload it. He also gave me a number to an excavator, actually a friend of his, so I took the liberty of calling him and gathering prices. He also said that digging a pit would be fine and that he actually preferred that option over the dump site, too." Then she presented the notes she took for Sierra to look over.

"Thank you for all your hard work, Carmen. I love you so much, woman."

"I love you, too, babe. So tell me about your day."

"Well, my day, hmm, where to begin," she smiled. "I met the group as intended, and, of course, we had to sit through all the safety films that contain vital information. They're boring but important. Especially in the event one of them were separated from the group or injured on the expedition. As in most groups, some fell asleep, and others took notes, so we'll see, I guess. Knock on wood so far, I have been mishap-free on any of my tours." After taking a sip of her wine, she went on to say, "I did get them up to your cabin and settled in. I need to be there at seven a.m. to begin our journey in the morning. I hope they're all ready."

"Well, I wish you the best of luck and will hope for a problem-free excursion," Carmen replied.

"Thanks, babe, I appreciate that. Listen, I hate to ask for any more of your time, but I wonder if you can get video footage of the burnt barn tomorrow, including my truck? Are you okay with that?"

"Yeah, sure, babe, I can certainly do that for you."

"Thank you so much. Carmen. I'll owe you big time for this, and after everything is over, I would like to do something special for you. Maybe we will take a vacation together somewhere special."

"Babe, that sounds nice, but you don't have to do that for me. Like I said, it's what partners do for each other; I'll always have your back. You mean so much to me," Carmen replied.

"I like the way you think, woman. You always warm my heart with the things you say and feel."

"Well . . . " she paused for a moment, "enough of that kind of talk; it's making me blush. But just so you know, tonight is our night, and I can't wait to spend it with you. Hopefully you're up for sharing a shower with me, and we can take it from there." Carmen smiled, then took her lover's hand and gently squeezed it. "I am so in love with you."

"Yes, and I am so in love with you, Carmen. The dinner was excellent, and after I clean up the dishes, I'll take you up on that shower and wherever the night brings us."

"No, baby, the dishes can wait. I feel so dirty," Carmen replied, then took Sierra by the hand and led her to the bathroom.

Sierra whispered, "So where are you feeling dirty at? Right here?" as she cupped Carmen's crotch in her hand, then moved up to her lover's breast. "Or right here?"

Carmen replied in a slow, seductive tone as she turned on the shower, "Everywhere. Wash me."

Sierra saturated the loofah with body wash and caressed it gently over her lover's wet skin. Her appetite grew with an insatiable hunger. She let the sponge fall from her hand and went to her knees. Carmen moaned with sounds of delight. She filled her hands with Sierra's hair and pulled her in close. She experienced the satisfying pleasure that was being received and could barely get enough. After Carmen had reached her climax, she gently coaxed Sierra up to her feet and pressed her against the wall of the shower. She kissed her with a forceful passion, then slipped her fingers inside her partner and pressed her knee between Sierra's legs. As the water sprayed over their bodies, it stimulated her senses. Every touch from her lover was electrifying. Sierra murmured sounds of a gratifying climax, while her partner held her tight. The magical dance ended with a powerful delivery of sheer satisfaction; they consumed the remainder of this perfect evening cradled in each other's arms.

Unlike others who harbor secrets of deception, John paced the hardwood floors of his home; he clicked his lighter lid while he contemplated his current situation. He paused for a moment and looked deep into a mirror, then removed it from the wall and set it aside. After taking in a long breath, John slowly exhaled as he dialed in the combination to the existing wall safe. He removed a small metal box and sat down at the kitchen table. After touching the top of it ever so gently, he remembered the day he had acquired it and the day his life changed. John had just turned twenty-one. He was sitting in class at the police academy when he received a message alert from Gifford Bank in Idaho. The email told him there was a safety box that contained his rightful property, and he could obtain it at the age of twenty-one. John also remembered being mystified; he didn't waste time acquiring the box and feeding his hungry curiosity. After reminiscing, John opened the box again for the first time in twenty years and took out the letter he had read back then. He sat quietly absorbing the words, just as he had the first time he ever read it.

Dear John, my only son,

I know this might come as a shock to you, and if you're reading this, then I have passed away, but I felt compelled to let you know the truth.

I met your mother when I purchased industrial land in Montana; we dated a couple of years while I worked there. She became pregnant with my only son, but she was in love with another man. She pleaded for me to walk away and let him raise you, so I did.

I was hurt but eventually moved on with my life. I met a woman who unfortunately died when giving birth to my only daughter and your half sister, Sara Tag; she is two years younger than you and was raised in Idaho with me. I often watched you from afar, when I was back in town working my land. I enjoyed seeing you grow up and especially enjoyed watching you and your team compete in grade-school basketball.

With all of this being said, I have written in my living will that upon my death you shall receive the deed to my land there, when you turn the age of twenty-one. This land is rich in oil; you can make a very nice living drilling on Hilltop, as long as you keep it in my name. I have supplied you with a number for a buyer, Gary Post, who offered to purchase the land from me on a couple of different occasions. If he is still interested in the land and you choose to sell the property to him, I have also left you with the deed and an account number to a bank in Switzerland for transactions of sales; this will keep your profit under the radar from the hungry wolves running our government.

The only thing I ask is that you find your sister when the ship comes in and share a quarter of the profit with her. You can make a private donation to her, or if you feel compelled to meet her and share our story, then by all means do so. Just promise me that you will follow through with my wishes as long as she is still alive and well.

Good luck in this life, son. You will find everything you need in this box to continue my legacy.

Love, Dad, aka Collin Tag

After John read the letter, he placed it back in the box. "Sara, where are you?" Then he picked up the phone and called the interested buyer Collin had left for him. He informed Gary Post that he was ready to sell the land and mineral rights, if he was still interested.

Gary's ears were wide open. "Yeah, I am interested in Hilltop, and you said your name was John? I thought Collin Tag owned and operated that property."

"Yes, I am his son. He left the property to me at his unfortunate early death, and I have been working the land ever since."

"I'm sorry to hear about your father passing away. How much are you asking for the land and mineral rights?" Gary asked.

"I'd like ninety million for land and rights, but would consider taking eighty-five, bottom dollar, if we can have the sale accomplished within thirty days or less."

"Hmm, I need to take a look at my schedule. Do you have the deed to the land?"

"Yes, I'm holding the deed in my hand as we speak."

"Okay, well, like I said, I'll take a look at my schedule and let you know when we can get together. I am interested.

Are you able to come to Dallas, Texas, to swap money for deed?"

"Yes, I could do that but would prefer that you transfer the purchase amount to a Switzerland account on the day we meet. Are you capable of doing that?"

"Certainly. A transfer is much easier than bringing that kind of cash, any day," Gary replied.

"Good. Well, I look forward to doing business with you and will be waiting for a date to meet with you."

"Thanks, John. I've been wanting this land for some time now."

When the call was over, John went to his office within the local police department, and for the first time in several years, he felt compelled to run a search for his long-lost sister. Before he could make it into his office that night, he saw Brittany standing outside, smoking a cigarette. "Hey, John, what brings you here so late this evening?" she asked.

"Just some research. Why are you here so late?"

She giggled, "Yeah, about the same for me. Did you ever find anything out about the missing articles that were in my lab?"

"Actually, that has been turned over to the feds and could be directly linked with an investigation. I'm sure we'll know something soon, but then again, the feds never move too quickly. However, I shared all the information with them," John replied with a fabricated explanation.

"Oh well, that's good, I guess, and so there is nothing for me to worry about then, right?"

"Yeah, just be sure to keep it quiet for now. I would hate to jeopardize the investigation."

After talking with Brittany, John continued into the building to begin his own investigation. During his search, he found court records of a Sara Tag that had been adopted in Idaho after her father had been fatally shot to death in Montana. The age sounded right, but the records were vague and the leads were slim to nothing. John decided to look further into the history of his alleged father, Collin Tag, in hopes of finding a lead to his sister. He learned his dad had a pretty long rap sheet of sex offenses but couldn't understand why his records were inaccessible. John was frustrated by the fact he couldn't obtain the information and was disturbed at himself for waiting so long to look up any records on either of them.

John's head was spinning with all this lack of information and the land sale that would be taking place soon. His eyes were tired and mind spent for the night. He felt like he just needed to process before he pushed further into Collin's history and the whereabouts of his sister.

CHAPTER SIX

Sprawled out on her stomach and dead to the world around her, Carmen was fast asleep while Sierra quietly tried to get ready for her day. She was able to accomplish her task without disturbing Sleeping Beauty. Just before she left, Sierra placed a note on Carmen's nightstand, then brushed her lover's hair back ever so gently and kissed her cheek. "Bye for now, baby. I love you," she whispered. Untouched by the sound of her voice, Carmen continued to rest peacefully.

Upon her seven o'clock arrival at camp that morning, she found a couple of guys still asleep by the smoldering campfire. Sierra walked up to them and gently kicked their feet, in hopes of stirring them awake. "Come on, guys, if you want to make the hike today, I'm out of here in five minutes." The others were up and raring to go on their day's adventure. After seeing a couple of empty bottles of whiskey near the two men, Sierra realized they probably weren't going anywhere. "All right, well, five minutes is up. Do yourself a favor—stay here and don't try to catch up; I don't want to be responsible in the event you get lost." Then she glanced at the group. "Okay, so is everyone else packed up with plenty of water and food supply for the day?"

The majority of the group nodded their heads, and others commented with a "yes."

"Great, let's do this," Sierra replied.

Unlike others who enjoy sleeping in, Jude was not among them. She has always been an early riser with a pleasant morning spirit. This made serving customers this early in the morning much easier for her than others. Just as she had turned the "open" sign around in her restaurant window, a familiar face appeared. This brought a smile to Jude. "Well, hey there, John. I don't mean to be rude, but you look like hell, hon. How about a cup of coffee on me?"

John smirked. "Yeah, it was a long night, to say the least. Do I really look that bad?" he asked.

"Nothing a hot cup of coffee won't fix and maybe a shower," Jude replied, then placed his coffee in front of him. "Can I get you some breakfast?"

"No, thanks, but maybe later. Listen, Jude, since it's quiet in here right now, do you think you can sit with me a few minutes? I have a couple of questions you might be able to help me with."

"Sure, be glad to help if I can," she replied.

"Do you recall anyone by the name of Collin Tag? He would have been around these parts in the early seventies."

"Hmm, yes, I believe your mother dated him for a little while back then before you were ever born, and I'm pretty sure he worked in the area. I want to say he was pretty hard on your mom towards the end, and she broke it off with him. I haven't seen him in these parts for several years."

John nodded his head. "He died in the early eighties, and according to records, he was shot to death in Montana. He left a daughter behind. She was just a couple of years younger than me; the information I received was vague. What I did find was in a brief court document regarding his daughter's adoption."

"I don't know, honey. I wish I could be of more help." Just then, a couple of regulars showed up for their coffee and breakfast. "Okay, I need to get busy, and if I think of anything more, I'll be sure to let you know." Before she walked away, a thought came to Jude's mind. "Have you tried asking Sadie for help? She's pretty good at finding out things."

"That's not a bad idea, Jude, and thanks for your time this morning."

"No problem. Always a pleasure, John."

John left the conversation feeling at ease. He was glad that Collin's letter had panned out and was looking forward to the sale of the land. But he was still curious about several things, like his father's past history and why the last few criminal records have been sealed. John felt convinced to do right by his half sister and willing to share the determined percentage with her. He was anxious to put this puzzle together and curious about the sibling he had never known.

Selling the land was John's main priority at the moment. He looked forward to ridding himself of the responsibility and any connection to it. He was tired of the worry and thought to himself, *After I sell the property, I'm going to wash my hands clean of it all. Maybe get married and have a kid of my own.*

A miserable, grumbling Piper lashed out harsh demands on his crew that morning, just as he did most mornings before. Whatever his reasoning may have been, Piper always had a productive crew. In the metal box Collin left behind for John several years ago, another note highly suggested Piper as the top crew leader. Collin explained that Piper was an old Navy Seal buddy of his. John had taken Collin's advice twenty years ago and hired Piper to maintain and operate the business, enabling John to keep a low profile in a shady business affair.

Piper was alerted when he felt his phone vibrating. After glancing at it, he realized he had an incoming text from his boss.

Boss: *Meet me behind the Laundromat just off Fifth Street in twenty minutes, don't be late.*

Piper: *No problem, Boss, see you then.*

Piper grumbled, "What the fuck does he want now, for crying out loud? He's a pain in my fucking ass!" Then he climbed down from his tractor and sounded a buzzer to capture his crew's attention. "I need to run into town and see the boss for a minute. I won't be gone long, so don't be fucking around, or I'll dock your fucking pay!" he barked out. After taking a shot of whiskey, Piper drove down the mountain to meet John and griped out loud, "He better not mention a word about that bitch's barn burning down. There's no evidence. He must think I'm an idiot! Well, I got his idiot right here!" then grabbed his crotch and spit out the window. As Piper pulled behind the Laundromat, he didn't see John there yet. "Oh great, that's just fucking great! I'm here burning good daylight, waiting on this prick to show up at his own leisure."

A few short seconds later, John pulled up beside Piper. "Shut your truck off and get in with me."

Piper followed John's cue and shut his truck down, then joined him in his vehicle. "What's up, Boss?"

"I talked to the buyer last night, and we'll be making a transaction soon. I look forward to the land being sold. I'm tired of the headache, and the payoff will be good for an early retirement for both of us. I wanted you to know that I appreciate all your hard work over the years, and you can expect double the bonus after the transaction is complete. You will be five million dollars richer, instead of the two point five we spoke of originally, and you deserve it."

Practically at a loss for words, Piper didn't know how to respond. Just the mere thought of being rich and retired sounded like paradise to him. "Wow, fucking wow, Boss. I don't know what to say. This is fucking awesome!"

"Make sure to keep this quiet with the other laborers, and when I lay them off, I'll be sure to compensate them with a nice-sized bonus check. That'll keep them occupied for a few months."

"Thanks, Boss. I couldn't have done it without a good crew on hand. They have worked their fucking asses off."

"While I have you here, Piper, how well did you know Collin Tag?"

"Fucking Collin and I were shipmates; he was a crazy son of a bitch. After our tour, we both went back home to Idaho. We had plans to buy land in Montana to work, but he got some bitch pregnant and had a kid. I never heard much from him after that, until you called and said he referred me. I heard through the grapevine that somebody capped the fucker but never did know for sure," Piper replied.

"Did you ever meet his kid?" John asked.

"No, he said he didn't want old buddies around his daughter. Probably afraid of her getting molested by some old horny bastard like himself. I bet he had his turns with her, though." Piper laughed out loud.

John was silent for a moment, while Piper kept rattling on about perverted nonsense. "Okay, I get the picture. So you know nothing else about Collin?"

"No, I guess not. How did you know him anyhow?" Piper asked.

"He was scouting some land here several years ago. He never did buy and wondered if he would be interested in it now. He's the one who suggested that you would be a good crew leader. But if he's dead, I guess my questions were useless. Besides, the buyer I have now is solid. I guess I just wanted to see if Collin would pay me more for it." John coyly misled Piper for his own reasons.

"Oh well, sorry I couldn't help you out any more than I did, Boss."

"Not a big deal. Just remember to keep our proceeds quiet from the crew, and I'll compensate them in due time," John replied.

"Okay, Boss, you can count on me, and thanks for making my day."

"We'll talk soon. Take it easy, Piper."

Piper's whole attitude changed after that visit. He was glad that the barn wasn't an issue and that he would soon be a millionaire. "Whoop, whoop!" Piper shouted out the window of his truck while he drove back to work. "A fucking millionaire! How you like me now!" He laughed a loud, vexatious laugh.

John was equally excited to see the payoff coming sooner than later, although he had hoped for a better return of information regarding Collin. Shortly after he left Piper, John called a friend, hoping for a little assistance. "Hey, Sadie, this is John; call me back when you get this message. I think I have a project for you." John went about his day and placed the sale procedures as a priority over his secondary concern of finding his half sister.

Later that morning, while Carmen was basking in the luxury of a hot tub, she used her handheld voice recorder to make a list of grocery items. The solitude felt nice, that is, until she realized she had a peeping tom of the feathered type. "Oh no, you don't!" She threw a towel at the screened-in window. "Get out of here, you freaky chicken cocker!" But the rooster stayed there, perched on the window sill, just nodding his head as he pecked the screen. Carmen was getting more unnerved by the second and still traumatized by the last encounter they had. After climbing out of the tub, she slipped into her robe and found a broom to chase the rooster away with. After a few good swooshes, directly aimed at the bird, he wasn't real happy and decided an eye for an eye and darted at Carmen. She jumped back just in time and hurried back inside. "That's it, you bastard. I've got something for you." Carmen saw the shotgun, and with intent, snatched it up. She went outside to reckon with this rooster for the last time. "Say goodbye, you fucking cock!" The gun blasted off, and feathers went flying.

Sadie had just pulled into Sierra's driveway when she heard a single gunshot sound off. "Shit, what was that?" she asked herself, then cautiously went around back. She found Carmen with a gun in one hand and a dead rooster in the other. "Hey, is everything okay?"

Carmen was startled by the voice that came from behind her. "Oh my goodness, you scared me," she said, then smiled. "Um, he was a bad chicken," Carmen replied, with a half- cocked grin.

Sadie let out a bit of a nervous giggle. "Ah, a bad chicken, eh?"

"Yeah, he was. He was actually very bad and noisy. I just hope he makes a good chicken soup; that will save me a trip to the grocery store." After Carmen set the gun down, she put the rooster in a bag. Sadie followed close behind and was curious about what she would do next.

"Go ahead; take a seat at the table if you have time. I'm going to clean dinner." Carmen smiled as she held up the bag.

"Oh my, you are wild woman, aren't you?" Sadie replied.

"Um, maybe a little bit. My father taught me survival skills, and he took it very serious. I've been hunting and cleaning prey since I was old enough to hold a .22 rifle. But enough about me; what brings you out this way today?" Carmen asked.

"Cabin fever. Figured I'd take a drive and check out the damage to the barn—an obvious total loss, from what I've seen. How's Sierra handling it?"

"She seems to be fine. I've been taking care of minor details for her. She's been staying busy with her tour."

"Aw, that's nice, I'm sure she appreciates that. Not to change subjects so quickly, but I was talking with John a few days back, and he doesn't think it's a good idea to probe around Hilltop. He said the feds are already suspicious of certain activities there, and they're under investigation. Did he mention any of that to you?"

"Yes, the day after the fire we had a similar talk. I guess it doesn't really matter, as long as someone takes that company down," Carmen replied.

Sadie nodded her head, then glanced at her phone, noticing a missed call. "Ah, speak of the devil, looks like I missed a call from John," she sniggered. Then she shared a past memory. "You know, John, Sierra and I had a lot of fun

174

in the day. We were all so mischievous but somehow always wound up on our feet. Mostly harmless fun, but then again, others might disagree."

"Yes, knowing Sierra like I do now, I can just imagine the handful she must have been. It's probably a good thing we lived miles apart until we were older," Carmen replied while she chopped vegetables for her soup.

"You could be right. So how's that rooster roasting over there? I must say, it smells good."

"That would be the sage and garlic with a touch of parsley; the combination is always an enticing aroma. I used to love coming home from school, and Dad would have homemade soup brewing. Always felt so homey."

"Yes, I still love when my mom or dad cooks." After a brief silence, Sadie asked, "So where do your parents live?"

"My parents have passed away. However, I've lived in Idaho most of my life," Carmen replied, then was distracted by an incoming call from Sierra. "Hey, I need to take this call; it's my sweetheart."

Sadie whispered, "No problem, nice visiting you. I should really get back to town; tell Sierra I said hello."

"I'll do that. Thanks for stopping by, Sadie."

On her drive back to town, Sadie took the opportunity to listen to the voicemail John had left for her earlier in the day. After listening, she was curious about the message he had left and was inclined to know more about the project he spoke of. Just a few minutes after Sadie left a return message to him, expressing her interest, he called her seconds later. "Hey, big guy, I'm so glad to hear back from you so soon. You certainly have my undivided attention. What's up?"

John replied with a hopeful enthusiasm, "Cool, glad you're interested and that it strikes your attention. I could really use some extra assistance with this project. I'm going to be pretty busy today, but if you have time in the morning, maybe we can get together over coffee. We could meet up at Jude's, say around eight-thirty?"

"Sure, that works for me. What is it about?" Sadie asked.

"I need help with a little research regarding a certain individual. I'd like to know more about this person but don't really have the time to invest of my own right now. If you'd like a jump-start on tomorrow's visit, I can leave you a detailed text message."

"Sure, that'd be great, John."

"Okay, well, thanks. I really appreciate it and look forward to seeing you in the morning."

After hanging up, John texted Sadie: *The person of interest would be Sara Tag. She was raised in Idaho. She lost her mother early in life and then her father when she was in her early teens. She was adopted by a family with the last name of Storm, but the records are sealed after that. Her father's name was Collin Tag, and that's all I really know right now. So I was hoping you could dig beyond that point and hopefully help me locate her.*

Sure, I'll see what I can find out, she replied.

Thanks, Sadie, and it's vital you keep this just between us; it could devastate my investigation if you were to share this information with anyone else.

No problem, John. I look forward to our visit tomorrow.

Same here, talk more then.

***

A rumble of dump trucks and excavating equipment roared up the driveway. Bear was alarmed and sounded off a repeating series of guarded barks. This captured Carmen's attention. "Bear, come on, it's okay, they're here to work." She encouraged him to come inside the house with an enticing rawhide bone, then went out to greet the group of laborers.

A tall, lanky, bearded man approached her with a clipboard that contained a contract for services that would be performed. He extended his hand. "Hi, I'm Dwayne Darling, but you can call me Bob. I take it you're Sierra Wolfe."

"No, she's working right now. My name is Carmen. I do live here and was asked to expect you, though," she said, then accepted his handshake. "It's nice to meet you, Bob, and glad you were able to get here so soon, especially on such short notice."

"Yep, no problem at all. The Buck family has always been good to us. Consider yourself lucky that John referred you because we've been staying pretty busy. I have a contract here; are you able to sign it for Ms. Wolfe?"

"Yes, we are partners."

"Okay, sounds good to me," then passed her the contract. "I need you to read this and sign it. We should only be here three days, by the looks of it," Bob replied.

"Wow, that's fast, but before I forget, Sierra wanted to know if you guys could dig a big pit out back; she'd rather have that than to pay for landfill."

"Sure, that'd be fine. It'll save me the trouble of hauling the debris off. But the price will stay the same, whether I dig a pit or haul it to the dump. It amounts to labor and time expense. Does she want me to cover it back over when we're done?" he asked.

"Sure, I understand. As long as you can dig that pit, Sierra can cover it back up. Just having it will make her happy." After looking over the contract, Carmen signed it, then passed it back to him. "There you go, it's signed. Now if you need anything, such as water, there is a hose over here on the side of the house; help yourself. As far as the restroom, well, your guys can do that outside or you may want to order a portable potty house. I'll be busy working inside and can't be disturbed. Oh, and one more thing, please keep the gate to the fence closed. Sierra would shit if her horse got out."

"That won't be a problem, ma'am."

Much later that afternoon, an exhausted Sierra finally made it to the sanctuary of her home. When she drove into her driveway, she was pleased to see all the progress the excavators had made that day. After opening her truck door, she sat there for a second, taking it all in. The long hike that day had taken a toll on her body. She thought silently, *I really need a treadmill for next winter. I can't believe how this first spring hike wore my ass out.*

A few seconds later, Bear alerted Carmen that his mom was home. He wanted out to see her. He pranced and moaned until she let him out. Carmen noticed Sierra was walking stiff-legged and went outside to greet her girlfriend. "Hey there, baby, welcome home. You look bushed. Are you okay, babe?"

178

"Oh yeah, I'm fine. I guess I'm getting old or lazy," Sierra replied, then sat on the front porch with her legs dangled over the edge. "Hey, come here," she said, and gently pulled Carmen close between her legs. They gave each other a warm hug. "Ugh, it's been a long day, and yes, 'bushed' is putting it mildly," Sierra smiled. "I'm glad to see the excavators made it here today; looks like they got a lot done."

"Yes, they sure have, considering they showed up later in the morning. Bob, the crew leader, said the project will take approximately three days and said the pit wouldn't be a problem. Although he did say the price would stay the same, and you get to cover it over when you're ready to."

"That's cool; thanks for helping out, babe," Sierra replied, then playfully smacked Carmen's butt. "How has your day been?"

"It was good. Come on, let's go in. After you take a hot shower, I have some homemade chicken and dumplings prepared for dinner."

"No shit. Wow, that sounds good. I haven't eaten that for years, Carmen."

Then while Sierra bathed, Carmen contemplated if she should tell her about the rooster incident that morning. She wasn't sure how Sierra would take the news and worried that it might upset her or even anger her. She ultimately decided not to mention it, thinking, *If the subject of his whereabouts came up, I'd just play dumb and say I haven't seen him since the excavators showed up.*

Like poetry in motion, Sierra lit up the room as she entered the kitchen, wrapped only in a towel. Her long, dark hair trickled down her back, and it glistened from the dampness. Carmen couldn't help but silently admire her lover's beauty, as she watched her fill a glass of ice. "Mmm, I'm making a glass of tea; would you like one?" Sierra asked.

"Sure, anything to watch you move around a little longer. What a beautiful sight you are, Sierra."

A blushing Sierra replied, "Thank you," then passed Carmen her cold drink. "Dinner smells so good, babe. I'm starving. Do you mind if we eat now?"

"Absolutely. Just take a seat, and I'll get you a plate."

"No, you don't need to do that. Seriously, I can make my own, babe."

"Nope, no arguing; I have this," Carmen insisted.

After retrieving a beautifully tossed salad from the refrigerator and rolls from the oven, Carmen filled a steamy bowl full of chicken and dumplings, then placed it on the table. "Hope you like it, babe, sounded good to me today."

"It smells delicious. Are you going to eat with me?" Sierra asked.

"Yep, I've smelled it cooking all day, vampire hungry for it," she teased.

"I was vampire hungry for you today. During a twenty-minute break from the hike, I got so horny thinking about us, I had to distract myself before I creamed my jeans in front of the whole team. I couldn't imagine explaining why I had a wet spot on the front of my pants," she giggled.

"Yeah, that may have been awkward to explain, naughty girl; you do look irresistible in that towel, though. Perhaps I'll be able to find that horn that was sticking you earlier," Carmen teased. She enjoyed watching Sierra eat her dinner and was thankful the rooster had cooked down tender.

"Mmm, perhaps you will; as long as you can keep me awake. This dinner may just knock me out. It's so . . . " Before she could finish her sentence, she bit down on something hard. "Ouch," she said, then pulled it from her mouth. "What the heck? Looks like buckshot."

"Let me see," Carmen replied. "Hmm, sure does. Imagine that." In an attempt to hurry and change the subject, she took Sierra's hand. "Oh, babe, you look exhausted. You must be, and your eyes are showing it this evening. Maybe I'll just spoil you with a good old-fashioned back rub and snuggles tonight."

"Oh goodness, that sounds heavenly, Carmen. I love you."

The girls turned in earlier than usual that evening, while others spent their time in a local bar celebrating things that have not yet come to pass. Piper had actually taken a shower and enjoyed spending some of the money he had put back on drinking and poker machines. After winning back a hundred dollars from one of the machines, he decided now was a good time for a smoke break in the alley just behind the bar. While he was outside, he glanced around to make sure he was alone, then peed on a brick wall. He was startled when he felt a hand touch his shoulder. "Hey, mister, I can help you with that for twenty bucks."

The look on Piper's face was priceless as he zipped his jeans. He turned around to acknowledge her, and after taking a quick look, it was obvious to him that she was probably a drug addict in need of a fix. He made a deep, grumbling sound, then replied, "Hmm, is that right," then quickly scanned the area with his eyes one last time, assuring himself they were alone. "My truck is just over there," he pointed. "Get in, and I'll be there in a few minutes. Don't touch anything." Piper went back into the bar and chugged what was left of his beer. He made certain the bartender knew he was leaving the facility alone. "Hey, Mitch, thanks for the drinks, but morning comes early, and I'm out of here."

"All right, man, thanks for coming in," Mitch replied.

After getting in his truck, Piper unzipped his pants and with a fistful of the girl's hair in hand, he guided her head to his lap. "Suck my cock while I drive." He kept the palm of his hand placed firmly between her shoulder blades. His intentions were of the worst kind and didn't want anyone to see her in his truck. Once he made it to his desolate camper at Hilltop, he turned to her and said, "Home sweet home. Get out; we're going inside."

"Seriously, I already gave you a blow job. That's twenty bucks. If you want any more, that will be extra," the girl said.

Piper tossed the girl a twenty-dollar bill, then forced her inside the camper. "Money is not an issue, and if it's meth you want, I have that, too," then pitched a pipe and baggy onto her lap. "Party up. It's going to be a long night, little girl."

"Sue," the girl said as she exhaled smoke.

"What?"

"Sue, that's my name."

Piper laughed. "Well, Sue, I don't really give a fuck what your name is. As far as I'm concerned it's 'whore.'"

She looked down at the floor with a look of humiliation and gently nodded her head. "Yeah, I guess that's what I am; I didn't want to be. I went to college and earned a bachelor's degree in science. Look at me now."

"Science, huh? Well, if you had any sense, you'd be cooking meth instead of smoking it," Piper replied.

She took another deep draw from the pipe. "Yeah," she giggled, then went on to say, "Thanks for the high; I appreciate it."

"Don't thank me; I'll have my payback," he scoffed. She didn't seem fazed by his comment, as if she were familiar with this harsh personality type and expected it, given her regrettable career. Piper took a few shots of moonshine, then offered her a swig. "Drink up; you're going to need it. My balls are so blue that I could fuck all night long. I'm going to enjoy myself and that sweet ass of yours."

"I hope you have the money because it's five hundred for a whole night. But since you got me high, I'll give it to you for a hundred-dollar discount," Sue replied.

Piper laughed, then backhanded her with a powerful blow, knocking her off the couch and to the floor. "Yeah, you don't say. Four or five hundred isn't shit for me to pay. I'm going to be a millionaire, you stupid cunt!" He proceeded to undo his belt from his jeans, then demanded that she take all her clothes off. Sue remained calm and followed his instructions. After she had undressed, Piper beat her with his belt with such force that it ripped into her flesh. He was aroused by her screaming out in agony and became fully erect. He snatched her up from the floor and threw her onto the bed facedown, where he raped and beat her continually into the early hours of the morning.

Around two a.m., Piper was exhausted and gave up. He glanced at her. She appeared to be passed out from the torment she had suffered and felt like leaving her unattended would not be an issue, assuming she wasn't going anywhere. Sue was well aware when he got out of bed to pee; she made a break for it. She dashed naked out the door in a desperate attempt to escape this lunatic and his brutality. Piper heard the door slam shut. He bolted from the bathroom and out the door after her. She could feel him closing in; the sound of his heavy breath and footfalls were just seconds behind. He took a leap and tackled her to the ground. In that second, her worries were indeed over. With a powerful impact, she hit her head on a boulder, which killed her instantly. "Sue, come on, you silly bitch, get up!" There was no response; she was lifeless. Piper rolled her over and slapped her face—still nothing. He listened for a heartbeat. "Fucking great, come on!" Piper knew she was dead. He stood up and paced. "Think, think, think," he mumbled, while he slapped his own head.

He knew he had to get rid of the body before the crew showed up that morning. After looking at the time, he was at ease knowing he had a couple of hours left to get it done. Piper fired up the backhoe, and it wasn't long before he had a six-foot hole dug. He picked up her body like a ragdoll and heartlessly tossed her into the pit, then covered it over. Piper spent additional time packing and raking the mound so it blended with the rest of the land, assuring himself his dreadful deed might go unnoticed. After he was satisfied with the results, he went inside and rested back in his recliner. He was exhausted by the whole experience; he didn't give a second thought to the death of a woman he barely knew. *(Personal note from the author: Salute to all the fallen women who have suffered abuse in any form, and a salute to all women who have made it through in a powerful way.)*

Early that morning, Sadie sat at Jude's Café, drinking coffee and researching any information she could find on Sara Tag. After running into small bits of information that led to plenty of dead ends, she felt a hand gently touch her shoulder. "Hey there, sorry I'm a little late," John said as he took a seat.

Sadie smiled. "Glad you made it. Although I hate to tell you that I'm stumped by information pertaining to Sara Tag. Like you, I am running into dead ends, but I assure you, I'll keep digging. It just might take a little more time and effort to achieve my goal." She smiled with a charming confidence.

John returned the smile and nodded his head. "I have no doubt that you'll succeed, my friend. Thank you for your time; it means a lot to me."

"So, what's the interest in finding this woman?" Sadie asked.

"Well . . . " John paused for a moment, "It's kind of a personal obligation I need to fulfill; it's very important that I see this through."

"Okay, well, okay, that will do, I guess. That's good enough for me. I'll see what I can do."

"That's cool, and I will owe you big."

"Naw, just a big hug," Sadie replied.

"Well, if you find her, I owe you a night out. But, of course, friends only."

"Deal, my friend." Sadie giggled, then placed her tab money on the table. "I have a million things to do this morning. Wish I had more time to spend with you, but I really need to get busy. My boss called, and I may be heading back to Idaho sooner than expected. I'll be in touch with you later regarding this mystery girl of yours."

"Sounds good. If you do leave town, have a safe trip, and it was nice seeing you again. I need to get my day started, too, and thanks again, Sadie." John watched her as she walked out of the café, then thought, *Yeah, it would be cool to find you, Sara Tag. A lot of questions I'd like to ask, and if you really are my sister, I need to know.* The peculiar drive that motivates certain individuals will remain a mystery to me—how some can appear harmless and even loyal, but within lays a dark cloud, filled with secrets.

That morning went on as many others; everyone seemed to have their own busy agendas. Sierra was forging her way through the overgrown trails on the misty mountaintop, and while leading her expedition of followers, she became weary of their constant complaints. "Good Lord, people, you whine more than children; aren't you supposed to be taking pictures and seeing the beauty that surrounds you, even with the fog?" She stopped and turned to look out over a cliff and into the great wide open. "What magnificent scenery, mist and all, don't you think?" Then she spread her arms wide open. "Beautiful, just beautiful—the serenity. Maybe you should capture that." In a playful gesture to lighten the mood of her group, she cupped her hands on each side of her mouth and yelled out, "I LOVE YOU, MONTANA!" Her voice echoed through the canyon brilliantly. The others enjoyed the exhilarating example and couldn't resist hearing their own voice resonate in a timed sequence. They enjoyed taking turns, as they echoed their own words.

While the others participated in their childish play, Ashley, one of the team members, figured now would be a good time to crouch behind some tall brush and relieve herself of an overdue, full bladder. Just a few short paces off the trail, she squatted behind a tree and exhaled a breath of relief as she peed. Then the horrifying sound of a shrill scream infected the atmosphere, alerting the group. Sierra's eyes quickly scanned the crowd, taking a head count, then screamed out, "Where's Ashley?" She heard the grumbling growls of an attacking bear, and without hesitation, she drew her shotgun and ran towards the disturbing call for help of the estranged group member. Sierra picked up a large stick and beat it against a tree to capture the bear's attention. "Hey!" she yelled repeatedly, then fired a shot in the air. The alerted bear released his victim, then stood on his hind legs and went back down on all fours. He smacked the ground with his big paw. He huffed while he displayed his territorial threats of dominance. Sierra didn't think twice and shot the crazed bear in the heart. After she assured herself that he was dead, the others rushed to Ashley's aid. Her facial lacerations were deep and severe. Sierra shouted, "Let's get her over to the clearing! Does anyone have alcohol on them?"

A man pulled a flask of bourbon from his back pocket. "Will this work?"

"Yes, give it here. Ashley, this is going to burn some, but we need to clean your injuries. Are you okay with that?" Sierra asked.

"Yes," Ashley frantically replied.

While dousing the alcohol onto her wounds, she cried from the sting. "I'm sorry, Ashley, but this will kill any germs from the bear's saliva," Sierra said, then looked at the team. "We need clean T-shirts to wrap around her head. Hurry!" As the other members grabbed shirts from their bags, Sierra worked hard to keep Ashley conscious. While one of the members wrapped her injuries, Sierra radioed the ranger station. "This is Sierra Wolfe, and there has been a violent bear attack up on Bluff Canyon. Requesting immediate medical airlift for the victim. Our location is ten kilometers northeast of the Pike Bluff. Please hurry!" After gaining the attention of the ranger station, Sierra demanded that everyone gather firewood and dry brush to build a fire that created lots of smoke, assuring the rescuers their location would be easy to pinpoint.

About thirty long minutes later, the sound of chopper blades filled the air. Team members waved their arms, guiding the medics. As it successfully landed in an open area, they rushed to stabilize the patient. Sierra assured the medics that she'd be fine hiking the rest of the group back to headquarters.

It wasn't long before the word spread through the mountaintops about the horrifying bear attack, and like many things that get passed down, the story will slightly change, as it goes from one person to another. Sierra's neighbor, Bryce, heard about it, and he ran straight up to her farm and found Carmen. "Is Sierra here?" he frantically asked.

Carmen could tell something was very wrong by the look in Bryce's eyes. "No, what's wrong?"

"My mom is a nurse and was on call today. They asked her to come in because some woman was viciously attacked by a grizzly in the Blackfoot territory. All I heard was the name Sierra Wolfe!"

"Oh my God, are you kidding me?" Carmen exclaimed. Without hesitation, she grabbed her keys and purse and hurried to the hospital. She ran through the emergency room doors and went to the patient check-in desk. "Where is Sierra Wolfe?"

The help answered, "We have not checked anyone in by that name today."

"It was a bear attack! Somebody said she was attacked and brought to the hospital!" Carmen replied.

About that time, Carmen felt a hand on her shoulder. "I'm here, babe. It wasn't me."

Carmen grabbed Sierra up in her arms. "Oh my God, baby, I love you. I thought you were attacked! What's going on?"

"It was a member of the team; her vitals are good, although she sustained some serious head injuries. I'm sure she'll pull through okay and thankful the rescue team showed up shortly after. Unfortunately, this will end the two-week excursion for the rest of the group," Sierra replied.

"Is that bear still on the loose?" Carmen asked.

"No, babe, I had to kill it. The rangers picked up the carcass and will have it examined for rabies or any other disease."

"Oh well, that's good. I've heard once they attack a human, it becomes a bad habit."

"Right, well, this one won't be attacking anyone else," Sierra replied.

After Sierra was certain Ashley was going to be okay and in good hands, she and Carmen stopped by to inform the group of the hopeful results and to let them know they'd all be going home in the morning. She explained that the expedition had been canceled indefinitely, due to the unfortunate event.

Sierra was glad to have made it home and especially glad Ashley would be okay. "Here's to life," Sierra toasted, as she drank a shot of bourbon. The more intoxicated she became, Carmen listened to her lover speak. "I wish I could have been there that day Piper attacked you. I would have shot him in the heart, like I did that bear today."

Carmen consoled her with words of encouragement as she held her close and watched her lover drink away all the bad memories that flooded her mind that evening. "You were there, babe. You did save me, and Piper will get his. I promise that." They held each other close that night, as they often did. Carmen could feel Sierra's tenseness, and her heart went out to her. She hummed a quiet melody, as she rubbed Sierra's hair and was pleased to see her finally fall asleep.

It's unfortunate the way some things can turn out. But like anyone, we can only do our best to see our way through any tragic situation. This night just happened to bond the girls even closer than before. Carmen was thankful Sierra was well and alive, and Sierra was just thankful Ashley lived through the gruesome attack.

CHAPTER SEVEN

One might find it hard to believe that waking up to the sound of loud power tools would actually be a pleasant experience. Well, for Sierra, it was music to her ears. Early that sunny, spring morning, Carmen hid her head under a pillow, hoping to drown out all the noise that was coming from outside, but Sierra sat up to peek out from the bedroom window. She smiled at the sight, then tapped Carmen. "Look, babe, they have almost got our barn built back. I can't wait; I have a surprise in mind for you after they're finished." Carmen heard what Sierra said but remained under the pillow, although her curiosity was making it hard to play dead. Sierra went on to say, "I found the perfect rooster at the Carson's farm a couple of days ago; they offered him to us as a barn-raising gift." Carmen cringed, as she removed the pillow from her face. Her long, blonde hair was tousled, and she stared at Sierra with a piercing glance, then covered her face with a blanket. Sierra knew that look and coyly replied, "Oh, don't worry, babe, I thought it'd be nice to name him after you. I'm not sure if you've noticed, but our beloved rooster is nowhere to be found. I felt like you were really growing attached to the little fellow, and I don't know where in the hell he went; maybe a coyote got him. But I'd rather think he just ran off and found employment assisting another family. We can call the new rooster Stormy. What do you think, babe?" Sierra asked with a straight face, while she secretly enjoyed antagonizing Carmen.

Carmen whipped the covers from her face and crossed her eyes. "Seriously, there is no need to replace the little bastard. I was not attached to him and found him rather annoying. I think the only time I found him useful and enjoyable was when we ate him in a pot of stewed dumplings."

"Stewed dumplings?" Sierra questioned curiously.

"Yep, chicken and dumplings or, in his case, rooster and dumplings," Carmen replied.

"Oh my God, we ate the rooster! Are you kidding me, Carmen?"

"Yes, we ate him, and I'm sorry for your loss, but I thought I was doing the bird a service by eating him. You see, they say it's a good thing to eat the things you kill; well, I honored his life in a pot of stew."

"Why did you kill him?"

"He was a very bad chicken cocker that day. He tried to attack me for the last time, and bang, from his standpoint, he got the wrong end of the shotgun blast," Carmen replied with a straight face.

"Well, I guess he was a handful and could be pretty aggressive at times. Hmm, I guess this means we're voting roosters out, is that correct?"

"Yes indeed, no more roosters," Carmen replied.

"Okay, well, just for the record, next time you feel the need to kill and feed me the victim, please let me know what I'm eating."

"Fair enough," Carmen nodded.

"Besides, I was bullshitting about another rooster anyways; I ran into Sadie a couple of days ago, and she asked me what I thought about the rooster and dumplings. I didn't get it, so she proceeded to explain. I found the whole scenario visually hilarious."

"I'm glad you had a good ole laugh on my account, especially with your ex-girlfriend," Carmen replied.

"Come on, Carmen, it wasn't like that. Never mind, I'm getting a shower. I have things to do."

"Whatever," Carmen replied and then covered her head back up.

Sierra noticed after her shower that her lover was still in bed and assumedly pouting from the conversation earlier. Without an ounce of hesitation or even thought of possible repercussions, Sierra took her wet towel and snapped it on Carmen's bare bottom. She screeched out a whelping holler. "Ah, what the fuck! That hurt, you bitch! Am I bleeding?" Then, without wasting a second, Carmen searched for a weapon in retaliation and found a suitable body pillow. Sierra could barely contain her laughter while recalling the recent lashing on her lover's behind and the reaction she got. Lucky for Carmen, she was able to get a good, old-fashioned zing on that body pillow and walloped Sierra a good one, with such force that it knocked her down and onto the bed.

Carmen jumped up and stood over her. She had her weapon in hand. "Ha ha, what, who's laughing now?"

"Okay, okay, I give." Sierra laughed as she held her hands and knees up in defense. Then with a sweep of her leg, she tapped behind Carmen's knees, knocking her off balance and down to the bed beside her. "Ha, ha, got you now, Fido!"

"Oh yeah, you certainly do have me now," Carmen coyly teased her submission, then by surprise attack, grasped a hold of Sierra and pinned her on her stomach. She pulled her panties down just enough, then spanked her lover with a couple of stinging blows to her bottom.

Sierra squirmed. "Ouch, hey! That's too rough!"

"Rough, my ass, you deserve it! You left a welt on my butt. I can still feel it!"

"Okay, okay, let's call a truce!" Sierra laughed.

"Wait, before I agree to that, I want to see if I left a red mark on your butt!"

"No, trust me, you left a whole fucking handprint on mine; it's still burning, Carmen!" Sierra exclaimed, then went on to say, "Fine, okay. we can call a truce, only because there's shit I need to get done today, otherwise . . . "

"Oh, oh, oh, I see, so I should indeed be prepared for a rematch later this afternoon; thanks for the heads up, babe," Carmen taunted with an intriguing sass that turned Sierra on.

Before leaving, Sierra went over to her lover, who was wrapped back up in the sheet, and hugged her close, then whispered, "Mmm, we'll see what this afternoon brings. I just know that I want to spend it with you."

Carmen watched Sierra leave from the bedroom window. She smiled, thinking, *I'm glad she is in better spirits today after the unfortunate bear attack. I should really try and do something special for her today.*

On her drive down the mountain, Sierra called a local quarter-horse rancher that has been a friend of the family for several years. "Good morning, Steve, this is Sierra. I was wondering if you were going to be around this morning."

"Yeah, I'll be around most of the day, if you want to come by. I'll probably be out in the barn or on the tractor."

"Good, I'm actually on my way now. I'll see you in about ten minutes." As she pulled through the entrance of the extravagant ranch, Sierra noticed a lot of yearlings playfully running about; the sight warmed her heart.

After parking her truck near the barn, she heard Steve call out, "Hey lady, come on in over here. I'm worming the mares."

"Hey, Steve, you're looking good. I heard you had some heart trouble this past winter."

"Yeah, I'm fine. Besides, doesn't help to complain; nobody listens any damn way," he replied.

"I was entertaining the thought of buying another mare, something older and somewhat trail-riding friendly. My horse Jess could use a companion, and I have a friend I'd enjoy riding with me; not real sure what kind of rider she is, so the horse should be fairly gentle and hopefully not too expensive."

"Hmm." Steve thought about her question as he chewed on a wad of tobacco, which was balled up in his cheek. "Well, I have an older paint, she's about fifteen, hasn't been much good for breeding the last two years, but she's good on trails and very gentle. I'd take five hundred out of her. She's over here; follow me."

Sierra touched the mare's nose. "Aw, she's a beauty. Does she have any major health concerns?"

"Nope, none to speak of. She's just cantankerous about breeding and not doing me a damn bit of good."

"So, for five hundred, could you have her delivered to my farm today?" Sierra asked.

"Yeah, it'd have to be around four this afternoon, though. I have a lot going on today," he replied.

After she passed him payment, she shook his hand. "No problem, Steve. You made my day, buddy. I look forward to seeing you this afternoon."

"My pleasure. See you then. Oh hey, how's that gal doing, who was attacked by that bear?"

"I heard she was going to be okay; recovery will be long, though," Sierra replied.

"I'm sure; well, glad she's going to be okay."

"I am, too, Steve."

Sierra was excited about her purchase, especially knowing it would be a gift for Carmen and an overdue companion for Jess. After leaving the ranch, Sierra was intent on shopping for a new saddle and other accessories for the new family member. While on her way into town, she noticed John's truck driving towards her. He put out his hand in a gesture to stop. As they pulled up alongside each other, John smiled. "Hey, stranger, what are you up to today?"

"Oh, I just stopped by Steve Taylor's ranch and purchased a horse from him today; it's a gift for Carmen. I thought it'd be a nice surprise for her and Jess."

"That's nice. Yeah, I was up by your place the other day and noticed they about had your barn rebuilt; I was glad to see that."

"No doubt me too. Now all I have to do is find another truck suitable for replacing Big Diggs."

"I'll keep my eyes open for you. Hey, if you're going to be in town for any length of time today, maybe you'll let me buy you some lunch at Jude's."

"Hmm, well, all I really need to do this morning is stop by Rural Farm Supply and Bair-Hill feeds. I'll be free to meet you at Jude's, say between eleven-thirty and noon, if that's good for you."

"Cool, that's good for me. I look forward to hanging out."

"Yep, I do, too, buddy."

On her way to the local farm store, Sierra saw Jed standing outside of his auto repair shop. She pulled up alongside him. "Hey, Jed, how are you doing this morning?"

"I'm good, enjoying the great sunshine. I saw Vern Martin yesterday; he was wondering if you'd be driving in the mud event this summer."

"Well, I doubt that, seriously, unless I can pull a rabbit out of my hat. But I am interested in finding a probable replacement for Big Diggs. I have my heart set on a Ford F350."

"Yeah, I know you like your Fords," Jed scoffed, as he was a Chevy man wholeheartedly. "Well, a buddy of mine has a 350; it's an eighty-six model, has a step side with a short bed conversion. I checked it out in the shop a couple of weeks ago, and it's a sound machine; he mentioned he may be interested in selling it, when he was in here. I can call him and find out more about that, if you are interested."

"That would be awesome. Could you call me as soon as you know for sure?"

"Yeah, no problem, I have your number. Hey, before I forget, regarding Vern—his brother Vince said he could use a driver for one of his trucks this year; he's been unable to drive since he broke his leg in that mining accident."

"Yeah, I heard about that, but I really have too much on my plate right now and need to focus on other priorities. I'll be back in the saddle next year," Sierra smiled.

"I'm sure you will, and imagine folks will miss seeing you run this year."

"I'll miss them, too. Okay, well, let me know when you find out about that Ford, and I'd love to stay and shoot the shit, but I need to get some shopping done. I purchased a horse from Steve Taylor today."

"All right, girl, talk soon," he said, then tapped her truck as she drove away.

Carmen was busy catching up on laundry that morning and frustrated by the lack of organization in Sierra's closet. After taking one look at the cluttered disorder, she gasped, "Oh my goodness, how in the hell does she find anything in this mess?" Carmen began removing items from the closet with the intent of putting things back in an orderly fashion. Upon her quest, she ran into an old, beat-up gym bag that was shoved back on a top shelf. With a curious nature, she opened the bag to find various sorts of medications that were used for livestock animals. One item that grabbed her immediate attention was a vessel, among several like it, labeled Xylazine. *Hmm, I'm not sure, but I think this is that drug I read an article on a couple of years ago, a tranquilizer that kids are abusing,* she thought. After checking internet resources, she verified that the medication was indeed a sedative for large animals. Carmen sat quietly for a few moments and thought, *I can use this on Piper*, then took four of the existing bottles, thinking, *She'll never miss these; there's so much more in here. I know she wouldn't mind, but I would rather do this on my own; I know she doesn't really want to be involved.* She then hid what she had claimed in her own belongings.

Later that afternoon, Carmen heard Sierra's truck driving up the lane. She looked out the window and noticed Sierra backing her truck into the new barn. A few minutes later, she started walking up to the house. Carmen called out from the front door, "Hey there, sexy, what do you think of that barn?"

"It's looking great. I see they still have a few things to finish up, but yeah, I love it," Sierra replied, then added, "Matter of fact, I think the barn needs more life, don't you think?"

"More life, ha, ha, don't you think the rooster story is getting old, babe?" Carmen replied.

"No, hon, I'm not thinking about roosters," she said, then stepped up onto the porch and grabbed Carmen up in her arms. "Yeah, more life. I think Jess is lonely."

"Lonely, I get that, so are you thinking another horse?" Carmen asked.

"Yes, matter of fact, I saw a buddy of mine today, Steve Taylor; he's a rancher a few miles from here, and he sold me a companion for Jess. But I was hoping you'd claim her for yourself, as in your own horse."

Like a young child, Carmen instantly became excited at the thought. "Are you serious? Oh my God, Sierra, thank you. I would love that!" After they hugged, Carmen took Sierra's hand. "Come with me, babe, I have a surprise for you, too—not as big, but hey, a surprise nevertheless. Okay, close your eyes," Carmen said, then opened the door to the closet that she had cleaned and organized. "All right, you can open your eyes now."

"What, wait, this is my closet! Wow, what a great transition from the land of the lost to this. Thank you, babe that was very thoughtful; I was dreading that project, as if you couldn't tell."

"I know, right, it was awful, to say the least," Carmen replied.

Then with excitement, Sierra grabbed Carmen's hand. "Come on, let's go to the barn and get a stall prepared for the new family member."

"Yes," Carmen replied, then let out a quirky little squeal. "I'm so excited; this is like my birthday!"

After the girls made way for the newcomer, Sierra patted a bale of straw. "Hey, you, come here and sit down beside me," then showed Carmen a freshly rolled joint. "Want to partake?"

"Heck yeah, where did you get it?"

"I saw John in town this morning; we met up at Jude's for breakfast. After John's mom died, he was surprised to find some doctor-recommended pot among her belongings. He said he didn't want to pitch it, so he gave it to me."

"That's freaking awesome. Go, John! What's he been up to these days?"

"I don't know. He's always so vague when it comes to his personal business; he's never been one to talk a lot about himself. I did get a pleasant surprise when my cousin, Brittany, and her husband, Billy, popped in for a cup of coffee, though. It's always nice to get a hug from her; she gives the best hugs ever."

Carmen poked Sierra. "Hey, watch it!" she laughed. "While on the subject of Brittany, did you ever get that sodium pentothal from her?"

"Oh hell, no, I forgot all about that with everything else that has gone on," Sierra replied.

"That's cool; I'm glad you didn't. I was thinking I'm not going to worry about it."

"Really, meaning?" Sierra curiously asked.

"Meaning, I'm having second thoughts about it, and even if I do decide to follow through, I wouldn't want to jeopardize you."

"Wow, I'm glad you have taken time to think this through some, Carmen." Before the girls could finish their conversation, a horn sounded as it was approaching the barn. "He's here! Come on, let's go see!" As Sierra exited the barn, she guided Steve to back up to the arena gate. "Let's put her in the round pin here for a little while; that way, she and Jess can get used to seeing one another before being put out to pasture together."

"Good plan," Steve replied.

Jess was as curious as Carmen; she whinnied and pranced around the perimeter of the arena, certain to let her presence be known. Carmen admired the beauty of this horse and thanked Sierra for such a majestic gift. While they watched the horse curiously investigate her new surroundings, Carmen asked Steve, "Does she have a name?"

"I got her when she was seven. They called her Chance, but I have so many horses, I usually refer to them by a number, rather than a name."

"Oh, well, I think I'll keep the name; I kind of like it." Then she turned to Sierra. "Babe, I want to pet her. Can you go in the pin with me?"

"Sure, she's gentle, but don't act timid with her, Carmen; she'll be able to tell if you are nervous."

Carmen approached Chance and gently touched her face. "You're beautiful, Chance. I think we'll be good friends," she said, then kissed her soft nose and couldn't resist the tempting urge to hug this creature around the neck. "I love her, Sierra; when can we go for a ride?"

"How about tomorrow? That'll give her time to get familiar with Jess."

"That sounds great; I look forward to it. What do you think about that, Chance? We can bond tomorrow, girl."

Later that afternoon, the women enjoyed sitting on the front porch and listened to country music quietly playing in the background. They sat in their wooden deck chairs, observing their latest family member. She was getting used to her surroundings and pleased that Jess seemed at peace with having another of her own species around. She stayed near the barrier that kept them apart, and they made subtle sounds of communication with one another. This made Sierra happy. As the sun slowly went down, the two horses touched noses several times and without any signs of aggressive behavior. "I think this was a great idea. Jess really needed a friend," Carmen said.

"Yes, I couldn't agree more. Horses are a herd animal by nature and enjoy having their own around; I should have done this much sooner," Sierra replied.

"Hmm, I think I'm a one-woman type creature and very pleased that I have you in my life."

"Mmm, yeah, I understand the concept. I've sort of mentioned this before but lacked detail. I've often thought of myself in some past life as a wolf that lived in a pack. I'm very loyal as well as dedicated to the ones I love, and yeah, I am very pleased to have you in my life. Welcome to my den."

Sierra glowed a radiant smile, then took Carmen's hand. "I love you and glad you like your horse. I'm excited about riding with you tomorrow."

"I can't wait; she's awesome." Carmen couldn't resist the thought of Sierra's theory regarding the pack life; the image etched in her mind was exhilarating. She was rather turned on by the lingering hypothesis and acted on her desire by going from her chair over to Sierra's. She straddled her legs over her lover's lap, facing her. They giggled as she seated herself comfortably. "Mmm, a wolf, huh?" Carmen seductively asked as she nibbled Sierra's neck.

Sierra replied by growling the words, "Mmm, hmm," while returning the love bites, her hands firmly caressing Carmen's inviting body. Their kisses became deep and passionate. Their hearts raced with a hunger, as they often did when they shared themselves with one another. Sierra began undressing her partner. She took her shirt off and buried her face in her lover's breast. She bit her nipples gently, then worked her hand into Carmen's shorts and placed her thumb inside of her and rotated it for a stimulating pleasure.

Carmen moaned the words, "Mmm, fuck me, you horny wolfie, own me."

"Mmm, you're so wet. Damn, woman, stand up on my chair and straddle my legs. I want that pussy in my face."

Carmen willingly complied to her request. She let her shorts fall to her ankles and then situated herself as Sierra suggested. After grabbing a handful of her lover's hair, she whispered, "Whatever you do, don't tip the chair. I'd have to kill you if I fell down."

"My feet are firmly planted. I promise we won't tip," Sierra giggled, then grabbed her girl's butt cheeks firmly and planted her face between Carmen's legs while she sucked her lover's clit. Carmen clutched Sierra's head, and she gyrated all over her lover's tongue, moaning with such pleasure as she experienced an exhilarating climax.

After she was satisfied, she climbed down from Sierra's chair and collapsed in her own. "Oh my God, that was so good," Carmen said with an exhausted expression.

Sierra looked at her and raised her brow. "Um, babe, me, my turn," then stood up and dropped her shorts down her ankles.

Carmen giggled. "Oh yeah, I almost forgot about you; come here, my wolfie, I'll fix you right up," then bellowed a couple of playful howls.

As the sun disappeared, the full moon was accompanied by an array of bright, shining stars. In the distance, they could hear some tribal members drumming for some spiritual intent. Sierra said, "It is believed that the rhythm is the portal into time, space and our creator. I remember joining my mother in similar drum circles. During the new moon cycle, Mom would make a thing called a vision board. This was carefully made up with things she believed the Lord would show favor on. With intent, she would burn it in the campfire, releasing her prayers to the creator."

"Wow, that's interesting, Sierra."

"Yes, the drum circles can be spiritually cleansing. With a full moon like tonight, it is believed to be the time to get rid of things that are binding, such as a bad habit or a personal affliction. Some people write these things on paper, then burn them during the ceremony. Sometimes the group will come together with a special prayer of intent." Before Sierra could complete her thought, she was distracted by a call from her grandmother in Florida. "Hang on, babe. I need to take this call."

Carmen sat for a few minutes, absorbing what Sierra had been talking about, then went inside and got a piece of paper and wrote down her thoughts of intent for this full moon. She wrote in bold letters GET RID OF PIPER! Then she folded the paper up and put it in her pocket. A few minutes later, she went out back and found an old tractor rim by the shed. She rolled it into the front yard, then loaded it with firewood and noticed Sierra gave her a wink, then thumbs up, as she continued to speak with her grandmother. Carmen doused the wood with fuel, then lit it up, thinking to herself, *I want rid of Piper, and I want him to pay for what he did to me. I want to make him pay, so he never does bad things to anyone ever again.* Carmen took the note from her pocket and tossed it into the fire. She smiled at the moon and thought, *Piper, you're mine, and you belong to me, and I have the drug to knock your ass out! I'm coming to get you.* Sierra watched her lover do this and was excited that she found interest, but she would have never shared these things with Carmen had she known her intentions and that she perceived them in the way of darkness. After she finished with her call, Carmen noticed Sierra looked concerned. "Hey, babe, are you okay?"

"Yeah, well, kind of. That was my grandmother. She said my grandfather has been rushed to the hospital with blocked arteries. He's stable but is scheduled for bypass surgery in the morning at four a.m. I should be there for both of them."

"Oh my goodness, baby, I'm so sorry to hear that. Do you want me to go along with you?"

"Actually, I think it would be better if you stayed behind. Somebody needs to tend to the horses and Bear; that would be a great help to me."

"Sure, I can do that, no problem, babe."

"Thank you. I love you Carmen. Hey, by the way, I saw you pitch a piece of paper in the fire. I hope whatever it was, is good for you."

"Yes, I am sure it will be wonderful, definitely a release of negative in my life. Hey, here is some paper and pen, if you'd like to do the same."

Sierra giggled, "Well, okay, I think I will participate." Sierra gave her concerns to God regarding her grandfather's upcoming surgery. She folded up the paper, then burned it in the fire and prayed.

After Sierra was done, Carmen placed her hand on her partner's back and said, "Come on, I'll help you pack."

"Thank you; I'm awful at packing."

"Oh yeah, imagine that," Carmen smirked.

After ordering a flight ticket online, Carmen drove Sierra to the airport. She wished her and her grandparents well. "I'll miss you, baby, and I promise to take good care of the animals while you're gone. Call me after his surgery, please."

"Thank you again, Carmen. I love you so much and will call as soon as I know something. Hey you, be safe on the way back home; the deer are plentiful."

Carmen spent her drive home consumed by thoughts of revenge and how she might go about ending Piper. She hoped to have him taken care of while Sierra was gone. She knew

Sierra really didn't have the heart, or desire, to assist in Piper's demise. After she made it back to the farm, she was exhausted but had a hard time falling asleep. She was unable to turn her thoughts off, and about four a.m., Carmen stumbled into the kitchen half asleep. She saw a note Sierra had left on the table, reminding her to call John. "Oh geez, seriously, he's not even family." After pouring herself a cup of coffee and smoking a cigarette, she grabbed her phone. "Hey, John, it's Carmen, Sierra's friend."

"Morning, what's up?"

"Listen, she wanted me to get a hold of you regarding her grandfather who lives in Florida. He's having open-heart surgery and wanted to let you know that she'd be gone, attending to family matters."

"Wow that sucks. I'm sorry to hear that. When will she be back?"

"I don't know for sure, but I'll be hearing from her soon and will let you know."

"Cool. If you can't get a hold of me, just leave a message; I'll be out of town myself." After John hung up with Carmen, he dialed Piper, only to receive his voicemail. "Hey, I'm on my way to close the business deal. I'll be seeing you in a few days. Be sure to keep shit intact. I don't need any problems fucking this deal up."

After Piper loaded his dirty laundry into the truck, he went back inside to get his keys and phone. He noticed a missed-call alert, then listened to the message. Like many things, it didn't take much to set him off in the wrong direction. He growled his opinion aloud. "Intact? You're a sorry son of a bitch. If I wasn't expecting my big payday, I'd tell you to fuck off." Piper drove down the mountain and headed into town. After throwing his clothes into a washer, he went to the local tavern and seated himself on a stool, up at the bar. He tapped the counter with his impatient nature and grumbled, "Hey, Mitch, you make any breakfast in here?"

"Well, let's see, I have chips, frozen pizza, a candy bar or liquid pork chops."

"Yeah, smartass, give me a pizza and a pitcher of draft, and can you open that front door? It's hotter than hell in here. Fuckin'-A, man."

"Yeah, the central air went out yesterday. A buddy of mine is supposed to be by to fix it sometime today." Piper just grumbled at Mitch's explanation and waited for his pizza.

Carmen was busy collecting throw rugs throughout the house, with the intentions of washing them, when she received a call from Sierra. "Hey, baby, I've been waiting on your call. How's your grandpa doing?"

"Hey, sweetheart, sorry I'm so late getting back to you. Grandpa came through the surgery fine, and the surgeon said everything went well. What have you been up to?"

"Oh, that's great, I'm glad to hear that. I've been doing a little spring cleaning. I'm gathering rugs now to wash."

"What rugs?" Sierra asked.

"Some throw rugs; they need washed."

"Could you do me a favor? If you want to wash them, please take them to the Laundromat in town and use one of those industrial washers; I don't think my washer can take that weight."

"Okay, no problem, babe. How's your grandma holding up?"

"She's doing fine. I can tell she's tired, but I'll make sure to keep a close eye on her while Grandpa is in ICU, recovering."

"Well, that sounds positive. I'm glad you're there for her, babe. I called John and delivered your message; he sends his regrets and hopes all is well."

"Thanks, babe. I appreciate that more than you know. Have you been out to see your horse this morning?"

"Oh yeah, spent time hand-feeding both of them grass. They seem to be getting along fine. Would you mind if I let Chance into the pasture with Jess? She seems cramped up in that round pen."

"Yeah, I'm certain they'll be fine. When you feed them, just make sure you put Jess into her stall first, then close the gate behind her. Then you can show Chance her stall, with her food in there. Close her in, too. After they eat, you can open their gates again. That should save any arguing over food, and Chance will get used to her own stall."

"That's a great idea."

"Okay, hon, I'm going to get off here and take Grandma for breakfast. I love you."

"Love you, too, and my prayers are with you all."

"Thanks, baby, talk soon."

Carmen eventually made her way to the Laundromat with the rugs; she didn't expect to see Piper's truck parked in front. Her first instinct was fear. She wanted to leave without being seen, but she felt compelled to grab the bull by the horns and make her presence known while she was in the safety of a public facility. She took her load of rugs inside and chose a washer near the exit.

Piper noticed her right away. "Oh my God, look what the cat drug in. You mean to tell me there isn't some kind of law in this pathetic town that prevents lesbians from washing their filthy laundry in public?" Piper rudely bellowed his opinion, then spit on the floor.

Carmen knew it was now or never. She calculated the fact that it was just she and Piper in there alone. She felt an adrenalin rush, then looked dead square at him from across the room and spit on the floor. "You seem to have a complex or maybe low self-esteem—who knows, you probably have both. I kind of feel sorry for you in an odd way. Hell, I think we should just have a drink one night and hash out our differences. Maybe there is a chance we could even wind up friends; wouldn't that be crazy?" Carmen's guts churned as she spoke those words, but her intentions of malice were driven by revenge. One thing for sure, Piper was no doubt shocked by her reply and was actually quiet for a couple of seconds, with the exception of a huffing sound he made. "Hey, cat got your tongue? What about that drink sometime? I'm open for Saturday, and I could use the company; my girlfriend is out of town."

Piper chuckled. "Well, you don't say, hmm, maybe you just need a man. Hell, maybe you've seen the light and are ready to rectify your wrongs." He chuckled again. "Yeah, hell yeah, I could have a drink with you Saturday. Where do you want to meet?"

"My place would be more private. Here, take my number, and call me around five Saturday. Maybe we could even go for a horseback ride together." Piper pitched his bag of laundry over his shoulder, and before he made it to the door, Carmen couldn't resist one last comment. "Oh, and Piper, I look forward to it."

"Yeah, I'll call you at five." After he was in his truck and heading back to camp, he spoke aloud to himself, as he often did. "What the fuck, this dumb bitch is ate up with the dumbasses. Well, one thing for sure, she doesn't know I was the man who fucked her senseless, but she will."

Carmen's heart raced. She knew what she had done and was anticipating the outcome of her justified vengeance. She knew she didn't have much time to devise a foolproof plan. Her mind was spinning with ideas, scenario after scenario, followed by what-ifs. "Fuck, Saturday is only four days away. I have to get this right. It's now or never," she spoke to herself, as she paced back and forth. "Shit, shit, shit. Think." She looked at the time and then the washer. "Oh, come on, you piece of shit, hurry up!" Then, in a tantrum, she kicked the washer. "Ouch, fuck, damn it to hell!" Her body slid down against the washer and onto the floor. She covered her face, then mumbled, "Shit, I need to call Sierra and make sure she's going to stay gone awhile. I don't need her involved." She convinced herself to relax and just breathe. "I can do this. He's just a man, a bad man. He's a vexation to society, and the world would be a better place without him." She silently chanted those words over and over until her laundry was done.

Wide awake—needless to say, it was another sleepless night for Carmen. She rolled over and looked at the clock that was boldly shining five a.m. "Oh shit, are you fucking serious? Five o'clock! I need sleep so I can think straight. I don't know who my worst enemy is—the rooster I killed or thoughts of Piper keeping me awake." After feeding the horses, Carmen sat on the front porch and left Sierra a voicemail: "Hey, babe, I know it's early. I was wondering how things are going for you and your grandparents. Give me a call when you get a chance; let me know what's going on. Love you." Carmen took advantage of the solitude that quiet morning. She collected her thoughts in a clear manner while she rocked. She had a full picture of what she wanted to do and how she was going to do it. A few minutes later, her phone rang. It was Sierra. "Hey, baby, glad you called back."

"Hey you, I miss you. My grandpa is hanging in there and healing as expected. Gram is tired, so I'm going to take her back to their house and sit with her awhile. She wants a bath and needs some rest. I do, too, for that matter. How are you doing, babe?"

"I am doing great and getting along well with Chance, and so is Jess. They are like ole chums out there, like they have known one another forever."

"Yeah, like I said, I should have got her a friend a long time ago."

"Not to sound like I'm pushing you, but I was wondering when you think you might be home?"

"Well, that's kind of hard to say at this given moment. Grandpa will probably be in the hospital a few more days, maybe longer. When he does get to go home, I'd like to stay there to help care for him, at least until he gets a little stronger. I know Grandma will need the help. We will play it by ear, but right now, it could be as long as a month, if other family members aren't able to step in and help out."

"Well, take your time and don't get into a rush. I know they are very important in your life, and if it were my family, I would take all the time needed, to make sure they were okay. I love and support you, and everything is going well here. No worries."

"You don't know how much this means to me, Carmen. I adore you, babe. Tell Bear Mommy loves him."

"Oh, I will. He's been sleeping with me the past couple of nights; I've enjoyed having him to myself," Carmen giggled.

"Hey now, he better not forget me."

"Oh, I'm sure he won't. I can tell he misses you; he waits on the porch and watches for you to drive up."

"That's just sad, but I'll be home as soon as possible. I love you, babe, and I'm going to go for now and get Gram home."

"Okay, be safe and send my best. I love you, too, Sierra."

Carmen spent the next couple of days methodically planning her vengeance. She planned out every possible scenario and was sure to cover all her bases. She watched the days pass by, as the time neared, to fulfill a dark desire.

CHAPTER EIGHT

Up into the wee hours of the morning, Sadie felt her eyes becoming tired. Her neck and back felt the stress from too many hours spent trying to open sealed adoption files on Sara Tag. She had hoped that her father's records would be of assistance, but she ran into the same problems with Collin's court records. After several attempts, she decided to call an old friend from college who prided herself in the art of hacking. She answered, "Hello," with a groggy and half-asleep voice. Sadie jumped right to the point, before her friend could yell at her for waking her up so early in the morning. "Hey Paula, it's me, Sadie. I'm sorry to be calling at such an early hour, but I'm not getting any sleep."

"Oh, you don't say, and?" Paula replied.

"I'm trying to open a file on a person that I've been investigating, and I can't do it. I keep running into lockouts. I'm having a lot of trouble with it and am completely beside myself. I was hoping you might be able to help out?"

"It's like three a.m., Sadie. This can't wait until later in the morning?"

"Actually, no. This is kind of a personal job or favor for a dear friend of mine; I feel better investigating it on my own time."

"Oh shit, well, okay. Are you back in Idaho?"

"Yeah, I've been back since yesterday afternoon. Should I put on a pot of coffee?"

"You're up this early, and don't already have coffee on?" Paula asked.

"Actually, yes, but if you're coming by to help me out, I'll make a fresh pot."

"Gee, thanks, how thoughtful of you."

"So, are you coming?" Sadie asked.

"Yeah, yeah, yeah, I'll see you in thirty minutes."

"Thank you. I'll owe you one."

"Yep, see you in a few." Paula staggered to the restroom of her dark apartment. She looked into the mirror and raked her fingers through her short, blonde hair. "Ah, fuck it, who in the hell has nice hair this early in the morning anyways? Not me, that's for damn sure." Then she grabbed her ball cap and placed it on her head backwards. After feeding her two small dogs, she looked at them and said, "Hold the fort down, killers. I need to rescue a damsel in distress. I'll be back soon."

It wasn't long before Sadie heard familiar taps on the door. It was indeed Paula, using her quirky, Morse code knock, like every other time before (.... . .-. .), meaning she was "here." "Hey you, come on in," Sadie said, then gave Paula a hug.

"So, what's up with the urgency? I'm kind of missing my beauty sleep, if you can't tell."

"Oh, you look great. First matters first—how do you want your coffee?"

"Of course black, with a ton of sugar."

"What's a ton?" Sadie asked.

"Five teaspoons of real sugar. I can't stand the fake stuff; it'll kill yah."

Sadie giggled. "Hmm, and you're not worried about diabetes?"

"Nope, I'm sure not. So, what program are we working with?"

"Confidential court records of a Collin and Sara Tag. I'm running an investigation for a friend, as I mentioned earlier, and I can't get past the block."

"Hmm, this type of program can be bitchy. Move over, and let me take a look at what we have here." An hour came and went, as Paula enthusiastically continued to tap away at the keyboard. She sat back in her chair and scratched her head a few times; it was certainly obvious she was aggravated by the difficult task at hand. "Come on, work, you bitch!" she grumbled, then as she made a last stroke to the keyboard, her eyes were wide open, and she flung her arms in the air. She succeeded and made it through the back door of the heavily secured site. "Who's the fucking boss, now?" Paula boasted. "There you go, all yours, and yes, you owe me big on this one. If you have a flash drive, I can download the pages for you."

"Oh my goodness, I do owe you! Thank you, Paula!" Sadie hugged her around the neck. "You totally rock, woman!"

"No problem. So like, there's a wedding party I'm supposed to attend next month, and the crazy thing is, I don't have a date, so how about it?"

"You don't have a date? What happened with you and what's-her-name?"

"Ah, we broke it off about a month ago; it's better that way."

"Sure, I'd be glad to go. Would this be considered payback?"

"Yep," Paula replied.

Sadie giggled, "Well, just for the record, I'd have gone without a payback, but definitely enjoy the fact, it will be considered payment."

"Seriously, that's cool. So, what have you been up to lately anyhow? I haven't seen you around much."

"I went back to my hometown in Montana for a long vacation. I enjoyed seeing old friends and family. I even got to see my little brother and close friend compete in an annual, preliminary mud digging event. They both placed, so that was nice."

"Sounds awesome. Glad you had fun. Um, if you don't mind me asking, are you seeing anyone special right now?"

"No, I haven't dated for a few months. My last experience was short-lived; she was crazy."

Paula laughed. "Yeah, I know that feeling. How would you feel if I added one small favor to the payback list?"

"Hmm, what would that be?" Sadie asked.

Paula stood up and said, "A real kiss."

Sadie kissed Paula with a surprisingly nice kiss, as if their lips were familiar with each other, then she whispered, "Seriously, you're making payback super easy, but it's tough at the same time. It's been awhile since I've had a kiss like that."

"I know, right?" Paula kissed her another time, then whispered, "Do you have hot water?"

"Hot water?" Sadie giggled. "Yes, I have hot water, silly."

"Well, would you be opposed to sharing a shower with me? I was in a rush this morning; I had to help a damsel in distress and didn't have time to take one before leaving."

"Oh, you don't say. Well, perhaps I could wash your back. Follow me." Just the thought of sharing a shower with Paula made Sadie wet. She was very attracted to her intelligence and her boyish charm. There was something about the way she wore her hat backwards that has always turned Sadie on, and she was glad they were finally single at the same time.

There wasn't much talk between the two girls during their shower, with the exception of body language and sounds of sheer pleasure coming from both of them. Sadie stood breast-to-breast with Paula. They kissed with a hungry passion, until Paula couldn't resist the thought of what Sadie must taste like. She had to find out; she followed her hands down Sadie's slick and soapy body. Paula eventually went down onto her knees, and with her hands firmly planted on Sadie's firm butt, she tasted the sweetest, most inviting pussy she had ever tasted.

Paula was a little nervous at first. She knew she only had one chance to make a first impression. She felt Sadie tugging firmly at her hair as she sucked her clit and worked her tongue firmly over her pussy. Sadie moaned wildly from the obvious skill Paula shared. After she was certain she had pleased her partner, she stood up and faced the shower wall. She wanted it from behind. Sadie knew exactly what to do. Sadie pressed her body close against Paula. She wrapped her hands around Paula's waist while she kissed the back of her neck. She fondled her clit with one hand, and with her other hand, she put her finger inside her partner from behind. The pleasant stimulation aroused Paula's g-spot, and she climaxed. She made her pleasure known by the erotic sounds she made.

They enjoyed bathing each other in the aftermath of an exquisite sexual encounter. Sadie whispered, "Wow that was nice, really nice."

"Yeah, maybe we can try that again sometime," Paula replied with a mousy grin, then popped Sadie's bottom. "Hey, do you have an extra pair of shorts and T-shirt I can wear, at least until I get back home?"

"I see—love me, then leave me, huh?" Then she tossed her a set of clothes.

"Don't want to wear out my welcome," Paula teased, as she pitched Sadie her wet towel in return.

"I enjoyed this morning. It was nice spending time with you, and hey, we're both single now. I like the thought of that."

"I do, too," Paula replied.

"Thanks again for your help; I look forward to reviewing the material. You're a lifesaver and greatly appreciated."

"Yeah, I know," Paula replied.

"You're kind of a sassy type boi, eh?"

Paula chuckled, "Mmm, maybe you'll stick around long enough to find out."

"Maybe; we'll have to see," Sadie replied with a curious smile.

After Paula left, Sadie's mood was very tranquil, and before she viewed the information waiting on the flash drive, she thought a nap sounded inviting. She was at peace knowing the information was at her fingertips and drifted away into a slumbering rest until the annoying sound of a missed-call alert kept antagonizing her. She tried to ignore it and continue her rest, but the curiosity was harder to manage than she thought. She couldn't help but think it might be Paula or something else that could be of significant importance. After flinging her blanket back, she sat up to address the alert. She noticed that it was a text message from John, asking how the investigation was going regarding Sara Tag.

She replied: *Hey John, it's going very well. I was actually able to obtain some records that I still need to review. I'll call you after I take a look at them. What are you up to today?*

A few minutes later, John responded to her text: *I'm in Texas but will be heading back home today. I'm waiting on a business associate to arrive at a meeting. Hope the news is helpful in regards to Sara. I'm curious to hear back. Oh yeah, did you hear about Sierra's grandpa? He had surgery or something, but I guess he's doing okay. Carmen told me Sierra went to Florida to see him. In case you want to send flowers or something, could you make them from both of us, and I'll pay you when I get home.*

Sadie: *Oh man, sorry to hear that. I'm glad he's okay, and yes, I'd be glad to send flowers from us, but just so you know, I am back in Idaho now. Work called and said the layoff was over, so looks like I'll be back on the clock starting next Friday.*

John: *Okay, well, I'll make sure to get you the money for flowers if you decide to send some. I'm also looking forward to hearing back from you. Thanks again for your help.*

Sadie: *No problem, hon, talk soon and good luck with your meeting.*

John's stomach rumbled from all the coffee, and he decided to make a quick trip to the men's room. He looked at the clock hanging in an elegant restaurant. He was glad to see he had at least twenty minutes before the probable buyer of Hilltop would be arriving. After picking up his phone from the table, he placed it in his back pocket and continued to the restroom. While he was sitting on the throne of relief, he received an incoming call from his client. After struggling to retrieve his phone from his back pocket while sitting on the toilet, he casually answered, "Hello."

"John Buck?"

"Yeah, this is John."

"Hey, it's Gary Post; I just arrived at the steakhouse."

"Okay, I'll be with you in a few minutes," John replied, then finished up. Just as he was pulling his jeans into place, he accidentally dropped his phone in the toilet. His face scrunched with disgust, then he grumbled through clenched teeth, "Oh fuck, are you kidding me?" as he hesitantly reached into the dirty stool to retrieve the item. He held it away from his body as if it were diseased and made a beeline straight for the sink. After washing up, he shook the phone off and dried it with a napkin. "Fucking great," was all he could say, then put the phone back in his pocket. After inspecting his appearance in the mirror, he went to greet the man who would be buying Hilltop and making him a millionaire. John saw him from a distance, sitting at the table they had reserved. When he approached him, John's heart pounded; he was nervous. He was ready to close this deal and be rid of Hilltop forever. He was tired of all the pressure and glad payday was just a few minutes away. He looked the buyer in the eyes. "Ah, you must Gary Post. I'm Collin's son, John; nice to meet you."

The two men shook hands. "Equally nice to meet a new business associate. Sit," Gary replied.

While the men waited for their dinner, they indulged themselves with a drink. Gary offered John another. "No, I'm good." Then he reached for his briefcase and pulled out the deed, along with a detailed property plat that described the boundaries of the property he was selling. As he pushed the information towards Gary, he said, "I also have a portfolio of photographs and the logged reports of oil harvest in the past few years. I believe you'll be impressed, all the way around."

"Oh, I'm familiar with the property; I did my research on that land back in the day, and after looking into it this past week, I see it's still rich. My father, God rest his soul, passed away the very day I was to attend a private auction for it. But as the cards played out, I was unable to make the closed meeting and therefore lost my opportunity to bid. So, your father was high bidder. I tried talking him out of the land back then, but he wouldn't hear of it." Then he raised his drink and toasted. "All good things come to those who wait."

"Well, as long as that transfer goes through as expected, then yes, the land will be rightfully yours, once and for all," John replied.

After dinner, Gary took the time to look over the property plat and signed a contract that John had provided, agreeing to sell the property to Gary for the stated amount of eighty million dollars. "Here is the account information to the bank in Switzerland. This is where you can transfer the money to," John said as he passed him a sticky note detailing the information.

"Eighty million, hmm." Gary hesitated for a moment. "Just for shits and giggles, I'm going to take a picture of the property deed and send it to my associate who verifies the authenticity of this type of thing."

"Sure, do what you feel you need to do. It's all on the up and up," John replied.

After a short wait, Gary received confirmation that the deed was indeed an original. "Well, looks like you're going to be eighty million richer today." Then he placed a call to his bank and transferred the intended amount of money to the account John had insisted on.

After showing him the transfer was complete, John smiled and shook Gary's hand another time. "I'll take that second drink now." The men talked a little more about business and then adjourned the meeting. They left that day feeling they both had gained. "I have a long drive back to Montana but have enjoyed doing business with you, Gary."

"It was my pleasure, John, and will look you up when I am in town. Maybe we can have some drinks then. Oh, and before I forget, I wonder if I could acquire your services, at least for a couple of weeks, until I can get there with my own crew to maintain the land."

"Hell yeah, I can do that, and look forward to the drink when you do come into town." John walked out of that place in a state of disbelief. He tried to hold his emotions inside and not appear overly excited as he left the restaurant. But after he was in the privacy of his own truck, his head began swimming with thoughts, his stomach churned, and he actually had to step outside of his vehicle and vomit. After composing his emotions and adjusting to his newfound sense of financial relief, he began his long journey back home from Texas.

Maybe I can actually find a good woman to start a family with, now that all of this is behind me, he thought to himself.

After a substantial amount of rest, Sadie woke up feeling energized and thinking about her encounter with Paula. She kept a lasting smile on her face, especially after she found a missed voice message from Paula that she had left sometime while Sadie was asleep: "Hey, I enjoyed seeing you, and look forward to another visit soon."

Sadie stretched as she sat up in bed, then fumbled through her laundry basket for a pair of shorts. She looked at her computer and the flash drive as she walked past the kitchen table that morning to make herself a cup of coffee, *Excellent, I have some reading material; let's hope it contains the information John's looking for*, she thought to herself, while she prepared to settle into her day. She looked picturesque, with her dark-framed glasses on, wearing a T-shirt that draped off one shoulder and her right leg drawn up to her chest. She sat studiously in anticipation of what she would learn from the files. After a few clicks, she opened the flash drive and began her research, just as she would with any other job she had done in the past. What she was about to find out would be life-changing for many who were involved.

Sadie opened Sara's file first, and as she read along, her heart went out to this young girl. She was thirteen years old when her father had been murdered in the state of Montana. Due to no other existing family members, she went into the system but was soon adopted by an older, well-to-do couple. Her name was then legally changed from Sara Tag to Carmen Storm. Sadie didn't make the connection at that time, between Sierra's Carmen and Carmen Storm. When they were first introduced, Sierra had done so by revealing only their first names to one another. Sadie jotted the name change down, in preparation of sharing the information with John.

After looking into Sara's file and learning more about her, she was curious and felt compelled to learn more about Collin. Before she could get anywhere of significance, Sadie received a call from Paula. "Well, hello there."

"Hi, hope I'm not bugging you right now. I just wanted to say hello and thank you for an awesome morning."

"No, you're not bugging me. Besides, thoughts of you have been tiptoeing through my mind all morning."

"Oh, yeah," she giggled. "I figured you would be hot and heavy into the files that I opened for you last night."

"Yes, I have certainly been busy today with that and have gained the information I needed, regarding the Sara Tag file, already. I will look into Collin's files in just a little bit. I really appreciate your help. I couldn't have done this without your brilliant mind."

"Ah, it was worth it. Besides, you're my date for that silly wedding now," Paula teased.

"I look forward to it. Seems like forever since I've been on a date, at least one that I really wanted to go on."

"That's awesome. I'm glad you're looking forward to it. Maybe we could get together later this evening for some dinner, that is if your schedule will allow you," Paula suggested.

"Sure, I don't see why not. Sounds good to me," Sadie replied.

"Cool. I'll call later, say around five, and we can figure something out from there."

"That would be perfect, and thank you again, Paula, for everything."

"Yup, catch up later."

Sadie didn't waste any time refocusing back on the task at hand. As she read through Collin Tag's file, she was horrified by what she discovered and why his records were sealed from the public. He was the man who had raped and killed Sierra's mother, and the same man Sierra had killed in return at the innocent age of thirteen when she witnessed her mother being raped. The records were sealed because of the Native tribal heritage and rights that the Wolfe family empowered. It was the right of discretion and honor. Sadie couldn't help but wonder what Collin's daughter must have gone through in her own life, living with a father like him. She didn't waste a second calling John and was aggravated that his phone went directly to voicemail. "John, call me as soon as you get this message. I found the information you were seeking, and it's chilling." Sadie wanted to call Sierra but didn't think bringing up the past would be suitable at that time, considering her grandfather was in the hospital. Besides, she recalled what John had told her when he first acquired her services a few weeks ago: "It's vital you keep this between us; it could devastate my investigation if you were to share this information with anyone but me." She tried calling John again, only to reach his voicemail for a second time. Sadie wondered why John's curiosity leaned more towards Sara than Collin. She thought, *This girl lived in Idaho and didn't have anything to do with Collin's crimes. Why does he want to find her?* Her mind was spinning, and she was determined to learn more about her and her adult life under her adopted name, Carmen Storm.

The day had flown by for Sadie, and before she knew it, she received her five o'clock call from Paula. "Hey there, I lost track of time. Geez, I can't believe it's already five."

"Hey, back. Do you still want to get together this evening for dinner?"

"Yes, I could use a break but would prefer dinner in, if that's cool with you; I still have some work I'd like to look into. Maybe you can assist."

"Sure, that'd be fine. How does Chinese sound? I can pick some up on my way over."

"That sounds great; I haven't eaten anything all day."

After Paula arrived with dinner, the girls enjoyed productive conversation during their meal. Paula could sense Sadie was still thinking about her investigation. "Hey, if you need a sounding board, I'm a great listener."

"Hmm, well, I hope you know what you're suggesting because my mind is truly reeling with thoughts; I could potentially bore you, or worse, run you off," she giggled.

"Seriously, I don't mind," Paula replied.

"Well, to be honest, the friend I am doing this investigation for is a cop; he asked me to keep this confidential. However, the things I have found out today directly involve another mutual friend of ours, who suffered a traumatic experience as a child. Can you pass me a soy sauce packet?"

"Yeah, here is some hot mustard, too, if you want it. So, I understand confidential, but the fact is, I don't know any of these people. If you kept the last names out of the equation, you might find that using me as a sounding board could help and clarify any unsettled thoughts you may be experiencing. I utilize this theory all the time with fellow hackers; it helps to see things from different perspectives."

"Hmm, well, if I share what I know with you, you can never speak a word of it. Promise me, Paula. I would die if John felt like I betrayed his trust in me."

"I understand, and I do promise that anything you share with me will remain in this room and in this time and space. Besides, it's a highly honored code of ethics that hackers never break," Paula replied.

"Well, in that case, I'll start from the beginning. Several years ago, when I was about thirteen, I had a close friend who was the same age; her name is Sierra. She witnessed a man rape her mother while she hid in a closet. In an attempt to save her mom, she shot and killed the man, but it was too late, he had already strangled her mother to death. After that incident, like many other things, it was swept under the carpet and forgotten by many over time.

"So recently, as I mentioned before, I went back to my hometown for a few weeks, and before I left to come back home to Idaho, I met with John. He was unable to retrieve certain information in a case that he had been working on and inquired about my services. So I agreed to help out. After reviewing the files you had opened for me, it was then I realized that Collin Tag was the man whom Sierra killed in return for killing her mother. Well, it turns out that the woman John is looking for is the daughter of the late Collin Tag. She was around age thirteen when she lost her father. Her name was Sara Tag until she was adopted by a family here in Idaho, who gave her the name Carmen Storm. Well, as I researched the available files on her earlier today, they stated that the child had undergone an extensive psychological evaluation. After that, the court and the adoption agency suggested she continue to receive treatment for behavioral issues. The thing is, John just wanted me to find her. He didn't want me to do any more than that. However, he did mention Collin Tag was her father, and if I needed to research him in order to find her, that would be fine. But since the information I have found on Collin directly involved Sierra, I can't help my curious or even nosy nature, in regards to the daughter this madman left behind."

"Well, I guess my question would be: What drives you to know more about her?" Paula asked.

"I'm not sure, other than the fact that by nature, I am just nosy and inquisitive. Hence I chose the profession that I am in now. I love investigative reporting, and the story never goes to bed until it makes a complete circle."

Paula listened, then asked, "So, what do you want to find out about Sara Tag or, better yet, Carmen Storm?"

"I don't know, but I am curious about the psychological evaluation. Not that it has any real significance to me; it's just me being me, I guess. A few years ago, I investigated a case that came to mind today when I saw her files. Not that her life would be anything like his, but it triggered that thought in my mind, and I felt compelled to dig further for my own satisfaction. If you'd like, I could enlighten you on that boy's case."

"Sure, I'm all ears," Paula replied, as she continued to eat her dinner.

"About ten years ago, I was chosen to investigate the history of a young boy. He had come from an abusive upbringing, then adopted at the age of twelve after his parents died in a home fire. It was unknown for certain if the boy had set the fire that killed his parents, but he was eventually determined to be innocent of any allegations that surrounded the investigation. The adopting family later had concerns with his behavior, prompting them to seek intensive, psychological therapy. He spent most of his teenage life in and out of mental facilities, until he was an adult. At the age of twenty-one, he refused any further help from psychiatrists and, one year later, was arrested for setting fire to the house his adopted parents lived in. This action killed everyone inside. Even though Sara, oops, Carmen, didn't murder her dad, and there's no evidence pointing to the fact that she ever tried to harm her adoptive parents, I have a suspicion that she probably suffered mental and physical abuse while being raised by her father; he was a known rapist. So, I'm just being me. I would like to know more about her medical records, sort of like some juicy gossip. Had I not known that her father was directly connected to my friend's past, I'm sure I wouldn't give two shits one way or another about what became of his daughter."

"I understand the connection and your desire to know more. I mean, who doesn't like a little gossip from time to time? Besides, I'm curious now myself," Paula replied.

After the girls cleared up their dinner mess, Paula passed Sadie a fortune cookie. "Oh no, I can't stand the taste of those things."

Paula giggled. "Well, you don't have to eat it, just crack it open and read your fortune. Personally, I like the lucky numbers they provide. I usually play them, if I think about it."

"Oh my goodness, check this out!" Sadie exclaimed. "Mine says, *Seek and you shall find.*"

"That's awesome! See, I told you, you don't have to eat the cookie to get a fortune," Paula replied. "So, would you like me to take a look and see what we can find out regarding Carmen's past medical history? Records like that are usually classified, but about two years ago, I had to help a friend of mine obtain similar information."

"Yes, definitely," Sadie replied, then turned her computer around so Paula could see some records she currently had on Carmen Storm.

After a careful evaluation, Paula jotted down a couple of notes: Check out mental facilities in or near Freemont County. Narrow down to facilities that specialize in children. When she was done, she passed Sadie the notes. "This is a good place to start."

"Yes, it is. Also, we can check local school districts that may have some useful information," Sadie replied.

"Okay, but I need to run out to my car and grab my laptop, so we can get some serious dual searches happening."

"This is exciting. Thank you for indulging me."

"Heck yeah, I love this kind of stuff," Paula replied with enthusiasm.

After Paula retrieved her computer, she suggested they start by locating the property address at which Carmen's adopted parents, William and Susan Stone, resided while they were raising her. From there, they were able to seek out public records that verified they had occupied the residence for over thirty years in Freemont County and still reside there. This information helped to narrow their search for school records and nearby mental facilities that Carmen may have attended.

While Paula was focused on narrowing down mental facilities, Sadie found the high school Carmen attended. Basic information, such as her attendance, grades and home address, were available to the public and coincided with the address her parents have occupied for the past several years. But they were unable to see the more confidential records. "Paula, can you hack the school's system in order to obtain the confidential and sealed information, such as mental, medical and disciplinary records they've maintained?"

"Yep, I'm pretty sure I can. Instant message me the link to the page you're on." In less than an hour, Paula found her way through the back door of the school's confidential files. After running a quick search for Carmen, they obtained the information they were looking for: many reports of misconduct, due to mental instability, that led to a permanent expulsion from school in her sophomore year. It was advised that she seek help at the North State Hospital for the mentally ill in Idaho. "Looks like I'll be hacking that site next, eh?"

"Right on, sister." Sadie couldn't resist her temptation; she got up from her chair and went over to Paula and hugged her from behind, then said, "You freakin' rock; we could get rich if we joined forces and worked as private investigators."

Paula giggled, "Yeah, I know, right?" While Sadie waited for Paula to get the medical records from the hospital, she made coffee, anticipating another long night ahead. But Paula was in before the coffee was brewed. "Hey, I've got her information on screen now, but it doesn't give in-depth detail, and I can't figure out how to surpass. I'll keep trying."

"Let me see what you have," Sadie replied. "Damn, she's labeled here as a sociopath with psychotic tendencies and was institutionalized until the age of eighteen. Poor thing, I can just imagine what she must have gone through with a dad like Collin. Well, this is good, says here she graduated with a GED during her stay, and she even earned some college credits. The release report states that she's functional in society and by law is required to stay on her prescribed medication."

"Yeah, that's cool," Paula replied. "So, are we going to search further, or have you quenched your thirst for knowing her history?"

"Oh, I'm fine, that's enough of that. I do need to find out where she's living, though. That was the main task John wanted me to accomplish, and now that we have her name, it should be easy."

"Yes, it shouldn't be hard to find out."

The search was indeed easy, but the impact of reality was shocking. All within a few clicks and typing in her name, a familiar face appeared. Sadie gasped at the visual. She knew this person. "Oh my God! No, no, no."

"What? What is it?" Paula asked.

"That's Carmen, the Carmen that my friend, Sierra, is seeing and that's living in her house with her. What the fuck is going on?"

"What the hell, do you think she knows who she is?" Paula asked.

"I don't fucking know. I have to call John!" After several attempts, the calls went straight to his voicemail. "John, answer the damn phone!" Sadie's nerves were rattled, to say the least. Her head was spinning with all kinds of thoughts. She knew better than to betray John's trust in her. He had been adamant about not sharing information she obtained with anyone. "Damn him, why isn't he answering the phone!" Sadie sat on the couch for a moment, trying to think things through. She spoke aloud as she tried to sort things out in her own head. "I met her, I've spoken with her, she seemed very nice, but hell, sociopaths are pros at that shit! What does she deem to accomplish by dating Sierra? I wonder if Sierra knows about her and her past. Or if she knows she's the daughter of the man who raped and killed her mother!" She paced back and forth, aggravated at John for having his phone turned off. "What am I supposed to do, Paula?"

"Do you think your friend Sierra is in any immediate danger?"

"I don't know for sure, but I do know she's not at home right now and thankful she's miles away in Florida with her grandparents."

"Well, maybe you could just call her and not say anything about what we have found out, but simply ask when she expects to come back home. That way you'll know she's safe, and in that time, hopefully, you'll have been in touch with your friend, John."

"Yes, yes, that's a good plan," Sadie replied, then without any delay called her friend.

Sierra smiled when she saw it was Sadie calling. "Well, hello, stranger, this is a pleasant surprise."

"Hey, back at you, stranger, just wanted to say hi and send my best to you and your grandparents. I heard your grandpa wasn't doing so hot."

"Well, you know Grandpa, he's a tough ole' bird. I don't think there's truly a lot that could keep him down. He came through surgery rather well, and his vitals are good. But that doesn't surprise me; he's a rascal."

"I'm so glad to hear that. When are you expecting to be back home, or are you planning to stay awhile?" Sadie asked.

"Not sure, although I'm going to wait until Grandpa is released back home and then stick around a few days after that. I'd like to make sure Grandma is able to care for him as needed. Grandpa would have a cow if he had to recover in a nursing home."

"Yeah, I could imagine that'd go over like a fart in church," Sadie giggled.

"I do miss home, and I miss Carmen. I love that woman."

"Yeah, I'm sure you do. Where's she from, anyhow?"

"Idaho. She was born and raised there," Sierra replied.

"Oh yeah, I think I remember her telling me that. Well, when you decide to come home, let me know. I can help keep you awake on your drive back; you know how I love talking on the phone."

"Yeah, I remember; however, I flew here this time."

"Oh yeah, I guess that would be the better choice, duh. Well, at least text me, and let me know when you decide to leave. That way, I can quit worrying about your grandpa so much and will know he must be doing much better," Sadie replied.

"I'll be sure to do that. Thank you for your concern; it means a lot to me."

"You know I'll always be there for you, no matter what."

"I know, and the feeling is mutual, my friend. Peace and hugs until later."

"Peace and hugs for you, too. Talk to you soon, Sierra."

After Sadie hung up with Sierra, she felt relief in knowing she was nowhere near Carmen right now. She struggled to understand why Carmen was in her friend's life.

She wondered what the possibilities were of it all just being a simple coincidence. But Sadie's gut feelings told her otherwise, especially knowing that Carmen had spent a few years in a mental institution and was still being treated for her mental disorder. "Paula, I wonder what the chances are that Carmen knows who killed her father and more so, why. What if Carmen knows Sierra killed her father, and what if she wants revenge?"

"I don't know. The records were sealed, and maybe, just maybe, they spared her the truth at that young age, regarding the circumstances that surrounded her father's death. Who knows, maybe it is simply a coincidence that their paths crossed," Paula replied.

"The crazy thing is, when I met her, I liked her, and she and Sierra seemed so happy and in love with one another. But there was this one time, I decided to pop in at Sierra's place, and she was obviously gone. When I got there, I heard a gunshot, and when I went to investigate, Carmen had just shot a rooster and commenced to cooking it."

Paula laughed, "Well, that's crazy. I've never heard of anyone killing a chicken before and then having the nerve to eat it. What kind of person would do that?" she teased.

"Ha ha, you're funny. But seriously, it was kind of freaky in a weird way."

"It's getting late, Sadie. I should probably head back home."

"Aw, I was hoping you'd stay tonight, but I understand if you want to get home."

"I have a lot to do in the morning but would love a rain check. If anything comes up, call me as soon as possible; I'm hooked now," Paula replied.

After the girls engaged in a meaningful kiss goodbye, Sadie ran herself a hot bath, then tried calling John another time before bed. "Geez, I wonder why he's not answering his calls. I hope he's okay." Sadie tried relaxing her mind from all the data she had consumed in that busy day and was thankful Sierra was out of state right now. She smiled at the thought of Paula and wondered where their friendship might wind up in the near future. She enjoyed the natural simplicity and interaction they were able to share; it was easy to be near her. After her bath, she tried calling John one last time before she turned in, only to get his voicemail, and with a note of aggravation, decided to leave him a detailed message containing everything she had found out that day in regards to Carmen and Collin.

John's eyes were tired and feeling the stress of night driving. As he pushed his way back to Montana, he swerved into the other lane and decided it was time to get off the road. He pulled over at the next exit that advertised a hotel and took advantage of a hot shower and a good night's rest. After taking his phone out from his pocket and trying to turn it on, he cursed. "Shit, I knew this fucker was trashed after it got wet. You think they'd make them waterproof," then tossed it into his backpack. "Oh, well, at least I have insurance on the fucker." After getting settled into a clean and crisply made bed, John had a hard time turning his thoughts off that evening. He could barely believe he was a millionaire. Many ideas of how he would invest it came to mind and, again, his wishes of being a family man someday warmed his heart. John was glad he didn't have to run a shady business any more but was thankful his father had actually left him something that financially benefited him. He had hoped to find his half sister, Sara. The thought intrigued him, and he felt there could be a chance that one day they might even be close.

Just about the time he closed his eyes, John was disturbed by a knock on the door of his hotel room. "What the fuck? Who in the hell would be knocking?" He pulled back the curtain just enough to see outside. "Oh fucking great— looks like a crack whore trying to drum up a little business," he mumbled, then opened the door just enough to address her. "What do you need?" he asked.

"I was hoping to find out what you might need," she giggled. "I can give you whatever you want for fifty bucks, or I can give you a blow job for twenty."

Against his better judgment, he opened the door and pulled her inside. "I don't know where that pussy of yours has been. Take a shower, and we can talk after that." The prostitute cleaned herself up and came out of the bathroom wrapped in just a towel, holding her clothes and shoes in her arms.

"You can put that stuff on the chair, then come here."

"What do you like?" she asked John.

"I like to watch. It turns me on," he replied.

"Well, okay, to each his own," she said, then began touching her wet pussy. "Does this please you?"

John didn't answer with words but pulled his blanket off and exposed his erection.

"Oh, I see you're the quiet type. I like that." As she continued to fondle herself, John masturbated. She seductively whispered, "You can cum on my breast if you'd like to." Still a quiet, cold silence, as John continued beating off, as if he was in another place and time. He reminisced, as he often did when he was aroused, about the first time he had seen a man having sex with a woman. He had been about fifteen years old then. He had gone to a friend's house and knocked on the door. There was no answer, but he had heard sounds. He remembered going from window to window until he saw somebody. He hadn't expected to see what he did. He had known it was wrong but somehow couldn't help but be turned on by it. He had crouched discreetly and masturbated, as he had watched his friend's mother being abusively raped, then strangled to death. He had witnessed the unthinkable, he had seen what happened, and he had seen his childhood friend, Sierra, come out from the closet and shoot the man dead. He remembered zipping his jeans up and rushing to her aid.

The flashback in time alone helped him to achieve an orgasm. Then he tossed the woman fifty bucks. "Okay, get dressed, and get out of here, you worthless whore."

She gathered her things, then stuffed the money in her bag and left. *Geez, some guys are just fucking weird,* she thought to herself.

The next morning, John headed out and was glad he only had about twelve hours left to drive. But little did he know that his arrival back home would soon be event-filled, that things were unraveling into a mess of truths, boiling over in a pot of deception.

CHAPTER NINE

The morning was tranquil, and the harmonious sound of birds chirping their poetic whistle just outside Carmen's bedroom window was calming to her soul. She took her time absorbing the comfort that surrounded her. The silence that allowed her to meditate quietly gave her great strength to see her day forward. Today was the day; Carmen had deliberated her overdue, but justified, vengeance, at least by her own sense of rationalization. She had spent the last few days preparing to execute a flawless and self-rewarding scheme on the man who had violently beaten and raped her. His worst mistake was thinking he had killed her that dreadful day, leaving her tattered body upon the cold and wet mountaintop.

Two days prior to that Saturday, Carmen spent her time researching and gathering things that would be of assistance in her diabolical plan of premeditated torture. She prepared the cabin she had been assigned to occupy during her job assignment there with things that would make Piper curse the day he was ever born.

Piper woke up feeling unusually good-spirited that morning as well. While naked, he cranked up his hard-rock music and gestured playing an air guitar in his tiny camper that sat desolately upon the land John had just sold. While singing along with the music, he heated a pot of water and sponge-bathed himself. After he dressed, Piper was entertained by looking into a dirty, broken mirror. He spoke aloud, as if he were talking to someone other than himself. "Ruggedly handsome, if I say so myself, dontcha think? Well, hell yeah, I have a date tonight with a lesbian whore that has nine lives—well, at least two," he chuckled. "The poor bitch has seen the error of her ways and needs a real man to bring her back to reality. She chose me, you know, to take on that task. I am the man for the job," he gloated. "But then again, I'm the man for every job out here, even the shit jobs my boss has me tending to. That poor bastard wouldn't have a dime to his sorry name if it wasn't for me slaving like a fucking dog. I'll show him my gratitude after he fills my bank account with the money I've worked my ass off for. Yeah, that's right, gratitude, with my foot dead up his ass," he laughed, then grabbed up a bottle of unopened whiskey. "You, my little friend, will be going along with me tonight. Pussy and whiskey always go well together. What's that you say?" he asked the bottle, as if it were talking to him. "Oh no, I can't drink you right now. I have to keep my wits about me, at least until I get there; but I promise you, my friend, we'll have a hell of a time tonight." After dousing himself with some strong, pungent cologne, he felt confident. "Oh yeah, women love this shit; it's fucking irresistible to them." Then he grabbed his phone and looked up Carmen's number. He stared at it for a couple of minutes before calling her.

Carmen was busy later that morning, preparing for her rendezvous with due justice, when she heard her phone ring. She wasn't surprised that the caller I.D. said it was Piper. She took in a deep breath, then exhaled before she answered the call. "Well, hello there, I'm glad you didn't forget about me. I've been looking forward to getting together with you."

"Naw, I didn't forget. So, what are we doing, and where do I pick you up at, or are we still going to meet at your place?"

"No need to pick me up. I think it would be nice to stay in this evening. I have my own cabin, a few miles down from Sierra's. I was thinking I'd make a pot roast. I imagine a man that works as hard as you do doesn't have a lot of time to enjoy a home-cooked meal as often as you should. Does that sound good?"

"Sounds freakin' awesome, and you're right, after busting my ass all day, I'm lucky to eat canned spam on crackers. Sometimes that shit tastes like a fucking steak. But lucky me, I'll be living the life soon, retired and plenty of green in my pocket, to do as I please."

"Yes, hard work always pays off, and glad you look forward to dinner. I can text you the address to my cabin. Do you have GPS?"

"Hell, yes. It's the chickenshit way to find things, but what the fuck, it saves me the aggravation of mapping it out."

Carmen giggled, "Yes, I guess so. How does five-thirty sound for you?"

"I'm ready now," he replied.

"Oh, well, I still need a shower and have some chores before you come. But maybe I can get done sooner, say about four-thirty instead?"

"Yeah, that'll work. Don't forget to text me your address, and I'll see you then."

"I couldn't forget that. I'm looking forward to our visit and the kindling of our new friendship, silly."

After hanging up the phone, Carmen felt nauseous. Just the thought of pretending to be nice to him was repulsive. She sat down for a moment to compose her emotions and focus on the task at hand. She utilized her time setting up the stainless-steel prep table that she had purchased yesterday from an auction. After lag-bolting the legs of the table to the wood floor, she wrapped a log chain around the top surface, one on each end, and padlocked them closed. She added wrist and ankle shackles to the chains, then stepped back to take a look. "This is perfect; he won't get away." She then attached a pulley to the ceiling beam just above the table. Carmen took time double-checking everything and rehearsed again and again how she would overtake Piper. Then she thought, *And to think that sorry son of a bitch actually thinks I'll have a pot roast waiting for him. Little does he know that as soon as he knocks on the door, this face will be the last one he will ever see.* Then she took the horse tranquilizer and loaded the syringe with just enough to knock him out. Afterwards, she went to the closet and pulled out a case that housed a sawed-off shotgun; it resembled the one her father used to have. She kissed the barrel of the gun, then loaded it. "Don't let me down, Lucy, I have one chance to get this right." Shortly after, she made a call to Sierra. "Hey, babe, how's it going?"

"It's going well. I have some good news. My cousin and her husband said they could stay with my grandparents for a week after Grandpa gets released. So it looks like I can be home Monday afternoon or Tuesday by the latest. I'm so excited; I can't wait to see you. I've missed you so much, babe."

Carmen was at a loss for words at that moment and hesitated before her response. "Oh, that's great, babe. I miss you, too. Be sure to give me plenty of heads up before you leave, so I can pick you up from the airport on time."

"No problem, that sounds good. How are the critters doing?"

"They're great. The horses are getting along well, and I've been spoiling Bear. We've bonded."

"Oh, geez, he won't even be happy to see me when I get back."

"Oh yes he will; he misses his mommy. Okay, well, I hate to rush, but I have dinner on the stove, and it smells very done. I should check it. We'll talk later, babe. I love you," Carmen replied.

"Love you, too, and hope your dinner works out."

"Oh, it will, trust me." After Carmen hung up, she sat down and covered her face with her hands. "Shit, I wasn't expecting her back so soon. Oh, well, I'll just have to make it work."

Piper spent his day looking at the clock while he watched some old porn videos that he had probably seen over a hundred times. He had experienced mixed feelings about Carmen throughout that day; he kept recalling her talk about making him dinner. It had been a long time since anyone cared enough to make him a nice meal. He actually looked forward to it and fought hard that afternoon to stay away from the booze, at least until he got there. "I wonder if she even likes whiskey; maybe I ought to call her and see if I should pick up some wine or something girls like." After mulling it over awhile, he decided to call and check with her.

Carmen's first reaction was, "Holy shit, he better not back out." Then she answered the phone and, with a cheery voice, she worked her magic. "Hey there, dinner is almost done. I can't wait for you to taste it. I'm getting excited."

"Yeah, a real meal sounds good. I'm bringing a bottle of whiskey for myself; do you want me to stop in town and get you some wine or something?"

"Sure, just surprise me, and thank you, that's very thoughtful. I'll see you soon." After hanging up, Carmen couldn't resist an afterthought that compelled her to run down to Sierra's place and scoop up a pile of Bear's poop. She certainly had an ulterior motive for such an action and looked forward to following through with it.

On Piper's drive into town, he saw some wildflowers growing just off the roadway. After he passed them, he thought about it and decided to turn back around and pick a handful. After tossing them into the passenger seat, he made his way to the liquor store. He took his time browsing the coolers and then called out to the store attendant, "Hey, can I get some help over here?"

"Yeah, what do you need?"

"What kind of wine do women drink most of?" he asked.

The help picked out a berry-type wine cooler. "Here you go. This has been selling very well; the ladies love it."

"Fuckin'-A, this shit's expensive enough. The businesses in small-town America seem to enjoy raping the fuck out of people."

"Well, we have to make . . . "

Before the man could defend his business, Piper cut him off. "Fuck that, I don't want to hear some bullshit sob story. I know how it goes." Then he tossed the money on the counter and left.

The store clerk was aggravated and mumbled aloud, "I hate that guy. Every time he comes in here, he bitches about something. Sorry bastard."

Piper seemed to thrive on upsetting people; it made him feel in control. His mood this afternoon was rare, in regards to his plans with Carmen; he was unusually excited. Unlike many other times before, the ladies he spent his time with were low-life drug addicts or whores that he held absolutely no respect for. He used them for his own self-gratifying purposes. Just as he was backing out from the parking lot, he saw John pull in behind him. "Fuck, I wonder what the hell he wants."

John rolled down his window. "Hey, I'm just now getting back into town. I closed the business deal. Our payoff is here, man. We just need to wait until Monday morning. I need to transfer the money into a bank account for you."

Piper's face said it all. He was on top of the world. "That's fucking great, Boss. Monday will be fine. Besides, hell, I've waited this long, and so have you. Did you wind up selling the land or just the oil?"

"The land and the mineral rights. I'm tired of this shit and getting too old to worry about it anymore. I'm ready to move on in my life and start a family, I guess."

"Yeah, I'm fucking over it, too. Funny you should mention starting a family; I've been thinking the same thing the last couple of days."

John bolted out a laugh. "Somehow I can't see you as a family man, Piper."

"Fuck you. I could be a good husband, to the right woman," Piper replied.

"Whatever. I'm just glad you stood by me on this job. I couldn't have managed it without you."

Piper appreciated the compliment. "Thanks. I'm glad you recognize that fact because I have literally sweated blood to see things rolled smoothly."

"Yeah, I know. It's all over now, and you'll be able to enjoy a new life, whatever it may be. By the way, don't bother trying to contact me. My phone took a shit, literally; I'll have to get another one Monday. I'll call you then."

"No problem. I plan on a busy weekend, anyhow," Piper vaguely replied. Knowing how John felt about him going around Carmen or Sierra would have gone over like a fart in church, had he told him of his actual plans for the night.

After the men separated and went their own ways, John was glad to see Jude's diner lit up. He was ready for a good dinner, and Jude was the person to make that happen. As he walked through the café door, his eyes locked with Jude's. "Hey, gorgeous, I've been missing you."

Jude smirked, "Oh, save that for the other girls. I know you're just hungry. Grab yourself a table, and I'll be there in a few minutes." After she was done with her other customers, Jude took John's order, then sat down with him while he ate his fried-chicken meal. "You look tired. Are you feeling okay?" she asked with a note of concern.

"Oh yeah, I'm feeling fine, actually great. I'm just tired; I've been on the road for the past five days. I had some business to take care of in Texas; that state is a freaking rat race, to put it politely," John replied.

"Well, glad you're home now. I heard Sierra was out of town, too; her grandfather, Ben, was having heart complications, from what I've been told. I hope that's going okay; he and his wife are great people. I've always enjoyed them."

"Yeah, I heard about that. Carmen called me and let me know. He's a tough ole guy; I'm sure he'll be fine." After John finished his dinner, he stood up and gave Jude a hug. "Thanks again for a great meal. I don't know what I'd do without you."

"I always enjoy feeding a man with a good appetite. Now get your butt some rest, mister; you look rough."

"That's where I'm headed now. See you later, and thanks again," John replied.

A few minutes after Piper left the liquor store, he called Carmen to let her know he was on his way to her place. She felt her pocket to reassure herself that the syringe was still there. Then she grabbed her shotgun and hid out of sight, just behind a pine tree near the front door of her cabin. She waited in anticipation. Her nerves were unsettled, and she tried hard to resist the urge of pissing her pants, a feeling she remembered well as a child when she played hide and seek with her dad. The thrill of it always made her want to pee. She heard the rumble of a truck in the distance; she imagined it was him. Her heart raced. As she mentally prepared herself for what was about to take place, she whispered, "It's okay. I've got this." Her adrenalin kicked in when she saw him coming down the driveway. Stealth mode was on her side. She took a deep breath and whispered again to herself, "Come on, motherfucker. Get out of that piece-of-shit truck." Carmen gripped the gun close to her and prepared to apprehend the man who had humiliated her in the worst way.

Piper gathered the flowers and alcohol, then stepped out of his truck and walked up to the front door of Carmen's cabin. Just as he knocked on the door, Carmen crept up close behind him. She buried the double barrels of this sawed-off shotgun deep between his shoulders and in a low, steady voice said, "You move, and I'll splatter your guts all over my front door, motherfucker. Now open the door and walk to the kitchen table and sit down."

The look on Piper's face was one in a million. Something inside his stomach told him he was screwed. He followed through with her request and sat down at the table. He couldn't help but think about the money John was going to deposit onto his card Monday. "I have money, a lot of it. My boss just closed a big business deal. I'm rich now. I'll give you half, if you don't follow through with whatever you're thinking."

Carmen was curious about what he said. "What's rich to you?"

"Five million dollars. My boss is making the deposit to my account on Monday."

"Monday? Do you think I'm stupid? Do you think I'm going to let your sorry, perverted ass just walk out of here and believe that you'll pay me half on Monday?" Then she went up close behind him and whispered, as she stabbed the syringe full of horse tranquilizer into his neck, "No, I'm not stupid, and I don't give a rat shit about your money. This isn't about money."

"What the hell did you put in me?" Piper asked.

"Just a little something; it will help you sleep, no worries. But in case you're interested, the information I found online regarding this drug—well, rest assured, it works quickly. If administered in the right dose, say about fifteen minutes, and you'll be sleeping like a baby. Oh yeah, and if I administer the wrong dose, it could kill you. But today is your lucky day."

Piper was becoming groggy. He slurred the words, "You stupid cunt, you were supposed to be dead." Then he slumped over, and his head fell onto the table.

Carmen waited a few seconds until his breathing changed, then poked him with the shotgun. After she felt certain he was out cold, she duct-taped him to the chair and rolled him into the bedroom that she had set up earlier in the day. After getting to the room, Carmen untaped him, then wrapped the chain that was attached to the pulley around Piper. She hoisted him up to the stainless-steel serving table that she had bolted to the floor. After a struggle, Carmen managed to accomplish that goal. After she stripped Piper of all his clothing, she shackled him by his hands and feet to the cold table.

She took a short break, then took a piece of baling wire from her back pocket. She wrapped it tightly around the base of his balls and twisted until she was certain the circulation had been cut off. Then she poured the whiskey he had brought all over his balls and scrotum. *I'm not completely ruthless,* she thought. Then she spoke to his limp body: "Hopefully that helps with any infection. I would hate if you died so quickly; we have a few things to talk about." While she waited for Piper to wake up, she took the dog poop she had acquired and placed it in a dinner bowl.

About a half an hour later, Piper started to move, and as he slowly came to, he realized he was shackled. But worse, as he felt a slight burning sensation coming from his balls, the look on his face was horrified. "What did you do, you crazy bitch?"

"Oh that, well, the research said that when castrating a bull with a band, much like I've done here, with the exception that I used baling wire instead, there shouldn't be a lot of pain," she smirked. "Well, hmm, imagine that. You can't believe everything you read."

Piper struggled, his face sweating profusely. "Please, I beg you, take it off. I'll do anything," he cried out.

"Anything, huh? I find this amusing. You must be getting hungry. A big guy like you must have a large appetite. Like I said, I prepared you a nice meal; surely you won't be rude to the host and not eat." Then she took a tablespoon of poop and shoved it in his mouth. "Mmm, isn't that just to die for?" she asked.

"It's shit!" Piper exclaimed.

"What, you're calling my food shit? How rude. I slaved over this all day."

"You fucking crazy bitch, turn me loose!" he exclaimed.

"Um, sorry, no can do. You see, I need to know who was with you that day, the day you climbed your smelly, nasty body on me and left me for dead."

"If I tell you, will you let me go?" he asked with a quivering desperation.

"Yes, I'm sure that could be arranged."

"It was my boss; he made me do it. He wanted to watch me rape you. He said you were here to start trouble for our business. He said we would lose everything. It was all his idea," Piper cried out.

"'Boss,' well, that doesn't tell me a lot. What's his name?"

"Buck, John Buck. He's my boss."

"John Buck? Well, imagine that. Let's get this straight—John Buck the cop, right?"

"Yes, that's him. Let me go, and I'll get him for you. He's the one that needs his balls cut off."

"Before I let you go, you must eat the rest of your dinner. I've always hated when guests leave and don't finish their plate. Seriously, that's just rude."

"Okay, give it to me. I'll eat it."

"That's so kind of you," she said, as she began shoveling spoonful after spoonful into his mouth. She took such joy when he gagged as he choked it down. "Now, that made me happy. I knew you'd like it."

"Let me go! You promised," Piper cried out.

"Oh yeah, about that, we need to talk about your balls. We really do need to wait that part out before you go anywhere. Let's see, according to wiki, they have a list of pros and cons here. I saved the page in case you were interested. I can see by your face that you have questions. Let's take a look-see. What do you think?"

Piper could barely speak. He cried the words, "Just read."

"Okay, here it says the advantages to banding, also known, as in your case, baling wire: 'This procedure is basically bloodless.' Oh, that's nice. Also a perk for you—there is very little chance of infection. Oh, and this is very interesting: It says that it's less painful than cutting them off because the area quickly numbs. I'm curious—are your balls numb by now?"

"No, it's painful. Please, just take it off."

"Hmm, that's odd; they said it's quick and easy if done properly. Go figure. But the part that impresses me, now listen carefully: 'Cutting off blood supply enables the testes and scrotum to gangrene and fall off on their own.' Wow, that's just cool and seems much more humane than whacky-whack. You know what I mean?"

Piper squirmed. "Please, let me go. I won't tell anyone. I'll get John for you. I'll give you all my money, all of it."

"You're not following the program too well. I told you, this wasn't about money, and I am completely capable of getting John on my own. Let's finish reading. Oh well, darn, it says here that it can take anywhere from ten to fifteen days before that shit falls off. Gee, I guess we are in a predicament here. You see, I only have until Monday before my girlfriend gets back home. I really didn't want her to know about all this; she has a much kinder heart than I do." Then Carmen took another syringe from her pocket and held it up. "Okay, time for a little nap; I have some research to do."

After Paula stopped by to see Sadie, she could tell her friend was growing impatient and aggravated by the fact that John was still not answering her calls. "What the fuck is he doing? Where is he at? Damn, I hate this shit. I have all the information he needed and more, and he can't answer his phone. If he doesn't answer soon, I'm going to Montana!" Sadie exclaimed.

"What do you hope to gain by going there? Didn't you say Sierra was out of town, and, for that matter, isn't John out of town on business, too?" Paula asked. "I don't think that's a good idea, Sadie. Surely John will return your call soon. Maybe his phone is dead, and he forgot his charger, or maybe it broke, or he lost it. There are a number of things that could explain why he's not answering calls. You even said his phone was going directly to voicemail. That means it's off, lost or broke, hell, maybe all of the above," Paula replied.

"Yeah, I agree those are good possibilities. But what if he's back home by now? According to our last conversation, he was going there and back. If he left after his dinner appointment, then he could be home by now. It's only a twenty-four-hour drive; I Googled it. I'm going to call Jude; she'll know if he's back in the area."

"Who's Jude?" Paula asked.

"She's like everyone's favorite aunt. She owns a diner there and gets all the firsthand talk from around town. If anyone knows, she will."

"Well, then, sounds like a good place to start," Paula replied.

Jude was busy that Saturday night, clearing up after a long day. She had just turned the sign around to say "closed" and locked the door. Before leaving out the back exit, she filled her go cup with coffee and grabbed her oversized purse. Just as she got into a dark car, her phone began to ring. "Well, shit, wouldn't you know, I don't get a call all day, and when it's least convenient, this thing rings," she grumbled as she dug through her purse to retrieve the phone. "Hello."

"Hi, Jude, this is Sadie. How are you this evening?"

"I'm fine, hon, just heading home; it's been a long day."

"I can imagine, everybody wants that good cooking of yours. I was wondering if you've seen John. I've had a hard time getting a hold of him."

"Yes, as a matter of fact, I saw him late this afternoon. He came into the diner with a big appetite. He looked wore out. He said he's been out of town for the past few days on some business trip."

"Oh. that's good to hear he's back. He had me look up some information that he was having a hard time locating. I've actually found what he wanted, so if you happen to see him tomorrow, could you please ask him to give me a call? It's kind of urgent. I've tried calling him several times, but it goes right to voicemail. Did he say anything about his phone breaking or losing it?"

"Sure, if I see him, I'll pass on the message, but he didn't mention anything about his phone. Are you in Idaho now?"

"Yes, I had to get back home, so much to do."

"Well, next time you leave, I'd like the opportunity to say bye and get one of your sweet hugs."

"Yeah, I'm sorry about that; however, I may be back in town soon. I'll be sure to see you then and give you that hug, and thanks for your help, Jude. Love you and hope you have a great evening."

"Love you, too, dear. Talk soon."

After Sadie hung up with Jude, she looked at Paula. "Well, at least we know he's back home. Maybe his phone is broke or lost, who knows. But I have decided that if I don't hear from him by tomorrow, then I'm taking a drive to Montana. I am also thinking about calling Sierra in the morning. I'd like to know how her grandpa is doing and when she might be home, without giving away any information, until I talk to John first. All of this just has me crazy right now."

"Yeah, it is a little weird, and I understand your concern. But don't you think Sierra will think it's weird if you call her again, asking when she'll be home?" Paula replied.

"Hmm, maybe you're right. Maybe I'll hold off on that. Hey you, just want you to know I appreciate all you've done for me lately. Thanks for stopping back by this evening."

"No problem, my pleasure. Besides, the motive is probably selfish, if I'm being honest. I kinda like hanging out with you."

"Yeah, the feeling is mutual," Sadie replied. "So if I go to Montana, do you want to ride with me? I don't expect to be gone too long."

"Depends. I would need to check with work and see if I can get someone to cover me. It sounds nice, the drive together, that is."

***

After Piper woke up, he was glad the pain had subsided and tried hard not to think about his balls being banded. But for an older man, he suffered, as many of us do, with joint pain due to working physically hard all his life. Unfortunately for him, being bound by his wrists and ankles to a cold steel table wasn't a pleasant experience. He lay there, still and quiet, and took advantage of being alone. He assessed the situation and pulled against his shackles; it was hopeless. A tear trickled from his eye. He knew he had crossed the wrong woman but felt no remorse for the things he had done to her or anyone else he had ever hurt. He was his own worst enemy. He was only ashamed of himself because he had fallen for her deceitful tactics. To fall into a trap like this was beyond his wildest dreams. He never imagined a woman would ever have the upper hand on him. The thought of dying didn't bother Piper, but the thought of Carmen killing him and gaining pleasure from it disturbed him. He didn't want her to have that satisfaction. He would rather take a knife to his own throat than let her kill him.

Piper cringed when he heard the screen door open and then close shut. He had hoped she would have just stayed gone and left him to die on his own. He couldn't bear the thought of what she might be up to. After listening to her clang around in the kitchen, as if she were cooking something, his imagination got the best of him, and he mumbled quietly to himself, "If that fucking whore thinks I'm eating shit again, she's dead wrong. I'll just play fucking dead, and she'll take these fucking cuffs off me; then I'll kill that bitch." A few minutes later, Piper heard footsteps coming towards the bedroom door that he was trapped behind. He took a deep breath and closed his eyes, then let his body appear lifeless.

As Carmen walked through the door, she was surprised he was still asleep. "Hey, wake up, I have more to share with you." No response from Piper. She poked him a couple of times and repeated herself: "Wake up." Still no response, so she felt the pulse in his neck and realized he was fine. Carmen quietly left the room and went outside. Piper just knew he had fooled her. He heard the sound of a four-wheeler start up just outside his bedroom window. He had hoped she was leaving again, but Carmen had other plans. She attached a set of jumper cables to the quad battery and then fed the other end through the bedroom window. They dangled there until she was back inside. Piper couldn't see what she was up to and continued to play dead. After attaching the other end of the cables to the steel table, it began shocking Piper. His body jumped, and his eyes were wide open. Carmen laughed after she released the cables from the table. "Oh my, that was entertaining."

"Fuck you, crazy bitch!"

"Oh, come on now, it was funny. I mean, seriously, were you trying to play dead?" she giggled. "Because if you were, you really suck at it. You see, look at me, for example. I had you and John both fooled the day you had a bag over my head. I choked up saliva and everything. Gee, I thought you would have learned something from that performance."

"Hey, I have an idea. Why don't you release one of my hands and give me a knife so I can slit my own throat?"

"That's just weird, and messy. Could you imagine the blood squirting everywhere if you sliced the carotid artery? And guess who would have to clean that shit up? Cleaning up your DNA isn't something I really want to do. But I give you an E for effort. I don't think I could do that to myself," then giggled at the afterthought of it all. "Piper, I was thinking . . . " Before she could finish her thought, Piper pissed all over himself. "Oh geez, I just told you, I didn't want to clean up your DNA. Men, they never listen. Looks like you'll just have to lay there in your own piss."

Piper begged, "Just let me go, or kill me now. I'm tired of this shit."

"Oh really, I'm curious—what part are you tired of? Would it be the humiliation of someone else trapping you against your will, or would it be finding yourself defenseless and unable to fight back?" She waited for an answer, but Piper just lay there with nothing to say. "Have you ever had a broken rib? That shit really hurts." Still no response. "Oh, the quiet treatment, I see. Well, I guess I'll just have to find out for myself how you feel about it. I'll be right back; don't go anywhere," she giggled.

Piper heard her in there, rooting around through something that sounded like a toolbox. He could just imagine what she was doing. "Fucking, wacked bitch, I hope she just fucking kills me."

A few minutes later, she entered back into the room. Piper didn't even bother to see what she might have brought back with her. He had his eyes closed and was unresponsive, as if he had drifted away somewhere else in his mind, perhaps to a place where he had hidden long ago when he was a child suffering the horrid abuse his father afflicted upon him. (One really never knows the extent of abuse people have suffered in their lives that made them the dreadful people they are today.) Carmen was amused when she walked in and saw his eyes closed. "Oh, come on, you already tried that. The whole dead thing didn't work for me the first time, but whatever floats your boat. You know, after Sierra rescued me, the day you and your boss heartlessly decided that my life was nothing but a threat to your business and I deserved to die because of it, she brought me to the hospital, where the good doctor determined the pain in my guts was due to a couple of broken ribs. That shit really hurt, by the way. So, here I am before you, with a couple of weapons of choice, one being a small sledgehammer, or second, a trusty tire tool." Piper stayed quiet, and his eyes remained closed. His lack of participation disturbed Carmen. "Oh, I see, you must be thinking, 'You didn't use these things on me.' Well, of course you didn't. You used your steel-toed work boots on me; I still remember the sound of my bones cracking. But the thing that stayed in my mind the most was the sound of your horrid laughter after you did it." Then, with a powerful blow of the hammer, Carmen slammed it onto his rib cage. She heard the bone fracture and hoped for more of a reaction from Piper other than a flinch and the obvious look of pain that had just been inflicted, which caused him to close his eyes even tighter. She yelled, "What is it, the bone breaking or me not giving a fuck about who you are, that hurts the worst? I demand an answer!" then delivered another blow to his ribs.

Piper flinched again. "I have never given a fuck about you! I enjoyed fucking you that day, and if I were free right now, I'd do it all over again. But this time, I would make sure you were fucking dead and rotting in hell!"

"Thinking I was dead was your worse mistake," she said, then, without an ounce of hesitation, Carmen repeatedly slammed the sledgehammer into Piper's skull, crushing the life out of him. She dropped the hammer and crumbled to the floor, and with her knees drawn up to her chest, she sobbed for a brief moment.

After she composed herself, Carmen went back to Sierra's cabin and took a long shower. She was mentally and physically exhausted. She was shocked when she heard the grandfather clock strike four times; she could barely believe it was already four a.m. on Sunday morning. She whispered, "I need some sleep before I get rid of his body." Then she tapped the couch. "Bear, come up here with me; let's take a little nap, big guy." Carmen was restless. She anticipated the cleanup from the mess she had made and having it done before Sierra came back home that Monday. But she couldn't fight sleep and eventually surrendered her body to rest.

That morning, Sadie woke up to a note on the bedside nightstand. "Good morning, Beautiful, last night was amazing. I wish I could have been there when you woke up this morning but was called into work. If you decide to go to Montana, understand I'll be here waiting for you. I tried getting some time off but looks like another person beat me to the punch. By the sound of it, I'll be working the next seven days. Call me and let me know what's up, and if you go, when you'll be expected back. Peace and hugs, my dear Sadie Lady." Sadie smiled and took a brief moment to reflect on the evening before. After getting a cup of coffee, she looked at her phone; still no response from John. After being an investigative reporter for several years, she had learned to follow her gut instincts, first and foremost. She had an awful feeling inside and made up her mind to pack a bag and head that way. She was determined to shed light on John and, in turn, hope to learn why he was investigating this woman, Sara Tag, in the first place. She couldn't help but wonder if he had a hunch about her all along, in relationship to Carmen Storm or what the connection was that triggered his curiosity.

Sierra struggled through the night; she missed Carmen and Bear. She was homesick and ready to sleep in her own bed. She was careful not to wake her grandmother as she made herself a cup of coffee. She wanted to call Carmen that morning, but then thought, *Maybe I'll just surprise her and come home today. Gram has relatives coming, and Grandpa is out of critical condition now. I'm sure she'll be fine for a day, until my aunt shows up on Monday.* And without further thought into the matter, Sierra had made her mind up. After looking at the time and considering the two-hour time difference between Florida and Montana, she booked the next six a.m. flight out, then said aloud to herself, "My estimated time of arrival home should be around eight-thirty a.m. That's if I drive a rental car from the airport to my place. I can't wait to surprise her, and oh my goodness, I miss Bear. I hope they're still asleep when I get there."

Sleeping in was not a concern of John's that Sunday morning. After his many hours of travel between Texas and home, accompanied by the full belly he acquired by dining at Jude's the night before, he slept like a baby. He found himself missing his phone and his inability to use it. After his shower, he glanced at his watch and noticed the date and time. "Shit, the damn cellular store isn't open today; that sucks," he grumbled. Then he had an afterthought. "I bet I still have a used phone here somewhere," and began searching through drawers for a replacement. "Fucking bingo, dude; I almost forgot about that." John had found an older android that he had used in the past and was happy he had saved it. After making himself an egg sandwich and another cup of coffee, he sat down at the computer and logged into his service provider's account with the expectation that it would be an easy switch. It wasn't long before John was aggravated. He had never been one to have a lot of patience with things of this nature. He decided to take a drive over to a friend's house. John knew his buddy would be able to get his phone transferred without a problem.

After a two-hour drive, Sadie made it to Montana around seven a.m. She was still unable to contact John, and Jude's didn't open until eight. She drove by John's place but didn't see his truck in the driveway. "Shit," was all she said, then got out and knocked on his door; there was no answer. She sat in his drive for a few minutes. "Fuck this, I'm going to see Carmen," and against her better judgment, she did just that. But before she left town and, with an ulterior motive, she stopped at the local gas station and picked up two cups of coffee and a box of donuts. She recognized the store tenant as a friend she had gone to high school with. "Hey, T.W., it's been forever. When did you start working here?"

"Since last week. My wife is pregnant with our second kid, so I decided we could use the extra income. How have you been?" he asked.

"Good, I've been good. Congratulations on the new baby. Hey, if John Buck stops in this morning, can you tell him I'm back in town? I'm going out to Sierra's place and tried calling him to go along, but I think something is wrong with his phone."

"Sure, no problem. Tell Sierra I said hi."

"I'll do that, and give your wife my best," Sadie replied.

After pulling into Sierra's driveway, Bear was alarmed and began barking. Carmen was startled awake and went to the window. "Oh, fucking great. I wonder what she wants." Before Sadie could knock on the door, Carmen had opened it. "Hey, Sadie, what brings you out this way so early in the morning?"

"I was bored and missing friends; thought I'd bring you a cup of coffee and enjoy a donut with you."

Carmen backed up and invited her inside. "That's thoughtful, but I don't have too long to spare. I have a shitload of stuff to do this morning."

"Oh, well, I can always come back later," Sadie replied.

"Don't be silly. Besides, that coffee smells great, and I'm always up for a donut."

Bear noticed the box right away and made sure they knew he wanted one. He pranced and growled as he often did when he begged for a treat. "Can he have a glazed one? I have a dozen here," Sadie asked.

"Yes, but he'll have to eat it outside," Carmen replied.

After Sadie gave him a donut, she sent him outside, then sat down at the kitchen table with Carmen. "So, how's Sierra's grandfather doing? I heard he had some heart problems."

"Oh, he's doing fine, I guess. Sierra is expected back sometime tomorrow."

"I think I met a nice girl from Idaho. Could be love," Sadie giggled.

"Oh wow, that's awesome. The best girls always come from Idaho, well, with the exception of my sweetie, Sierra."

"Yes, they do. Hey, you said you were from Idaho. Where were you raised, what area of Idaho?"

"Actually, my dad was a businessman, and after he served his time in the Navy, we never really had a chance to settle down in any one place too long before he died. But we spent a lot of time around the Boise area."

"Oh, I'm sorry your father has passed away. That's never easy. Was he ill?"

"No, he was shot to death. I heard it was a case of mistaken identity. I was in my early teens when I lost him, and yes, you're right, it was anything but easy."

Sadie was certain that Carmen had to be Sara Tag and went further with her inquisitive questioning. "I can imagine so. I assume your mom missed him, too."

"I never knew my mother; she died giving birth to me," Carmen replied.

"Oh man, wow. You really had it tough. I'm so sorry, Carmen."

"Ah, no biggie. I've learned to deal with it. I was adopted by a family who actually paid for my college education. They were a bit uptight during my teen years. They sent me away to a private school. I graduated there, and after I turned eighteen, they eventually lightened up, I guess."

"Did you ever live in Montana prior to coming here for work?" Sadie asked.

Carmen became wary. "Wow, you're full of questions this morning. Is there something . . . "

Before Carmen could finish her thought, Sadie received a call from John. "Damn, hold that thought, I really need to take this call," Sadie replied. Then she got up from the table and went outside to talk privately. Carmen had a bad feeling about all this and eavesdropped on her conversation through the kitchen window. "Jesus, John, it's about time you called."

"Yeah, that's not important. What the fuck are you doing there after the messages you left me? Are you fucking crazy? Are you even sure all this is factual?"

"John, easy. Yes, it's factual, and I'm talking to Carmen now, and most of it is adding up."

"Don't ask any more questions, Sadie. I'm on my way."

Carmen couldn't hear what John said to Sadie, but she knew something was boiling, and it wasn't good. She felt things unraveling in the worst way, and without clear thought, she grabbed the iron skillet from the stovetop and acted on impulse. She waited for Sadie to walk back through the door. Without an ounce of hesitation, she caught her off guard and bashed the heavy skillet over her head, killing her with one blow. Carmen didn't waste time. She knew by the sound of the conversation that John was probably on his way there. She struggled while dragging the lifeless body to her vehicle. She ran back into the house and made sure Sadie hadn't left anything behind. After placing her coffee cup and box of donuts in a bag, she took them along and tossed the items into Sadie's car. Carmen drove the vehicle, with Sadie in it, down to the pit the excavator had dug, then grabbed a brick and placed it on the accelerator. After she put the car in drive, she stepped back and watched it disappear into the abyss. She knew she was playing against time and feared running into John. So many things were spinning through her head. She panicked for a moment; then she thought, *I need to get Piper's truck in that pit, too.* She raced the four-wheeler back to her cabin and got in Piper's truck. She squealed the wheels and rushed back to Sierra's place. Her heart pounded with anxiety, and adrenalin pumped through her veins as she raced against time. Just as she dumped Piper's truck into the pit, she heard a vehicle coming. She ran up the hill and hid behind the shed. She peeked to see who it was, but she didn't recognize the car. She stayed still for a moment and watched with clandestine eyes. It was Sierra. "Oh my God, what the hell is she doing here right now?" Carmen thought about approaching Sierra, and just before she revealed herself, here came John's truck down the lane. "Fuck, I knew that bastard was coming." Carmen remained out of sight. "Think, think, think," she repeated to herself time and time again. She paced back and forth behind the shed, while John and Sierra stood outside of their vehicles and talked. Carmen couldn't hear what they were talking about and feared the worst. She was able to sneak behind Sierra's house and enter through the back door. She fumbled through a bag that she kept with her belongings and took out a handgun. After placing it in the waistband of her jeans, she noticed the silencer that attached to it and placed it in her pocket. She had to struggle to push Bear away from the door, as he knew his mom was home. "Stay, Bear, stay," she insisted. Finally, after getting past the dog, she walked out the front door, as if everything was normal. As she walked up towards John and Sierra, she nodded her head. "Hey, baby, welcome home."

"Hey you, I thought I'd surprise you, but wow, John's surprising me," Sierra replied with an obvious look of concern on her face.

John had his own agenda; he was fearful after Sadie had informed him of all she knew regarding Sara and Collin Tag. Unlike John, Sadie's fear and concerns surrounded her friend's safety and wondering how and why Carmen had shown up in Sierra's life after all this time. But John was out to save his own ass, and Carmen knew it. She was curious about what he was feeding into Sierra's head and listened intently as John rambled on, "I think Carmen is a danger to you. I recently found out her father, Collin Tag, is the one who raped and killed your mother."

The expressions on Carmen's and Sierra's faces were priceless. They both looked shocked and, for a moment, at a loss for words. Carmen shook her head in disbelief. "He's a liar, Sierra. He's trying to tear us apart," she responded with a desperate plea, then turned to John and pointed her gun directly at him. "I should just shoot you where you stand, you perverted sack of shit."

Sierra's heart raced; she was torn and confused. Her lifelong friend had just sent her head spinning with his accusations. "Carmen, don't. Please just stop waving that gun around. John, how do you know this?"

Before John could reply, Carmen stepped in. "He doesn't know anything; he's a liar. He's trying to tear us apart."

"I had Sadie help me with the research. She found out all of this for me. Carmen's father is Collin Tag, the same man who raped and killed your mother and the same man you shot to death all those years ago. Open your eyes, Sierra, her being here is not a coincidence," John replied as he kept a watchful on Carmen. "Where's Sadie at? She was supposed to be here, and I don't even see her car. What did you do with her, Carmen?" John asked.

Sierra's eyes focused on Carmen. "Sadie was here?"

"Yes, she stopped by but left in a hurry after she received a call from somebody," Carmen replied, then reached out for Sierra. "Please, trust me, babe, my dad could have never done such a thing. He was never an angel, but he would never do something like that. You have to believe me."

"What did you do with her? Huh? I want to know!" John insisted.

"Why would I do anything with her? You're crazy, John."

"She came here to see you, and she knew more than you bargained for. What did you do? Did you kill her?"

Carmen was shaken by John's questions. She knew she had killed Sadie but was torn about telling the truth of the matter. Sierra locked her eyes on Carmen for a response. "Talk to me, Carmen. What's going on here?" Sierra asked, hoping for some logical response.

"Like I said, John's a liar, and Sadie left on her own free will," Carmen replied.

"Sierra, listen to me. Carmen is a bad apple. The coincidence of her showing up here for work, then accidentally becoming a big part of your life, is staged. I can feel it! Her name is Sara Tag, and she's the daughter of Collin Tag!" John yelled.

Before John could say any more, Carmen interrupted him. She answered as calmly as possible, "Yes, my name was Sara Tag before my father passed away. I was adopted and

271

given the name I have now. At that young age, I was told my father was shot. I never had an explanation. But what I do know is; John has his own secrets. He is a dangerous man that stood by while I was being raped by his flunky, Piper." She then turned to John. "You clicked your lighter lid over and over again. The sound has stayed in my mind since that day, you dirty bastard. He was there, Sierra. That's why he is here now and determined to fill your head with his lies."

"What are you talking about?" John asked.

"I just found out a few hours ago who you really are, Boss. It's just crazy what people will tell you when they're under extreme pressure, and I mean extreme."

"You've lost your mind. You don't know shit, bitch."

"STOP this!" Sierra shouted. "Just stop. This is all really crazy. Carmen, please just put the gun down; I can't think."

"No, Sierra, I can't do that. He was the one who stood by that day. He watched me being raped, and Piper referred to him as 'Boss.' He would kill me now if he had the chance to. I have Piper's confession all on voice recording." While holding the gun on John, Carmen said, "Here, get my phone out of my back pocket and listen to all Piper said. Sierra, I love you. You have to believe that."

Sierra took the phone from Carmen's pocket and listened to Piper's confession. John heard it, too, and blurted out in desperation, "I don't even know this guy. I have no idea who he is or how she got this confession!"

"When you were away, I ran into Piper at the Laundromat, the day I was washing rugs. He was being his normal rude self, so I took advantage of the situation and turned it around to benefit myself. I encouraged a truce between us and invited him over for dinner that coming Saturday. Little did he know, but he walked into his death sentence. That's right, he's dead—I killed him. But not before I got his confession."

Sierra was at a loss for words and felt a certain churning in her guts. "Oh my God, this is all so crazy. John, tell me you're not this monster."

He was silent. He searched for an answer but was unable to respond with a good explanation. He lowered his head and simply replied, "This is a setup. I'm being framed."

"What reason would she have to frame you, John?" Sierra asked with an obvious look of desperation on her face.

John huffed, "This is crazy. I'm leaving, and Carmen, you're a crazy, delusional bitch."

Carmen held the gun firmly and aimed it at John. "No, you're staying right here. Matter of fact, sit down on the ground; you're making me nervous."

"Just let him go," Sierra pleaded.

"Sierra, he stood by and watched me be raped and beaten. It was by his order and his words that he demanded that his flunky kill me and leave me for dead that day. He was the second man. This guy Piper—well, John was his boss."

"She's crazy, Sierra, don't listen to her. She's a liar!" John pleaded.

Sierra processed all that had been said. She knew John had a nervous tick and would click his lighter lid from time to time. Then she remembered the note she had left for Carmen on the table, the one she had found crumpled up on the floorboard of John's truck. She recalled what Carmen had said about a nightmare she had that day—she felt as though someone had been watching her and clicking a lighter lid while she was resting. Sierra knew Carmen had to be telling the truth. She looked at Carmen with a sorrow-filled expression and just before she could speak her mind, Bear came crashing through the kitchen window from inside the house; he was determined to see Sierra after what seemed like a long separation. His collar hooked onto a piece of the window frame, and without hesitation Sierra ran to his aid in order to free him.

While Sierra was distracted, Carmen kept John at gunpoint. "Get up on your feet and walk over towards the pit; I want to show you something," she commanded.

"Just let me go, Carmen. We can forget about all of this, and nobody has to know about Piper."

"You think it's that easy, John? Do you really think I can just let you walk away like that? Just shut up and keep walking." After they made it to the edge of the pit, John was horrified by what he saw. "No, no. You didn't. You fucking, crazy bitch! That's Sadie's car," John gasped. "What the fuck have you done?"

"Oh, I see that you must not recognize that Piper's shitty truck is in there, too. Or maybe you don't give a hairy shit about him. Geez, what a shitty boss you are."

"Sierra will never forgive you for this!" John exclaimed.

"Trust me, Sierra will be fine. She loves me. The funny thing is, John, we both have a terrible distaste for rapists. The world is a better place without guys like you."

"I didn't rape you! I've never raped anyone," John replied.

"Yes, you raped me that day when you stood by and ordered Piper's every move. I might have been blindfolded, but I wasn't deaf. You're a sorry asshole, and you deserve to die."

Just as Carmen pointed the gun and took aim, in a desperate attempt to save his own life, he yelled, "You're my sister, Carmen! Collin was my father, too."

"Hmm, well, imagine that. So my brother is a perverted motherfucker, just like daddy was. That's just sick and sad at the same time."

Just as Sierra freed Bear's collar from the broken window frame, she glanced up to see Carmen and John standing near the pit. She couldn't hear what they were saying but saw John lunge at Carmen with a powerful force that knocked her to the ground. Sierra screamed out, "John, no!" Carmen kept a tight grip on the gun, and in the midst of the struggle, the gun went off. John collapsed lifelessly on top of her. She tried desperately to push him off, but his body weight was more than she could manage. Sierra ran to Carmen and rolled John's body off her. "Are you okay?"

Carmen cunningly replied to benefit herself, "Yes, I'm fine now." After standing up to brush herself off, she rolled John's body into the pit. Then Carmen pointed out Sadie's car that was buried in the rubbish. "He confessed to me that he killed Sadie. He said she knew too much. He was trying to make a deal with me to set him free. He thought if he told me he had killed Sadie that we would be even for me killing Piper and that somehow we could just put all this behind us."

Sierra broke down in tears. "This is awful, everything. Sadie was innocent. She didn't deserve to die."

"I know. I'm sorry John felt like he had to kill her. She was a nice person," Carmen replied, then went onto say, "Look, I need to get some gas and catch this pit on fire. We don't need to leave any evidence that any of them were here."

"I'm going to be sick. I can't help with any of this," Sierra replied.

"Go inside with Bear and get yourself a shot of whiskey and try to relax your mind. I will clear this mess up, and then we can talk."

After Carmen gave the cabin a thorough cleansing, she went back to Sierra's and lit the pit on fire, then walked up to the porch and sat in a rocker. Sierra came outside and sat with her in silence while they watched the blazing inferno burn away their past nightmares. "I'm glad you're okay and sorry John was there the day you were raped. I can't believe it; I really never knew him. It's sad. This whole thing is a fucking mess. People are going to be missing Sadie and John. There will be questions."

"Sierra, just breathe; we'll work this out," Carmen replied. She reached out to take Sierra's hand, but she pulled away. "Sierra, please, I just set out to do away with Piper. I didn't anticipate John or Sadie getting involved."

"Yeah, that's what you said. So is there any truth in what John said about your dad being the one who raped my mom?" Sierra asked.

"I can't answer that question for you. I was just a kid when I found out he died. I was always told it was a freak accident and that he was in the wrong place at the wrong time. I swear I never knew anything about that. Yes, if that is true, then it is an eerie feeling. But my meeting you was somehow fate, and I don't regret that. We were both kids; we didn't have control over the situation. I just know how much you mean to me and hope we can get past this fact, if it is fact at all."

Sierra sat quietly for a moment, absorbing what Carmen had said then she quietly spoke. "After the fire cools down, I'll cover it over with the backhoe early in the morning. I was thinking we need a pole barn that sits on a concrete slab; a big one that I can store hay in and some other things; that would give me more room in my new barn. Brittany's husband, Billy, does that for a living, and it would be perfect, built over the top of that pit. I'll be sure to have him get right on that."

"I made sure to get rid of all the evidence from the cabin," Carmen said. "I'm sorry, but we'll make it through this. I do feel bad about Sadie. I hate that John felt like he had to kill her."

"I don't want to ever talk about this again. Not Sadie and not John. I just want that pit covered over and the shed built as soon as possible, before people start missing either of them," Sierra replied.

"I do have something else to tell you," Carmen stammered.

"Oh? What would that be?" Sierra asked.

"We are eighty million dollars richer. I received a call a few nights ago from a bank in Switzerland; he referred to me as Sara Tag. The man wanted to verify a deposit that was made into an account that I was a mutual account holder on. It turned out my half brother was on the account, too. I was confused because I don't have a brother, and just before John tackled me near the pit, he confessed that Collin Tag was his father, too. I believe he was telling the truth. I found out through Piper that John had just sold Hilltop Drilling to a buyer out of Texas. Turns out my father willed that land to John to own and operate, if anything ever happened to him. He sold it for eighty million large just a couple of days ago."

"Are you freaking serious? That's a ton of money," Sierra replied. "Wow, I can't believe all of this. Brother, he was your brother? I'm so sorry."

"Yeah, I know. Maybe after we get that shed built, we could get away for a couple of months and let things blow over. I was thinking of Australia—I've always wanted to go there. I even have a good friend who lives near Queensland. Her name is Em Gee. What do you think?" Carmen asked.

"Yeah, it's not a bad idea, but I need to take care of first things first. I don't need anything linking me or us to this mess."

"I agree, Sierra. Besides, just for the record, if anything would ever come of this mess, just know that I would take the fall on my own. I love you."

"I love you, too, Carmen, and I hope that one day we can get past this," Sierra replied.

"I'm sure we will. We are a team, and together we can prevail through any obstacles in our path," Carmen said, then reached out for Sierra's hand once again. Sierra took Carmen's hand in hers this time, and they watched the fire dwindle away into the wee hours of the morning.

By: Tosh Baker, Author

Justified Vengeance; or was it?

Thank you for reading. I hope you enjoyed the story. Feel free to visit & follow JVTwisted, Discussion Club on Facebook. Also if you could leave feedback on Amazon I'd really appreciate that. Peace & HUGS

,fied Vengeance, Twisted by Tosh Baker

Made in the USA
Monee, IL
01 September 2021